THIRTY FIFTEEN

PHIL TOMLINSON

Matador
9 Priory Business Park
Kibworth Beauchamp
Leicestershire LE8 0RX, UK
Tel: 0116 279 2299
Email: books@troubador.co.uk
Web: www.troubador.co.uk/matador

ISBN 9781785893100

British Library Cataloguing in Publication Data.
A catalogue record for this book is available from the British Library.

Typeset in 11pt Book Antiqua by Troubador Publishing Ltd, Leicester, UK
Printed and bound in the UK by TJ International, Padstow, Cornwall

Matador is an imprint of Troubador Publishing Ltd

donation from   EAS
Jan   the
2017   author

W/D

Get **more** out of libraries

Please return or renew this item by the last date shown.
You can renew online at www.hants.gov.uk/library

Hampshire Libraries
Tel: 0300 555 1387

 Hampshire
County Council

To my sister and all of my family.

For Allan, Christian and Linzi with thanks.

To everyone at the Hare and Hounds in Whitwick,
Leicestershire.

CHAPTER ONE

Zoe awoke and – in a hazy half world between sleep and wakefulness – shook her head to clear the mass of thoughts and visions that cluttered up her brain as they swam back and forth through her turbulent mind.

'This is so weird,' she muttered languidly to herself. 'I feel as if I'm still asleep, yet dreaming I'm awake. Either that, or I'm stuck in the aftermath of some nightmarish dream – or some obscure unknown reality which my mind has entered while I was asleep.'

Zoe rolled onto her back, eyes shut tight as she tried valiantly to wrestle with the task of deciphering the confused mess that floated around inside her head. She quickly gave up the fight, as the process was too much for her brain to cope with when she had just awoken. She did however manage to reach a decision that of the observations she had just made regarding her current state, she would prefer either the first or second. After all dreaming she was awake meant that when she did wake, life would be back to normal. Similarly if what she had experienced *was* a nightmare, she at least had the chance of feeling better once she had woken up properly and begun the daily task of going about her business. Whereas if she found herself in some dubious situation, events could well be beyond her control.

A few minutes later – yet a lifetime within her tired, troubled mind – Zoe opened her eyes. Now at least partially awake and with senses fairly settled, she was ready to face daylight and tackle the day that lay ahead. Yawning and stretching, she blinked as she looked around expecting to see the familiar pink and lilac pattern of her bedroom wallpaper, as well as the brightly illuminated red numbers on her bedside alarm clock. Instead, she couldn't see much at all. She was surrounded by a semi-darkness, much as one might find between evening and night time or perhaps just before dawn.

'It's still dark,' she grumbled. 'That dream must have woken me up too early. Now, I feel grumpy … and I'm cold too.'

Zoe rolled back so that she lay on her side again. She reached out an arm as she turned in order to grab the duvet, so she could pull it tightly around her against the chill of the night. She hoped the warmth would help her get back to sleep. Zoe's grasping hand felt nothing but fresh air. She tried again but there was no duvet. Opening her still sleep filled eyes once more, Zoe suddenly realised that she wasn't in her bedroom. She was outside in the open air. She could feel the wetness of the grass beneath her. She assumed this was either from evening dew or rain. *But what am I doing lying on grass?* she thought.

The shock of this discovery caused Zoe to wake up properly. Eyes now wide open and brain on full alert, she sat bolt upright and looked about her again. In the gloom she could just about make out the silhouettes of trees standing tall against a brooding night sky. But it was a sky that bore no resemblance to any night sky she had seen before.

Some distance above her hovered what appeared to be a large illuminated ball. A similarly well-lit but substantially smaller spheroid floated alongside this.

Zoe twisted her neck sharply so that she could look behind her, then wished she hadn't as she realised that her head was sore. She rubbed it, slowly at first, to try to ease the pain. She grimaced as she massaged the scalp beneath her matted hair, all the time staring upwards as she took in the amazing sight that was manifest above her head.

Now she was sitting properly upright, Zoe could see several other illuminated spheres hovering at various points in the sky and stretching far away into the distance. It was as if someone had created a haphazard pathway of moons around the Earth, all of differing sizes. Their presence generated a light pollution that all but extinguished the natural candescence of the stars and planets with which she was familiar. The light radiating from this array of globes – whilst far from brilliant in comparison to sunlight or light from a full moon – nonetheless obliterated clear visibility of the heavens, to the point where even the commonplace and somewhat comforting sightings of The Plough, The Great Bear, and The Milky Way were no longer visible to her naked eye.

Surprised by this vision, Zoe once again dug deep into the muddled cluster of thoughts that had returned to plague her mind. She was vaguely hoping to find some clue in there that might help her understand where she was and how she got here.

For some reason the clock that she'd expected to see at her bedside was still prominent in her thoughts. *But why?* thought Zoe, frowning. She screwed up her face in deep concentration. It took a while before she remembered! Then it all came flooding back. *She had been with DI Benson and Professor Tompkins in Cristelee Safari Park. There was a clock there too. But where was it now? And where were DI Benson and Professor Tompkins? Had they gone and left her? Was she still in the park? If so, was she in danger of being attacked – or perhaps even eaten – by wild animals?*

'So many thoughts and questions, and no answers,' said Zoe out loud to no one in particular as she slumped heavily back onto the grass, exhausted from the effort involved in trying to think.

Her head still hurt. She was cold, wet and worried. Worse still, she had no idea where she was or how she came to be sleeping outside.

After a few minutes of fruitless conjecture, Zoe became aware of what seemed to be muffled voices in the distance. She cocked her head and listened hard. The sound came floating on the still air, breaking through the silence of the night.

People, she thought, with a sense of relief washing over her. *Maybe they can help me. It might even be Benson and the Professor coming to find me.*

She sat up again and was about to shout out when another thought stopped her, and with an increasingly sinking feeling she lay back down abruptly.

4

What if it isn't Benson and Tompkins? It could be anyone, and if it isn't them then who will it be? They might not like me being here, and if so they could harm me.

Zoe was instantly apprehensive and fearful. She had a vague memory that all had not been well when she was in the safari park.

The voices got louder as the people got closer. Zoe could see lights flickering against the darkness of the trees. She didn't know whether she should run or stay put. She hesitated.

'Over there,' said a voice.

Immediately Zoe saw the outline of several shadowy figures heading towards her. They seemed to be surrounded by flames. It was too late for her to run now. She stood up shakily. Her legs felt weak and wobbly and her muscles ached. She began to rub her hands up and down the back of her calves and thighs in an effort to ease the tension in them.

The figures were almost upon her by now. She could see they were definitely people, but not people whom she recognised. The flickering lights and flames she'd seen came from old fashioned fiery torches that several members of the group – now fanning out so that they cut off any chance of escape – held in their hands. Zoe stood up straight. She stared at the crowd of people who had by now formed a tight circle around her. As far as she could make out, most of the gathering looked to be in their late teens or early twenties. She couldn't say so with any degree of certainty though, as every one of them had dirt smeared across their face. She could see there was a mix of males and females, most of whom

5

had long, lank, unkempt hair hanging down their backs or across their shoulders. Clothes were a hotchpotch of animal skins, furs and scruffy shabby garments that seemed to be no more than coarse bundles of untreated wool and rough natural materials. These had been stitched together crudely to form what Zoe supposed were meant to serve the purpose of jumpers, blouses, shirts, trousers or skirts. Footwear seemed to be an assortment of roughly hand-made fur or fleece mules, although Zoe noticed that some of the people had merely wrapped furs – tightly tied – around their bare feet. One or two others had fashioned animal skins into coarse shoes.

Zoe's eyes shifted from one person to another as she scanned each member of the group. She was alarmed to see that no one displayed any outward sign of friendliness.

A young man stepped forward. He seemed to be the leader. 'Name yourself and state your business here,' he said in a clear stentorian voice.

Zoe opened her mouth to speak but no words came out, just a weird croaking, rasping sound emerged.

'You will answer,' said the young man, continuing to assert himself in a similarly severe tone to the one he used in his previous statement.

Just for a moment the phrasing and the clipped monotone stirred a distant memory in Zoe. An involuntary shudder ran right through her body as an image of herself lying on an operating table with a well-dressed humanoid standing alongside her appeared in her head.

The vision faded from Zoe's head as quickly as it had appeared, leaving behind an uncomfortable feeling deep down in her stomach, which seemed to be knotting itself up with fear.

'My name is Zoe,' she spluttered, before asking. 'Where am I and who are you?'

'Zoe?' queried the young man. 'That is not a name I am familiar with. Are you from the South?'

'I am from Cristelee,' Zoe answered.

'I have not heard of this Cristelee,' said the man. 'Where is it?'

'It's in the Midlands,' Zoe replied, 'somewhere between Birmingham and Nottingham.'

A hubbub of voices greeted this statement as everyone in the group began talking rapidly to each other. The young man held up his hand and silence descended.

'You are lying,' he said, turning back to Zoe. 'I will ask you again. And this time you will answer truthfully. Have you come from the South?'

Fear gripped Zoe's stomach even tighter than before. She was unsure of what to do or say next.

Who are these people? And how come they don't know about Cristelee? she thought, before hesitantly replying to the young man.

'Er … er … I'm not from the South. I … I … I told you I'm from Cristelee.'

'There is no Cristelee in Lowlands,' said the man, now clearly getting impatient at what he saw as Zoe's reluctance to answer his question satisfactorily. 'It *must* be in the South.'

He turned to face the others as he completed the sentence. Then in a voice that held more than a touch of menace he pointed at Zoe whilst issuing his orders. 'Seize her! Bring her to the camp … but blindfold her first. We don't want her knowing the way in … or out.'

Four or five individuals broke away from the impenetrable ring of human beings around her. They advanced quickly towards Zoe. She turned to run, but there was no way through the rest of the people who had rapidly closed ranks, securing the tight circle around her. Besides, Zoe's legs were unable to respond to the frantic urgings of her mind. Almost before she knew it, she had been overpowered by her assailants. Each one secured a grip on a part of her arms, dragging her forward. Zoe's arms were quickly pinned behind her back. Someone tied a dirty, smelly piece of cloth around her head and across her eyes – which were now wet with tears – before spinning her body round roughly for six or seven times until she was quite dizzy. She was then led unsteadily across the long grass to a well-trodden path that lay nearby.

As she was pushed and pulled on the journey along the flattened dirt pathway, Zoe cursed silently under her breath. Her unspoken oaths were accompanied by shrieks and cries as she frequently stumbled, tripping over sprawling tangled tree roots, while getting her face and hair alternately caressed or whacked by what she assumed must be overhanging branches.

Zoe was cold, wet, bruised, and terrified. She had no idea who these people were or what they intended to do with her. She wasn't absolutely certain whether they *would* harm her, although their actions so far suggested that they weren't about to throw her a party either. No one spoke to her during the journey. However, she could hear whispering and spasmodic bursts of conversation break out between some of her captors. Zoe knew there was no way of escape at present. Her survival instinct might be strong, but her body felt far too weak to comply. She tried to gather her thoughts and remember how she got to this unfamiliar and scary location. The clock still played on her memory, as did the vision of the humanoid she'd just glimpsed. She felt sure that they both somehow held the key to her memories.

After a lot of hard thinking Zoe had a clear picture in her head. She saw an image of herself holding something in her hand. She was pointing it towards a clock which had red numbers on its face. The numbers were spinning around in a blur. Then out of nowhere the initials RSMM leapt into her head. It took a few more minutes before the penny finally dropped and she remembered that the acronym stood for Remote Sensory Magnetic Manipulator. It was this that she had been pointing at the clock as she tried to turn back time in the safari park. Everything came tumbling back into her head as she regained a complete memory of the past – the Soul Snatcher, his attempts at getting his spaceship back. The children, Benson, Professor Tompkins. Finally, she remembered how she'd fallen into the time vortex.

She could see the blackness even now. She could still feel the pain and terror she had experienced within the plummeting, twisting spirals of darkness inside the vortex as her body was tossed and buffeted about. She'd been hurled sideways, upwards and every which way, before the final corkscrewing downward dive that had deposited her with a painful jolt onto something rough and solid, which she now knew to be the grass on which she'd lain when she regained consciousness.

There was something else she remembered too. She had been holding on to something, or someone, when she was inside the vortex. Zoe racked her brain in an effort to recall this missing part of her memory and when it reappeared she wished she hadn't bothered. *It was him! Kazzaar, the Soul Snatcher! But he'd been in the guise of a human.* Zoe searched further into the deepest recesses of her mind until the name of this human finally came to her. *It was Zak Araz!* All was clear now. In her mind's eye she could see herself and Zak Araz clinging tightly to each other as they tumbled through the vortex.

But if I was holding on to him and he was holding on to me. Where is he now? she thought.

CHAPTER TWO

Zoe had no time for further thinking, as she was unceremoniously grabbed by her shoulders before being spun rapidly around another five or six times in an effort to further disorientate her.

'We're here,' someone said in her ear. 'We need to make sure you have no chance of finding your way to this place again.'

There was an ominous rider to this statement as the voice added. 'That's if we ever let you go, of course.'

When the blindfold was removed, Zoe blinked her eyes several times to get them accustomed to seeing again. She looked around at her new environment, trying to focus her eyes to see through the flickering glow emitted from the fiery torches. She was in what appeared to be a clearing, surrounded by trees that – as far as she could make out in the poor light – were not yet in full bloom. Zoe guessed it must be early springtime, unless she was on another planet, in which case the time of year was anyone's guess. In the centre of the clearing burned a large open fire that was contained by a bricked rectangular surround. The light cast by this fire allowed Zoe to get a better picture of her surroundings. She could see what appeared to be cooking pots stacked neatly at one side of the brickwork. More people – of similar age to the others – had joined the group around the fire. They were staring at her with expressions ranging from curiosity to hostility.

In the firelight Zoe could see the shadowy shapes of a number of buildings and makeshift shelters standing haphazardly on the perimeter of the clearing. The erections had been sited to form a vague circle, creating a protective barrier around the edge of a large field that was itself surrounded by forest. At first glance they looked to be rough primitive constructions. Some of the buildings were made from wood. Others seemed to be made from metal sheeting combined with bits of old clothing. The crude basic assemblies produced the overall effect of a small village compound within the clearing. The circular formation gave it a neat appearance despite the ramshackle nature of the dwellings.

Zoe was still feeling scared. She had no idea who these people were or what they were going to do to her. They all seemed to speak English and – although it was unfamiliar to her – the landscape suggested she was still somewhere in Britain. However, the questions they'd asked – along with their lack of geographical recognition when Zoe said she was from Cristelee – made no sense to her. She was also extremely concerned that her own attempts at giving answers didn't seem to satisfy any of *them* either.

The young man who had spoken to Zoe earlier jerked his head in the direction of the fire. Immediately, Zoe felt herself being roughly propelled towards the flames. Her heartbeat quickened noticeably as she thought about the horrible injuries that such a fire could inflict, should someone still not like her responses to further questioning.

Forcibly pushed to the ground very close to the blaze, Zoe struggled to get herself into a sitting position so she could face her captors as they once again circled around her. The glow of the firelight reflected eerily off the faces of the encompassing group members.

Zoe could feel the heat from the flames. The warmth made her relax a little, even if it didn't remove all of her fear and trepidation.

'Right Zoe … that is what you said your name was?' It was the young man who spoke again. Zoe nodded her confirmation. He was calmer now, his voice controlled. His breathing much more even. 'Talk to us. Tell us who you are … where you are from … and what brings you here. We know you are a stranger. We've not seen you before and your clothes are strange. We have no clothes like that in Lowlands so we know you are not from down here. Besides, you were seen to appear from the skies. You arrived out of nowhere, so you must have come down on a teleport beam. That suggests you come from the South. So what have you come for? Are you here to spy on us and report back?'

Zoe looked earnestly around the group, hoping to find a sympathetic face but all she saw was suspicion and belligerence. She was feeling lost and helpless. She didn't know where she was or who these people were. Zoe was disorientated, as she thought, *they could yet turn out to be friendly, even though they don't look that way at the moment. On the other hand they might decide to kill me, so I need to be careful what I say.*

She had no way of knowing which of these thoughts would turn out to be the right one, so Zoe decided she had to tell them everything and hope that at the end they would understand. If so perhaps they would show her some leniency and give her some support. She took a deep breath and began her story.

The group sat in silence as Zoe told them about the exploits of Kazzaar, from the kidnapping and removal of souls from the children, through the force field and time reversal, to the moment she fell through time.

'… and the vortex spat me out here, wherever that is,' she concluded, looking around the sea of faces once more as she tried to gauge the mood of the group from the expressions of people who were staring in her direction.

Zoe wasn't exactly buoyed by what she saw as her gaze was met with a sea of blank, gawping faces.

After a few seconds of silence the young man spoke. 'That's an incredible story Zoe,' he said.

Zoe could see other heads nodding their agreement as the man continued. 'It's really hard to imagine you could have made that up, so it must be true. It would certainly explain the way you just turned up here and why you talked about a place we'd never heard of … Cristelee, wasn't it?'

Zoe nodded.

'You say you fell through a time vortex?' asked the young man.

Zoe nodded again.

'In what year did this take place?' he queried.

Zoe looked puzzled. 'Um … 2015,' she replied hesitantly, aware of gasps from within the crowd.

'Welcome to our humble home.' The young man proclaimed. 'We are the mid Lowland people. We live here in the forest. My name is Heron. I am leader of this tribe. It is not a role I took on unilaterally. This is a democratic unit. I had to win votes from the others in order to achieve this position. We believe in equality so we share everything. As you can see we are not wealthy, but you are welcome to join our tribe and stay here with us.'

Heron paused before adding in a sympathetic tone, 'but I have to tell you Zoe, I cannot see a way in which you can ever get back to your own time and your own people.'

'What do you mean by my own time?' Zoe queried. 'What year is this?'

'It's 3015,' answered Heron. 'You've travelled a thousand years into your future.'

'A thousand years,' echoed Zoe. 'I didn't think the time vortex would actually take me to a different period in time. Well, certainly not one this far into the future anyway. Tell me, do you have time travel in this millennium?'

Heron shook his head.

'I'm afraid not,' he said. 'We don't even have electricity or any other source of energy or power.'

Zoe felt her hopes fading at these words, but nonetheless tried to summon up a little of her normal determination. *There must be some way I can get back,* she thought. *I just need time to suss out the situation. I'm not going to give up.*

She turned to Heron. 'Thanks,' she said. 'It would

be good to stay here, but I'm afraid I will probably drive you all mad as I have so many questions.'

Heron smiled. 'Save them for later,' he said. 'We need to sleep for now. We rise early in the morning.'

He jerked his head towards a young girl with straggly, matted, dirty blonde hair. 'You can move in with Lake over there,' he said. 'She has room in her house.'

Lake smiled at Zoe, beckoning her over. She was dressed in a home-made full length skirt. It was anybody's guess as to the original colour, as the material was now badly faded. It was also shabby and very grubby. The scruffy lumpy sweater she wore as an accompaniment to the skirt was full of holes. This too was badly faded. Zoe could see that at one time it had been patterned with alternating thin yellow and black hoops. These were now almost invisible to the eye as well as being covered in dirt. She couldn't help but think that close up the garment gave Lake the appearance of a rather bedraggled and sickly bee or wasp.

Zoe followed Lake as she led the way to the tumbledown shack that passed as her home. Once inside Lake gave her an old blanket and a small cloth bag filled with leaves and chunks of rough wool.

'Here,' she said. 'You can use this as a pillow. There's plenty of room for you to sleep over there.'

Lake pointed to a dark corner away from the shack entrance. Zoe – feeling very tired and emotional after her recent experience – took the items offered, mumbled her thanks, then prostrated herself on the ground in the spot indicated by Lake, who lay down on her own blanket just a few metres away. Despite her tiredness Zoe couldn't get to sleep. It wasn't just the hardness of the bare ground that served as a floor that kept Zoe awake, her mind was racing as it worked overtime trying to come to terms with her current situation. She wasn't helped by a deepening feeling of depression as she wrestled with the thought that she might never get home and would probably have to spend the rest of her life in this unknown, unattractive environment.

Zoe did sleep eventually, but it was fitful. Her dreams were filled with disturbing images of Zak Araz, her family, her friends, and a group of monkeys – all swirling around in a whirling black void. They flitted through her subconscious mind like patterns in some cataclysmic kaleidoscope.

On awakening next morning Zoe found herself alone in the hut. She could hear voices and other sounds of activity from outside so she got up and wandered out.

Lake was standing in the middle of the clearing with two other people. When she saw Zoe she came across to talk to her. 'Did you sleep okay?' Lake asked.

Zoe nodded, answering 'Yes thanks … eventually.'

'Come on,' said Lake brightly, 'I'll show you around our little village.'

Zoe trailed behind as Lake, after introducing her to everyone, led the way down the track to the river.

'This is where we wash and bathe,' Lake explained. She turned, pointing to a nearby clump of bushes, adding, 'We use those for other ablutions and toileting.'

Zoe nodded her understanding. She asked, 'What is this place?'

'It's the forest,' replied Lake.

'No,' said Zoe. 'I don't mean that. I mean what forest? What town? What area of the country? I assume we are still in England?'

Lake smiled. 'Yes we are,' she said. 'But it's not the England you know, or remember. We are in an area called Lowlands, which is all that's left of the original British Isles. It stretches from where Central England used to be to a point just north of the Pennines. There is no North East anymore, or Lake District either. Well I suppose you *could* say there is, but it's actually all one big lake now. Scotland is no more than a small group of islands, as is Wales. The coastal boundaries on the east and west sides have been squeezed as the sea has risen, resulting in land/sea borders now being much further inland. A lot of what you might remember as the British Isles has long since disappeared. The South East, West Country, and East Anglia have all gone as well.'

'What about London?' Zoe asked. 'Does that still exist?'

Lake grabbed Zoe's hand as she spoke, pulling her through the trees until they reached a small open field surrounded by more woodland. 'There,' she said, pointing upwards into the distance.

Zoe's eyes followed the line of Lake's finger, settling on the object targeted by the digit. It was the large sphere that she'd first noticed on the previous evening when it was all lit up. It now hung in the sky like an enormous silver ball. Zoe stared at it intently. She was fascinated by both its presence, and its proximity to Earth.

'What is it?' she asked Lake.

'That's the South,' was the answer.

Zoe looked puzzled. 'The South?' she queried. 'I don't understand.'

'Well,' Lake began. 'It's all to do with climate change … oh and I guess wealth and greed too. My father said it started with global warming which was aided by human waste and selfishness. Then came a thing called fracking, which he said involved drilling into the earth to inject liquid at very high pressure. This broke up rocks so that gas sources would be revealed.

'That practice didn't help at all. The land became unstable. There were lots of floods. Eventually, large parts of the country disappeared underwater. The rich powerful people in London and the south – I think from the area that used to be called the Home Counties – decided to break away from the rest of the UK. They secured Government finance along with technological support and expertise, until they managed to make their own planet. Well they call it a planet, but I guess it might equally be called a space station as it's artificially constructed. Anyway, whatever it is, it's up there in the sky. That's London and the south, but it's just called the South. It's now the home of rich people and working professionals, some of whom actually lived in the north until they joined forces with the southerners and conspired together to build their dream world.'

Zoe was amazed. 'How can you make your own planet?' she asked.

'It was to do with something called Higgs-Bosun and particle physics,' replied Lake. 'I don't really understand, but I think you might remember the start of it, as it was about a thousand years ago. Some scientists had a thing called the Hadron Collider with which they were trying to find the particle that created the Universe, or the Earth or something like that. They did so too. Since then scientists have carried on experimenting over the years. Apparently, it is now relatively easy to create planets.'

Zoe nodded. 'I do remember Higgs-Bosun,' she replied.

Lake smiled. 'All of the rich countries in the World have their own planets now. I said you wouldn't recognise our World, didn't I?'

'How do the planets stay up there?' Zoe asked.

'I'm not really sure,' Lake replied. 'But you must have had space stations in your time, so I guess they use the same technique. Keeping them within the limits of gravity must also help I guess, so I assume gravity holds them in place. In any case planets have their own gravity ... don't they?'

'I've no idea,' said Zoe, shaking her head. 'I learnt about both Newton and Einstein's theories of gravity when I was in school, but I've long since forgotten them. Not that I could ever really understand them anyway.' She smiled at Lake, then asked 'Did you get all of your knowledge in school?'

'Goodness, no!' said Lake emphatically. 'There are no schools in Lowlands. There haven't been any for a long time. I learned what I know from my parents – as does everyone else here. But some parents are better than others at passing on information and mine were very good.'

'What about work?' Zoe raised another question.

'There is no work in Lowlands, well at least no paid work,' Lake answered. 'We are the underclass … the forgotten people. No one wants to know about us. We are an embarrassment to the Government. We are not allowed to work even if work was available. We cannot leave Lowlands, so we have to look out for each other.'

'Surely the Government help with benefits, food, finding somewhere to live? Surely they help people raise and educate their children?' Zoe queried. 'Otherwise how are they going to get anyone from here to vote for them?'

Lake shook her head. She looked half-pityingly at Zoe before giving her response.

'The Government don't pay benefits or give any support to anyone … let alone people in Lowlands. We have no schooling because they say we don't need it. Also Lowlanders are forbidden to have children … as for voting, there is no official voting anymore, certainly not in Lowlands.'

Zoe was stunned by what she was hearing. She stood there with her mouth opening and closing like a fish stranded on a river bank, as she tried to form the words she wanted to say. Lake waited patiently for her to speak.

When she did so all Zoe said was, 'How long has this been happening?'

'Since long before I was born,' said Lake, 'probably for a few hundred years.'

'You said that Lowlanders are forbidden to have children,' said Zoe, finally finding her flow. 'That can't be true. You and the other people I've seen in the camp are all young. Some are still in their teens, so you must all have been children quite recently. How can that be if what you say is true?'

Lake gave Zoe the semblance of a smile, but it bore the weariness of someone who had already seen too much of life and wanted a rest from it.

'It's a long story,' she began, 'but I'll try to be as brief as I can in my explanation. Many many years ago Lowlands became the dumping place for all of the people that the Government hated. They were good people really, caring, kind, helpful, but not what the Government wanted. They wanted well educated, healthy, intelligent, and rich people – or at least fairly well-off people – who could work in professions that would make lots of money. People who would work hard at anything without asking questions or showing dissent. People who would look out for themselves and their families only, and not care about anyone else.

'The Government helped these people with jobs, houses and tax benefits. They were well rewarded for their work and their continued support of the Government. The economy became strong. As a result, everyone got richer and richer. Banks and businesses thrived so much that bankers along with the wealthiest businessmen also created their own planet. That's it there.'

Lake pointed to the smaller sphere alongside the South that Zoe had also seen last evening. She continued with her story as Zoe's gaze settled briefly on the miniature planet.

'Meanwhile, people in Lowlands adopted a lifestyle in which they grew their own crops and vegetables. They hunted for food too. Locally we have the river for fishing. There are also a number of animals living in the woods. Food is plentiful all over Lowlands.

'Even though they lived rough, communities developed and thrived as generations passed. Then the Government in the South got wind of what was happening. They must have seen it as a threat to their stability, despite Lowlanders having no way of getting to the South. Soldiers were sent down to hunt Lowlanders, who were rounded up and imprisoned. Then a group of surgeons came down. They performed operations on all of them, men as well as women … sterilisation I think it was called … it meant they couldn't have children.

'When the soldiers and surgeons went back to their planet, they believed that they'd operated on everyone. They were unaware that some of the Lowlanders had avoided capture by hiding in the forest. These people could still have children and did so, thus continuing to populate Lowlands with fertile inhabitants. We are descendants from those people. Hopefully, we will eventually have our own children too so we can carry on the population line.

'Of course we have to be careful. It gets more difficult as the Government has started to banish Southern people to Lowlands if they have committed a crime or if they are unable to work. Also if they have become financially unstable. When that happens, we tend to keep out of each other's way as we have nothing in common. Besides, the people who have been sent down here can still communicate with the Security Police in the South. If any of these exiles gives information that leads to anyone in Lowlands being captured, they get rewarded by being taken back to live in the South. Lowlands is regularly raided by the Security Police. They hunt for us. If they catch us we are taken up there.' She pointed to the new planet. 'If that happens … no one ever comes back.'

Zoe gave a huge sigh as Lake finished her tale. 'How do they get here?' she asked.

'Sometimes they come down by teleport, sometimes through light beams that they shine onto Lowlands. That's why we thought you'd come down from the South when you suddenly appeared from the skies as we were walking home last night.'

'This is a strange World,' said Zoe. 'It's nothing like I imagined the future would be. I envisaged that a thousand years into my future, everyone would be enjoying the benefits of technology. I thought there would be prosperity, peace and harmony, with no poverty or hatred. This is primitive. It's like going back a thousand years instead of forwards.'

'We're used to it,' sighed Lake. 'We were born into it so it's all we've known, but we do want to make it better and we won't give up. All of the power lies in the South. That's where all of the decisions are made. Our biggest problem – besides having no access to the South – is that we have nothing to help us learn to do things better. We have no technology or books.'

By now the pair had walked full circle. They were almost back at the camp. Zoe could see the crude collection of buildings up ahead. She changed the direction of the conversation by saying. 'Why do you all have unusual names like Heron, Wolf, Vixen, Rainbow, Cloud, and Lake?'

'They aren't unusual to us,' Lake responded. 'We name ourselves after things we find in our environment, creatures or other natural phenomena. It seems quite normal that our names should reflect nature as we live in the forest.'

'Did your parents give you your name?' asked Zoe.

'No. We pick our own when we are still quite young,' said Lake.

'I've only seen young people here,' said Zoe. 'Where are your parents?'

'They're dead,' replied Lake quietly. 'No-one in the current group has any parent who is still alive. Life expectancy is short. We have no doctors, no medicines, no form of heating except our clothes and blankets … oh, and the open fires we make. Although food is plentiful it is also seasonal. Our diet is dependent upon our crop growth, the availability of animals we hunt, also the fish stocks. All of these are variable as they are vulnerable to severe weather patterns – especially harsh winters – as are the seasonal fruits we eat. Our diet is often frugal. People die from illness, from cold, from starvation or malnutrition. Sometimes the fruit we eat poisons us. Sometimes our hunters get killed by the animals they hunt. Or they might drown whilst fishing in the river. It is a dangerous existence for much of the time. Very few people in Lowlands live beyond the age of thirty-five.'

CHAPTER THREE

Zoe found it hard to believe what Lake was saying. In her mind she saw a picture of people dying at what to her seemed a very young age. She tried to imagine what it must be like to hardly have time to really get to know your parents, and to perhaps never have known your grandparents.

She looked at Lake, then said, 'I'm sorry.'

'Thanks, but no need,' Lake replied. 'It's a fact of life. We are all aware of our limitations. I am twenty-two. My hope is that I can live for at least another eighteen years so I can carry on the fight, and also raise any children I might be lucky enough to have. I'd love for them to be able to continue what we've started down here. However the reality is that I might get killed at any time or I might die naturally in my thirties.

There was silence for a while. It was broken by another question from Zoe. 'How can animals kill people?' she asked.

'What?' Lake's response conveyed her bewilderment at Zoe's words.

'You said people sometimes get killed by animals that live in the forest,' explained Zoe. 'As I remember it, Britain's mammals were hardly killers. To my knowledge foxes, badgers and deer don't kill humans. Well occasionally they do by accident perhaps, but extremely rarely.'

Lake gave another deep sigh. 'If only it were that simple,' she said. 'The forests are full of all different kinds of animals these days. It's not just foxes, badgers and rabbits. Creatures such as big cats, wolves, apes, and large snakes are now inhabitants of Lowlands. Over the years they have either escaped or been released by zoos, safari parks, or private collectors and have reproduced to the extent that they are now native to this island. We have packs of wild dogs roaming around the forest too. They are the descendants of domesticated animals that have been abandoned to their own devices. Different breeds of dogs, that in the past either fought or kept away from each other, have in the course of time joined forces. They now form large hunting packs which are sometimes big enough to take down and kill any animal, irrespective of size. Tame animals no longer exist in Lowlands. Every creature is a potential killer. There are even herds of cows and horses that have been living in the wild long enough to revert to their most primeval instincts.

'All of these creatures have long since lost any connection or empathy with humans. This is nature in the wild, red in tooth and claw. We humans are now well and truly part of the food chain, seen as both predator and prey. In fact it's not only the animals that you need to watch out for, some of the humans have become quite tribal and primitive too. There are groups out there that are cruel and dangerous. So beware Zoe, never venture into the forest alone. You have no idea what might be in there waiting for you.'

Zoe shuddered at the thought. She was liking this World less and less with every minute she was in it. The thought that she was now here, possibly for the rest of her life – which by all accounts would be far shorter than she could expect to live back in her own time – filled her with dread and despondency. She told herself firmly that she had to find a way out somehow.

'What about buildings?' Zoe asked, recovering some of her composure. 'Are there none left? Houses, libraries, museums, factories, shops? There must be something?'

'Nothing of note,' said Lake. 'I can remember when I was a very little girl I did see some ruins, you know, bricks, shells of buildings, foundations, but there were only a few around here. These have now mostly fallen down, rotted away or been submerged and lost within the density of trees, bushes and undergrowth. I haven't seen anything that resembles a building for some years, although there may well be some building remains in other parts of Lowlands, unless the soldiers have destroyed them to stop people from utilising them. My parents told me that my grandparents once found an old factory building filled with different kinds of material from which they were able to make clothes. I'm still wearing some of the things they made, but I'm afraid they are not going to last for much longer.'

The smell of roast meat suddenly wafted on the air. Zoe noticed that she and Lake were back at the point from where they had started their tour. 'That smells good,' said Zoe.

Lake smiled. As they entered the circle of shacks Zoe could see an animal carcass being turned slowly over the flames of the big open fire by a youngish boy. She couldn't tell what kind of animal it was, but as she approached the sight of a deer skin with fresh blood on it made her think that venison was on the menu tonight.

'Badger caught it,' said one of the girls. 'It's a big one so there's enough for everyone.'

Zoe sat with Lake as she ate with the group. It was the first time she had tasted venison. She liked it, even though it had a stronger flavour than she was used to. Venison wasn't the sort of thing her mother would buy. Her parents' tastes were quite conservative and conventional when it came to food, with traditional roast beef, lamb, or chicken the limit of their culinary creations.

Zoe felt the tears pricking her eyes at the thought of her parents and her home. A lump formed in her throat, making it hard for her to swallow the food. She hadn't always got on well with her family. To be honest, there had been times when they really got on her nerves, but she wished she was with them now. They would all be dead by now. She wondered how they had coped with her disappearance. *Had they been told what really happened to her? Did they think she was dead? Had they thought about her? Had they missed her as much as she missed them?*

'Not eating?' said a voice from alongside her, breaking into her thoughts. 'Don't you like the food?'

Zoe turned to see another of the girls to whom she'd been introduced when out with Lake. Zoe remembered she was called Rainbow.

'Just thinking about home,' said Zoe, her thoughts quickly snapping back to the here and now as she answered the question. 'I do like the food though, it's delicious.'

'It must be difficult for you,' said Rainbow, 'being in a strange World so far into the future where you don't know anyone, and you know nothing about the place you're in. I'd be scared rigid if it was me.'

'It is difficult,' said Zoe. 'And yes I *am* scared.' She took a bite from the lump of meat she held in her hand and began to chew it slowly.

'Try not to worry,' said Rainbow. 'We'll look out for you and help you through.' She placed a hand on Zoe's arm and smiled.

Zoe smiled back. 'Thanks,' she said. 'It's Rainbow isn't it? That's a lovely name.'

'I picked it myself,' Rainbow replied. 'I was four years old and we'd just had a massive thunderstorm. I remember I was really scared. The thunder was so loud. The lightning flashes were so bright and ferocious that I clung tightly to my mother. I honestly thought the world was going to end. I couldn't look at the rain or lightning anymore so I buried my head in my mother's bosom. She stroked my hair and sang to me until it was all over. Then, when I lifted my head from her chest after the storm, I looked at the sky and there was this beautiful arc of colours stretching from one side of the earth to the other. It was so magnificent, so calming. I was awestruck. I felt so relieved and happy that I cried. I pointed to the arc. My mother told me it was a rainbow so I said "that's what I want to be called. I want my name to be Rainbow". So it is.'

Zoe saw tears in Rainbow's eyes as she recounted

her memories of her mother. It did nothing to help ease Zoe's internal aching to be with her own family. Rainbow blinked her tears away as Zoe squeezed her hand. The pair ate the rest of the meal in silence, each deep in their own private thoughts.

It was Zoe who broke the spell of emotionally induced muteness. 'How do you cope with living in such primitive conditions?' she asked.

'We know no different,' came the reply from Rainbow. 'To us … well certainly to me, it's something I've always done and it's all I know, so I just get on with it.'

'Lake said that there are no schools in Lowlands, yet everyone I've spoken to is articulate and knowledgeable about the place you live in and about your history. How is that possible? You must learn these things, but how?'

Zoe was keen to find out as much as she could about this strange World, but she was also worried that her new found companions would soon tire of her endless questions and ask her to shut up or to leave, so she added 'Please tell me if my constant questioning is becoming a nuisance.'

Rainbow shook her head, smiling as she did so. 'It's okay,' she said. 'I'd be just the same. I don't mind, honestly … I guess it's helpful to you as you're not from these times. Anyway, when you've done I've got loads of questions I want to ask you about your World. But to answer your last question, our knowledge and learning has been passed down from generation to generation by parents and other adults. That's what we'll do with our own children too. It's important to know why things happen and what changes have taken place in your environment. After all, this is our home. It's all we've got. We have to make sure it survives. We have to keep on trying to change it for the better. Then one day, hopefully, either our children or our children's children may get the chance to join with the people up there ...' Rainbow pointed to the Southern orb, '...as one planet and one race.'

For the rest of the day Zoe hung around with Rainbow, who showed her the art of skinning animals. She demonstrated how to remove pelts from carcasses before making them into clothes and shoes. True to her word, Rainbow bombarded Zoe with questions. Zoe told her all she knew about what life was like on planet Earth in the year 2015. Then, as much as she could remember about the previous history of the planet.

During the evening Zoe sat around the fire with everyone, eating and chatting. That night she slept in Lake's shack again. She found sleep hard to come by once more, so she lay in the dark listening to the noises of the forest. The faint sound of Lake's even breathing arose from the far end of the room, mingling with the shrieks, growls, screams and cries that filled the air outside. Zoe shivered slightly as the animal calls echoed back and forth, resonating across the night sky. She thought about the variety of creatures that Lake said now inhabited the woods. Creatures which – in the cloak of darkness provided by the night time hours – sprang into life, becoming animated and dangerous as they prowled the forest, hunting their prey in the blackness.

Zoe recognized some animal calls from her own

World. It gave her a small crumb of comfort to know there were still sounds that were familiar to her. But there were many more nocturnal noises she found to be completely alien. These unfamiliar howls, roars and barks filled her with a sense of dread, as well as an overwhelming sense of isolation and loneliness.

Zoe must have drifted off to sleep at some stage, because she awoke with a start as she felt a movement at the foot of her makeshift bed. She peered into the darkness but couldn't see anything. Her body tensed. She could hear her heart thumping out a loud rhythm, as she strained eyes and ears for a glimpse or a sound that might confirm her worst fears.

After a few minutes Zoe decided she must have been mistaken. She felt the rigidness in her body begin to subside. In an attempt to relax and get back to sleep she rolled onto her side to get more comfortable. As she did so her heart almost leapt from her body. At the side of her bed she saw a white face with black lips and hollow black eyes. *Kazzaar!* The name sprang immediately into Zoe's head as the face moved closer to hers. She tried to move away but her body was paralysed. She couldn't move! Zoe opened her mouth to scream but nothing came out. Her breathing quickened sharply. She felt as if she was choking as the face – now huge – loomed above her. She was helpless. The face was so close she could feel hot breath on her cheeks. She closed her eyes, waiting.

Suddenly Zoe's survival instincts kicked in, breaking her terror-induced paralysis and sending her body into a paroxysm of panic. Her torso began to shake violently. She thrashed her arms wildly as she tried to beat off her assailant.

Zoe found her voice as she flailed about. 'No! No! No! ... Get away from me! Leave me alone!' she screamed.

A hand closed on her shoulder. She screamed again.

'Zoe! Zoe! Are you alright? Wake up! What's the matter?'

Zoe sat up, eyes wide open in fright. Lake was shaking her by the shoulders. There was no-one else around. 'You scared me,' gasped Lake. 'I heard you shouting, then when I looked over to your bed you were waving your arms and bouncing all over the place as if you were fighting with someone. I thought you were ill or hurt.'

Zoe gulped in the fresh night air as she struggled to catch her breath. She realised that she'd just been dreaming. Even though she'd thought she was awake when she saw the face, it must have been a dream. Yet it had seemed so real.

'Bad dream,' she said. 'It was really scary, something from my past. Do you remember I told you about the Soul Snatcher? Well I dreamed he was here beside my bed and he was coming for me. I saw his face as clearly as I'm seeing yours now. It was horrible. I'm still shaking.'

Lake sat down beside Zoe. She gave her a hug. 'It's okay,' Lake whispered 'There's no one here but you and I. Here, have a drink. It might help calm your nerves.'

Lake handed Zoe a water bottle. Zoe took a long swig from it. She could feel her body settling now. In her mind she tried again to tell herself that what she'd just experienced *was* a dream. Yet it had felt so real that deep inside Zoe wasn't entirely convinced it hadn't genuinely happened. Lake hadn't indicated that she'd seen Kazzaar when she'd looked across at Zoe thrashing about, so Zoe decided it would probably be best to try and forget the incident.

Turning to Lake she said, 'It's probably because I'm a bit unsettled right now. You know … with being out of my comfort zone. My brain has brought up an image of something that scared me in the past and planted it in my dream. It doesn't have enough information yet about what I might be scared of here, so it's dug up a scary thing from way back. I have to admit that I've been a bit worried about what might be out there in the forest. I've also been wondering where Kazzaar has got to, so I guess my brain has put the two things together and come up with that nightmare.'

Zoe smiled as Lake hugged her again. 'Goodness knows what it will conjure up in my head when it does find something that *really* scares me while I'm here,' she concluded.

CHAPTER FOUR

The rest of the night passed peacefully enough for Zoe despite the fitful uneasy sleep that followed her nocturnal terrors. Tiredness and lethargy accompanied her waking, so she reluctantly arose before venturing outside to look for Lake, who was nowhere to be seen.

Zoe decided to wander down to the river to wash herself in the cool flowing waters, thinking along the way about what she would do for the rest of the day, which stretched long and empty in her mind. The idea that this was how her life would be from now on added more grief to her already miserable mood. Depression hung around her so thickly she felt she could easily slice it up if she only had a knife.

Back at the camp after her ablutions Zoe breakfasted on fruit, after which she set off to find Lake or Rainbow so she could help with whatever it was they were doing. On leaving the camp she headed across the clearing towards the far side of the forest.

Once inside the forest Zoe noticed how dark it was. It was cold too. The trees were much closer together here. They were also much taller than those in the area where the settlement lay. Looking up she saw how closely the branches intertwined. The foliage was thick and heavy, blocking out not only the spring sunshine but most of the daylight too. The woodland was eerily silent. In fact the whole landscape gave off an ambience of spookiness that caused Zoe to shiver. She could feel goose pimples rising on her skin, formed partly from cold and partly from anxiety.

Zoe followed the rough pathway as it wound between the trees. Every now and then she stopped to call out. 'Lake? ... Rainbow? ... Are you there? ... Is ANYONE there?'

On the third occasion she called out, Zoe thought she heard a reply. It was very faint – almost inaudible – but she had no reason to doubt her ears. She'd definitely heard something. There were no recognisable words in the response, just a muffled, guttural noise. The sound came from somewhere to her right. Zoe changed course, heading in the direction of the cry. She continued to call out as she walked. Each call was followed by a similar rough brusque reply, deep, rumbling and growing louder as she got nearer. Zoe became a little more anxious at the lack of clarity in the responding cries when she reflected that they didn't sound much like Lake or Rainbow. But she convinced herself that the density of the trees might cause some distortion, or that any of the males from the group could be shouting the response.

Zoe was now deep inside the forest. The return calls were quite loud, suggesting she was near to the group. She stopped briefly to listen, aware of a tiny voice inside her head that was telling her to go back. Zoe – convinced she would soon meet up with the others – chose to ignore the advice. In an effort to be positive she urged herself forward.

It had grown extremely dark in this part of the forest by now, even though it was still morning. Zoe could barely see the path as it wound between the trees ahead of her. A mist had descended too. It covered the treetops, spreading long grey fingers downwards through the branches as if reaching out for something – or someone – to grab hold of. There was no birdsong here, nor any sound at all except for the occasional creak of a tree swaying in the breeze that had suddenly sprung up. Even the two beautifully patterned butterflies that danced together in front of Zoe looked somehow drab and out of place. Their now subdued colouring added to the grimness and eeriness of the surroundings.

Visibility had shrunk to less than twenty metres. Zoe called out again, but this time there was no answer. There was just the sound of the wind whining and moaning through the trees, accompanied by the swishing and rustling of leaves and grasses. The feeling of apprehension in her stomach gradually turned into a full-blown fear that gripped her insides ever tighter. The voice in her head was still nagging at her. This time Zoe listened. She decided it would now be wise to go back to the camp rather than continue her quest – however near she might be to finding her recently made friends.

She turned, retracing her steps as she began the return journey. Her pace quickened as she headed back in the direction from whence she came. In the grey mist everything looked different. Zoe's imagination began to play tricks with her mind – producing more heart stopping moments – with each illusion adding to the terror that was building up inside as it threatened to engulf the poor girl.

Whorls and knots on tree trunks swiftly became faces – grotesquely gnarled, distorted gargoyles – that leered and grimaced at Zoe. Branches were now hands with fingers that poked and pointed as she passed, while twisted tendrils of tree roots took on the form of slithering, sliding serpents that seemed to come alive with the sole purpose of tripping and trapping her.

Panic rose in Zoe's chest, quickly climbing upwards until it stuck in her throat causing her to gag. She stood still with eyes closed, breathing deeply for a moment or two in an effort to calm herself as she tried to tune her mind into more rational thoughts. When she opened them again she caught sight of a movement in the long grass about ten metres ahead of her.

It's just the wind, she reassured herself. *Stay calm and concentrate on following the path home.*

Zoe's attempt at being brave dissolved like ice in boiling water when she saw the grass moving again, this time away to her right. Almost simultaneously the grass to her left began to wave and sway too. Zoe couldn't help but notice that both movements were diametrically opposite in direction.

That's strange, she thought. *The wind can't be blowing in two different directions at the same time. Or can it?*

All alone in the dark deserted forest, Zoe was now extremely scared. She was once more aware of her heart pounding like a steam hammer beneath the old, worn and very thin sweater she had borrowed from Lake. She felt the cold – yet contrastingly clammy – hand of fear tighten its grip on her body, forcing the hairs on the back of her neck to lift themselves until they bristled and prickled like quills on a warring porcupine.

Zoe began to walk slowly forward but was stopped in her tracks by something shining in the long grass ahead of her. Zoe peered in the direction of the glinting light, trying to fathom out what was causing it. She soon realised that whatever was glistening within the dark blades of grass wasn't just one single thing. Whatever it was, there were lots of them, little lights sparkling brightly like highly polished gems. It was as if each strand of grass was covered in tiny raindrops which were sparkling in the sunlight. Except there was no sunlight. It may have been dark inside the forest, but whichever way Zoe looked she was confronted with row upon row of twinkling lights.

Zoe's fear temporarily gave way to curiosity. She tried to get her thoughts in order. She couldn't work out what the gleaming buttons were – or why they would be in the forest. *Maybe it is some kind of genetically modified grass that glows in the dark. Or perhaps the light is caused by colonies of insects, like glow worms – after all I'm a thousand years into the future and I have no idea of life forms or scientific advances that could make such things possible.*

Peering intently through the gloom, Zoe tried to acclimatise her eyes so she could properly identify the source of this sparkly, shiny phenomenon that had suddenly appeared before her.

However, when her eyes did finally pierce the surrounding darkness sufficiently for her brain to provide an answer, Zoe found no comfort in the image that was planted into her mind. In fact her fear levels increased substantially, as she realised the truth, sending her body into convulsions of terror.

The bright shining lights weren't raindrops or buttons. They weren't insects either, or even special grasses. They were eyes! Zoe could now see that each sparkling gem came in matching pairs. *But whose eyes were they? And why were there so many pairs of them?* Zoe's thoughts ran deep. All at once, the full realisation of her plight struck her. But it didn't fill her with confidence, nor offer any hope that she could get out of this situation alive. Her position was very clear. She was in imminent danger, standing all alone in a misty grey forest – lost within a strange unknown World one thousand years into her future – surrounded by creatures with eyes that burned like bright orange/yellow circles of fire ... with every single one of those fiery orbs very firmly fixed on her.

CHAPTER FIVE

Zoe stood stock still, breathing hard. She tried to keep the short, sharp gasps as quiet as possible as she considered her situation. She had no idea what kind of creatures were watching her as she could still only see their eyes.

This unfamiliar forest was home to any number of wild beasts Zoe had only ever previously seen in a zoo or on television. She knew there could be any species of animal within the pack that was closing in on her. Zoe's heartbeat leapt off the decibel scale as she surveyed the scenario that was unfolding around her, the loud thumping sound revealing the terror she was feeling inside. She was convinced the animals could hear it too. Her brain still wrestled with the question as to which creatures they might be. At the same time she was scared of what the answer might be.

In a matter of seconds Zoe discovered the truth. She could see several shapes – dark shapes – moving slowly towards her. She nervously watched the outlines – shadowy bodies that exuded menace – as they drew closer, creeping, slinking, crouching and crawling. The silhouetted bodies moved in unison, carefully choreographing their movements, until they had formed an impenetrable barrier around her. Their actions succeeded in closing off the pathway and imprisoning Zoe inside their trap. Zoe felt the freezing fingers of fear clamp firmly around her insides. Suddenly her brain lit up as it recognised her would be assailants. It quickly flashed its message in the form of a loud, clear warning. *Beware! They are dogs! Wild dogs!*

Wide eyed and totally helpless, Zoe stared about her. It was true. They *were* dogs. Not all the same size or breed, but that was unimportant. It was a pack of dogs and Zoe knew full well that packs of animals were dangerous. She remembered what Lake had told her about domesticated dogs that had become wild. She was now looking at a large group of them. She could see Terriers, standing alongside what must have started out as Bulldogs that had now evolved into even bigger, fiercer animals through cross-breeding. Zoe's eyes scanned across the group, picking out other breeds. She saw Alsatians, Wolfhounds, Great Danes, Corgis, Poodles, and the odd Jack Russell. These silent, would-be assassins that formed this hungry canine pack had successfully manoeuvred themselves into a position whereby they had Zoe well and truly cornered. Furthermore, it appeared that she was the main item on their dinner menu.

One of the dogs began to growl. Zoe recognised the sound as being the call she'd been following through the forest. The snarling got louder before becoming a bark. Other dogs joined in until, instead of a band of patient secretive stalkers, they transformed into a vicious unified hunting pack. Moving as one, they closed in rapidly on the helpless girl.

The dogs were clearly relishing what was to come, each one showing fangs that dripped wet with saliva at the thought of the feast that lay ahead. The yellow eyes that had appeared to Zoe as twinkling fairy lights were now blood red. The gore glazed eyes burnt with a deadly fire, as the animals closed in for the kill that would provide their food for the day.

Now they came! Leaping, running, growling and barking. Each one competing with the others in an attempt to win the race to strike down their petrified prey, in a ferocious, brutal, gory contest that would end with the winner tearing off the first piece of flesh from Zoe's young body. Such an act would begin the process of satisfying the hunger of the entire pack, ending only when there was nothing left but bones.

Zoe wanted to run. But where to? There was nowhere to run. She was hemmed in on all sides by the dogs, which were now so close that she could smell their foul breath. Zoe prepared herself to die. *Is this the way my life ends?* she thought. *In a strange World in the future, and with no one in my family ever knowing what happened to me?*

A tear fell from Zoe's eye. She closed her eyelids tight shut as she braced herself for the first of what she knew would be many vicious and painful bites, hoping that one of the creatures would execute a killer blow very quickly, so she wouldn't have to suffer the long excruciating agony or the shock of being eaten alive.

As Zoe – terrified, cowering and unseeing – stood there awaiting her grisly fate, a mighty roaring noise suddenly rent the air, drowning out the din from the dog pack. The roaring was accompanied by the sound of snapping branches and pounding, thudding footsteps. Zoe opened her eyes to see what was happening. Then immediately wished she hadn't. She didn't know which was worse, being torn apart by the wild dog pack or being ripped to pieces and eaten by what she now saw crashing through the trees as it raced full pelt in her direction.

Zoe did a double take just to make sure. She couldn't believe what she was seeing as she stood there terror-stricken at the sight of the huge creature that was thundering through the trees towards her, sending twigs and branches flying everywhere as it exploded into the clearing. It was an enormous brown bear!

It seemed that the dogs couldn't believe it either. Every one of them ceased the leaping, running, growling assault charge – abandoning the snapping, biting disorderly procession that had fought to get a taste of Zoe's flesh. The snarling pack turned as one, temporarily discarding their intended quarry. Collectively they charged headlong toward the rampaging bear. The dogs may have fought with each other for the right to rip Zoe to pieces, but none of them intended to share or give up their meal to this marauding interloper. This ursine scavenger, who had so rudely gate-crashed and intruded on their dinner party, had no claim on their dinner. He needed to be driven off.

The dogs were brave and fearless. Driven by ravenous hunger, they attacked the huge brown creature. But despite their numerical advantage they were no match for the bear, which stood up on its hind legs fighting off the canine onslaught with flailing extended claws, strong wide jaws and gnashing teeth. Its thick fur coat absorbed everything that the dogs could offer, without showing any sign of injury or even disturbance.

Zoe was fascinated. She stood watching the battle that had unfolded in front of her, marvelling at the bear's strength whilst at the same time wondering what a bear was doing roaming the English countryside. She assumed it was one of the escaped wild animals that Lake had talked about, yet she couldn't quite get her head around the fact that such creatures lived in the same forest that she would be using regularly while she was in Lowlands. Somehow it was unreal.

Zoe's mind snapped sharply back into focus as the dog pack began to thin out before dispersing altogether. Some of the creatures lay dead or injured, while others still fought. But the majority were making their escape into the surrounding trees, appetites now supressed and all thoughts of tearing Zoe to shreds now expunged from their heads. As the pack began to disintegrate, scattering to all parts of the forest, Zoe was suddenly alert to the new danger – the bear. If it decided to attack her she would have no chance of survival. She had to make her escape quickly while the beast was still occupied with the final few dogs. With a last glance at the still upright bear, cuffing and clawing at the remaining handful of fighting, biting canines, Zoe ran, desperately hoping that the path she was on would lead her back to camp.

It did, and when she rushed into the village

compound Lake was waiting. Anxiety was registered all over her face.

She sighed with relief as Zoe approached. 'Thank goodness you are safe,' Lake gasped, giving Zoe a big hug, then quickly pulling away embarrassed. 'I've looked everywhere for you, where have you been?' The words tumbled rapidly from Lake's lips. 'You haven't been seen in camp since this morning so I guessed you'd gone for a walk or something. Then we heard the dogs. The barking was so loud and fervent we assumed they were chasing something … I was scared Zoe, I thought it was you. I thought you were dead. I had visions of you being killed, perhaps eaten, and it would have been my fault because I left you alone this morning as I thought you might need to sleep. I'm so sorry, Zoe.'

Touching Lake's arm, Zoe smiled. 'It's kind of you to worry about me but I'm okay, Lake. Even if I wasn't, it wouldn't be your fault. I'm a big girl. Legally I'm an adult in my World. I have to take responsibility for myself.'

'But you're in our World now,' Lake responded. 'A World that's very strange for you. A World that's filled with hidden dangers. We have to look after you. You're one of us now.'

For a brief moment Lake's words brought back the feelings of despair and loneliness that Zoe had experienced earlier. She'd had a difficult day. Besides, she was feeling quite emotional after her narrow escape. Zoe felt tears pricking at her eyes again. Making an effort to blink them back, she told Lake all about her day in the forest, ending her story with her escape from the dogs and the bear.

'A bear?' questioned Lake, when Zoe had finished her tale. 'Are you sure it was a bear?'

Zoe nodded. 'No question,' she said. 'It was brown and very, very big.'

'That's new,' said Lake, anxiety returning to her face. 'We've never had a bear around here before. I wonder where it's come from. I'd better tell the others so we can decide what to do. We don't want it wandering into the camp.'

After Lake had reported Zoe's adventure to Heron, she and Zoe spent what was left of the day in the camp. Zoe got fed up of relating her story to everyone who called her over to ask her about it. But she understood that they were curious. They were probably more than a little scared themselves about this new, dangerous creature that had appeared in their environment.

'We'll have to be extra careful,' said Heron. 'If there *is* a bear in the woods it could mean trouble and not only when we venture into the forest. Bears don't stick to woodland, they roam about a lot. When they're hungry they invade human territory. No one should go into the forest alone. We should make some weapons and take steps to make our camp safer. We need to mount a guard all of the time. I suggest we can take it in turns to keep watch. Perhaps we ought to dig a trench around the camp, and cover it with branches and grass to form a trap for the bear if it invades the settlement. At the very least it would provide us with some sort of warning, as well as allow a bit of time for escape, should the bear fall into it.'

Everyone set to work immediately and soon the trap

was set. A wide, deep trench, fully disguised, that encircled the camp. A small portable bridge, far too weak to take the bear's weight, was laid across the trap so that people in the settlement could still go about their usual business. A rota indicating times for guard duties was also organised.

Zoe's name was on the rota. She had helped to dig the trench and make weapons too. It was hard work – especially with the primitive tools available in the camp. Her hands bled as she worked, but Zoe ignored the blood, the blisters, and her aching body until the tasks were completed. By the end of the day she began to feel for the first time as if she belonged in the group.

CHAPTER SIX

Days turned into weeks without any further sightings of the bear. The fear of attack that had cranked up tensions among the residents of the camp subsided as they began to relax again, although everyone still remained watchful. Zoe had become far more settled within the group. She helped with cooking, building, hunting, even making clothes. Her body had become accustomed to the tough manual work, and the skin on her hands had hardened to the point where she felt she had the hands of a builder or a labourer. Her face too had acclimatised to the weather as she spent most of her life outdoors. No one used makeup in Lowlands. "Only the savages in the more aggressive tribes, who use it as war paint," Lake had told her when she asked about it. There were no moisturising creams or oils to keep skin soft. There were no mirrors in the settlement either, so Zoe was unaware of how tanned and toned her body had become.

Although reasonably comfortable in her new life, Zoe was still mindful of a deep ache that remained in her heart. The yearning she'd had for her past existence had lain dormant for a while as she tried to fit into village life. But the latent longing continued to fuel an inner desire for Zoe to be with her family in her own World and time. Every so often this urge to go home would rise up inside, causing her to reflect ever more gloomily on her present predicament. At such times she would struggle to find anything positive in her current situation. Then Lake would find some way of raising Zoe's spirits and Zoe would rediscover her earlier resolve, vowing to get back to her family when she could find an opportunity to do so. She would then carry on with whatever it was she was doing and make the most of her life in Lowlands.

Zoe's changing moods – along with her fluctuating yearning – wasn't helped by the planet South being visible from Lowlands. Every day she was haunted by the sight of the globe suspended in the sky high above her. At night she would sit gazing at it for hours as it glowed with a greenish blue light that she assumed was given off by the illuminated townships of the South. The more she looked at it the more convinced Zoe became that the key that would open her way back home lay somewhere on that man-made planet.

Occasionally she would see shafts of light beamed from the orb, and stretching downwards in a straight line to shine on Lowlands. They always seemed to settle at some point in the nearby forest. She asked Lake about this.

'That's the Southern Security Police,' Lake told her.

'Who are *they*, and what do they do?' asked Zoe.

'They come down at night looking for us,' said Lake 'You remember I told you that the soldiers come down to try to find us? That's the light beam I mentioned.'

'Do they only come at night?' Zoe queried.

'No, as I said before they come in daylight too, but

that's when they use the transporters. We can usually see the light beams, so it gives us time to hide if we need to, but if they use the transporters we get no time or warning.' Lake explained. 'There are hidden locations in Lowlands that serve as transporter stations. We've searched around but so far we've been unable to find any. They are very well camouflaged, but we're hopeful we might stumble across one someday.'

'So there are soldiers *and* Security Police?' queried Zoe.

'No, they are the same thing,' Lake replied. 'I've just got used to calling them soldiers I guess.'

'How do those light beams work?' asked Zoe.

'I'm not sure,' answered Lake. 'But I think they either climb down or slide down inside them. Whichever it is they can get here pretty quickly. If the beams are close by we run and hide as soon as we see them, but why all of the questions? All you have to remember is to avoid them.'

'I guess so,' sighed Zoe. 'But I have this dream, Lake … a dream that one day I'll get back home to my family … what's more, I'm sure that the path to my doing so lies in the South. I *will* do my best to avoid the beams … and the police, but there may come a day when I need both.'

It was Lake's turn to sigh. She squeezed Zoe's hand. In a voice that was choking with emotion, she said. 'Oh Zoe … it must be very hard for you, and while I would love to think that you *can* be with your family again someday, you should know by now that *we* are your family too. Everyone loves you here. They would miss you if you left us. I can understand that you want try to get back, so if you think that going to the South will help you then that's what you have to do. But please … please, don't rush things and please be very careful … you could get seriously hurt, or even killed if you go up there.'

Zoe returned Lake's squeeze, giving her a smile too. 'I'll be careful, I promise,' she said.

Night time brought little in the way of peaceful sleep to Zoe, as her dreams were filled with vivid images of glowing spheres and dark dense forests in which shafts of bright light criss-crossed starless skies of midnight blue. It got worse as the glowing orbs interchanged with images of Kazzaar's grinning face before merging into faceless soldiers who inflicted severe wounds to all parts of her body.

A few days later, Zoe's nightmares became reality as she was awakened from yet another troubled sleep by the sounds of shouting and running feet. At first she thought the bear had invaded the camp. She leapt from her bed and seeing daylight outside, assumed she had overslept. She was about to rush outside when a voice from behind her said 'Come with me, we need to hide.'

It was Lake. She too had been awakened by the noise. Zoe could hear her breathing heavily in the shadows at the rear of the shack. Lake spoke again. 'They've found us,' she whispered. 'We knew they would get lucky one day and this is it. But we do have a plan. Come on, time is of the essence. They'll be down here in a minute.' She reached out, grasping Zoe's hand, before leading her outside.

'Who are *they*?' Zoe croaked hoarsely as the pair emerged into the central clearing inside the camp.

Even as she spoke the answer to her question became obvious. It wasn't daylight after all. The brightness came from two thin shafts of white light illuminating the clearing and the camp. The twin strands of light reached skywards as they traced a path right back to the orb that was the South.

The Southern Security Police, thought Zoe at exactly the same time as Lake whispered the words to her.

Heart thumping loudly, Zoe allowed herself to be led by Lake. Soon they were on the edge of the forest, beyond the beams of light.

'Get down,' Lake hissed urgently. 'We must hide. Quickly … lie down over here. The grass is long and these thick bushes will hide us from anyone in the clearing.'

She pulled Zoe to the floor where they both flattened themselves as close to the ground as possible. The grass was wet, but that was of secondary importance compared to being captured, tortured and possibly killed. They only just got down in time, as two men appeared at the base of the light shaft. The men were armed with what looked to Zoe to be a miniature version of the speed guns used by police to catch speeding motorists back in her world. They searched through the shacks in the camp, but everyone had gone.

'Is there just two of them?' whispered Zoe.

'That's as many as we've ever seen,' Lake whispered back, 'It seems to be the norm.'

'Couldn't you all have overpowered them?' asked

Zoe. 'There's a lot more of you than them. You could take their weapons. They might help with your hunting.'

'We could I suppose,' said Lake. 'But what would be the point? We don't want to antagonise the people up there. They might decide to send down an army and destroy us all. Anyway if we did overpower them, what would we do with them? We're not killers, and we wouldn't be able to guard them forever. It's better this way. They come down. We keep out of the way. They go back. It keeps the status quo, everything stays in balance. It's a bit like a game really. As for weapons, well we do okay with our own.'

'The people in the South wouldn't know if their policemen had been captured. They might think they'd been killed by wild animals,' said Zoe. 'I presume they know there are wild animals down here?'

Lake nodded. 'That's why they're not too unhappy about us being here. They hope the animals will eventually finish us off and save them a job.'

From their hiding place the two of them watched as the men – finding nothing of interest in the camp – set about dismantling the already rickety shacks by kicking them and pulling them apart. When this was completed they began to walk across the clearing in the direction of where Lake and Zoe were hiding.

'They're going to fall into the trench,' gasped Zoe, clasping her hand to her mouth as she spoke.

'No they're not,' said Lake as the two men spied the bridge and ran across it. 'Shush now … they'll hear us.'

Lake and Zoe pressed themselves further into the ground. Suddenly a twig snapped nearby with a cracking sound that resonated loudly through the still night air. The men's footsteps were now clearly audible as they crunched on the loose shale that lay strewn across parts of the well-trodden path. Zoe raised her head slightly to risk a look.

One of the policemen was quite close. He had on a tight-fitting one piece uniform, which in the shadows cast by the light beams looked to be light grey. The top half of the uniform had SSP emblazoned across the front in bold dark lettering. The man's face was covered by a black helmet that fitted tightly. This appeared to have a dull red visor attached to the front. Zoe assumed that he was able to see through this, as he didn't lift it up when he turned his head to look around the area. The man held his gun in his right hand. She was about to whisper to Lake to ask about the visor when Lake, as if reading her thoughts murmured, 'Infrared, for night vision.'

Zoe felt her body stiffen as the man edged slowly towards their hiding place. She held her breath. He was now so close she was scared he might hear her exhaling.

'No one here, William.' It was the other policeman. He was searching among the bordering trees.

'I can't see anyone about over here either, Damian.' The loud reply came from somewhere just above Zoe as the nearest man answered his companion.

'Looks like they either ran away, or the camp is an old one that no one uses,' shouted Damian, adding in a voice laced with laughter, 'they certainly won't be able to use it any more now that we've redesigned it. There's nothing here for us. I think we should go home.'

'Let's give it a few more minutes,' William yelled

back, 'Just in case. That fire was still burning, which suggests that someone was there quite recently, so let's look around for a bit. We might get lucky.'

The voice was even closer now. Zoe lifted her eyes. Fear ran down her body at what she saw. William was standing so close that she could have touched him. She pressed herself lower into the grass, not daring to look or breathe. She hoped he couldn't hear her heart beating.

An excruciating pain shot abruptly through her left hand and up her arm. William had moved slightly. He was now standing on her hand. Zoe wanted to pull it away. She wanted to scream in pain. But she could do neither. Either action would result in discovery. She bit hard on her lip in a bid to divert her mind from the real source of pain.

William – sensing the small lump beneath his foot – began to stamp up and down as he tried to figure out if it was caused by uneven soil, an animal, or perhaps unexpected treasure trove.

Zoe could stand the agony no longer. Every stamp of William's foot brought a new wave of pain, each spasm accompanied by a surge of nausea. She fought back the urge to be sick, but with lip bleeding profusely, eyes filled with tears and pain shooting up and down her arm she could hold back no longer. Zoe screamed.

Immediately William looked down. Seeing the distraught girl he grabbed her by the arm, roughly hauling her to a standing position. 'I've got one, Damian,' he shouted. Zoe immediately saw the other policeman running urgently towards his colleague.

Despite the throbbing, stinging hurt she felt in her

hand and her concern at being caught, Zoe remembered Lake. It wouldn't help anyone if *she* were caught too. Zoe looked down at Lake, indicating with her eyes and a shake of the head that she should stay put. Zoe shuffled forward, trying to lead her captor away from where her friend was lying. William kept a firm grip on Zoe's arm, but fortunately he pulled her across the grass to meet the onrushing Damian. The move took them away from Lake.

Zoe knew she had to try to make her escape. She calculated that if she could somehow break from the policeman's grip she could run the short distance to the dense part of the forest. Once inside she might have a chance of finding another hiding place. The trees that grew there stood very close together. In the darkness it would be very hard for the two men to find her inside that overgrown wood.

She did briefly toy with the thought of letting herself be taken to the South – thinking that she might be able to find a way home from there – but quickly dismissed the idea.

I can't go like this. I need to be in control when I get there. I need to be fit and strong, not in intense pain. I also need to go there unannounced, not as a captive. Anyway what's to stop them from killing me here? she thought. *No, I have to escape. Hopefully I'll get another chance later.*

Damian was now close at hand. At his approach, William half turned in order to greet him. Zoe saw her chance as the grip on her arm relaxed ever so slightly. She twisted away, kicking out at William's legs as she spun around. The movement caught the policeman by surprise. He let go of Zoe's arm, trying to steady himself as he fought to keep his balance. Taking advantage of this temporary respite, Zoe ran full pelt towards the cover of the trees. She was almost there when she felt a stinging sensation in both legs. Her legs gave way, causing her to collapse to the ground. Zoe realised that she had been shot. Her body trembled, then shook violently as she lay on the grass. Among the panic and despair she felt, it suddenly dawned on her that the policemen's guns didn't fire bullets. They released volts of electricity designed to temporarily immobilise an assailant or enemy. Zoe's legs were now paralysed. Terrified, she looked over her shoulder from where she lay. She saw William just a few metres away. He was grinning. Damian was behind him. He too was smiling broadly.

'Oh no you don't,' said William. 'Thought you'd get the drop on me did you? Well my little friend here soon sorted *you* out eh?' He pointed to his gun. 'Now my girl, you're going to come with us. There's some people waiting for you on that globe up there and they're going to ask you lots of questions … and if your answers don't match up with what they want to hear there will be a few nasty surprises in store for you.'

Zoe sighed, inwardly cursing herself for not being quick enough to make her escape. She wished in afterthought that she had zigzagged her run to avoid presenting the men with such an easy target. Now she was going to be taken to the South but had lost any chance of her visit being a surprise, instead she was a prisoner. Zoe was terrified of what might await her when she arrived on the planet, but she was determined not to show fear to her captors. At least she found a little comfort in the fact that Lake was now safe.

William was standing over Zoe once more. He reached down to grab her, intending to throw her across his shoulder, but before his hands could make any contact a mighty growling noise rent the night air. It was accompanied by the loud thudding of pounding feet. Zoe felt a sudden rush of wind. She saw a dark shape flash across her vision. Rolling over on the grass she looked up. William had gone. He was no longer standing over her. He was on the ground several metres away, being savaged by a huge brown bear.

Damian rushed over to help his colleague, rapidly firing his gun at the ferocious animal as he ran. The bolts of electricity from the gun had no effect on the bear, which was now turning its attention to Damian as it left William seemingly lifeless on the ground. Damian turned tail, running as fast as he could back towards the light beam with the bear in full chase behind him. He managed to get to the light before the bear, disappearing into the shaft at rapid speed. The bear stood at the foot of the beam, looking upwards for a minute or two before loping off into the forest.

As the creature departed, William got unsteadily to his feet, his uniform shredded and bloody. He looked across at Zoe. She held her breath as he began to stagger towards her, raising his gun. A further loud roar emanated from the bear which had stopped and turned around. William quickly lost interest in Zoe. He lurched towards the twin beams, limping as he tried to run. The bear watched until he disappeared from view inside the light.

Lake ran over to Zoe. 'Are you okay?' she asked anxiously.

Zoe nodded, then replied. 'My arm hurts, so do my legs. They seem as if they don't belong to me. They are still paralysed. In fact I don't think I can stand up yet, but apart from that I'm fine. It was a close call though. I'm grateful to that bear. That's the second time a bear has saved my life.'

'Come on, I'll help you back into camp,' said Lake. 'That was really scary. You were so brave, Zoe. I thought they were going to take you. It was lucky the bear chose that exact moment to appear … it was even luckier that he went for the soldier rather than for you.'

'Yes.' Zoe was reflective, puzzled as to why the creature had chosen to attack and then not eat or drag away its prey. 'Even though I was the nearest and also the most helpless. It would have been so much easier for the bear to take me than to fight with an armed policeman, especially with another one close by.'

'I don't suppose the bear knows much about guns,' Lake laughed. 'Anyway, who cares? You're safe. That's all that matters to me.'

Zoe shrugged. 'I guess so,' she said, trying to stand but falling down again. 'See, I told you my legs weren't working. I wonder how long before the effects wear off … if they ever do! I hope it's not permanent.'

Lake looked concerned. 'If it is, we'll look after you.' she said.

Zoe puffed out her cheeks as she levered herself into

a sitting position. Then with a frown she said, 'Do you know Lake, the more I think about it the more suspicions I have about that bear? I'm sure it could have caught up with the other policeman, bears move very quickly especially where food is concerned. Yet it let him go. Also, if it's the same bear as the one I saw before, that's twice it has spared me when I could easily have been its dinner.'

'Perhaps it's used to humans. Maybe it was in a zoo or something,' Lake speculated. 'As long as it doesn't come looking for you in camp, we've got nothing to worry about. Now come on, let's get you back before it *does* decide to find you again.'

Lake helped Zoe back to the camp. The others were already there carrying out temporary repairs to the damage done by the security policemen. It was still dark, so proper repairs would have to wait until daylight.

Lake told the group what had happened, which resulted in everyone fussing over Zoe before taking her to Lake's shack where she was told to lie down and rest. The hut seemed to have survived most of the destructive actions of Damian and William.

Zoe didn't feel good. Her head ached, her lips were swollen and bloody, and her legs still throbbed painfully, even though she could feel them gradually beginning to regain their usefulness. She lay down on her rough bedding, closing her eyes she tried hard not to think about the pain as she struggled to get to sleep.

It wasn't long before she drifted off, but her uneasy sleep was troubled by weird dreams yet again. During a night filled with fantasy and hallucinations, Zoe found herself angrily and aggressively confronted by Ella and Amy from her secondary school. Next she was surrounded by a chattering, scratching, grabbing troop of monkeys that quickly became a pack of snarling, biting dogs. Then as she tried to run away from the pack in her dream, her legs became too heavy to carry her. Just as the dogs caught up with her she saw a shaft of bright light. Zoe dragged herself into it, scrambling up inside the beam only to find the dogs had turned back into monkeys which were now clambering up behind her. She tried to climb faster but slipped, falling backwards. As she fell she began to spin quickly. She was now tumbling around in the time vortex, trying to hold onto Zak Araz, but he slipped away from her grasp. Flailing wildly as she felt herself grabbing at fresh air, Zoe plunged downwards in freefall.

It was at this point that she screamed. She woke up abruptly, her eyes wild and staring. Lake was quickly at her side, hugging her tightly.

'Zoe. It's alright, you're only dreaming,' Lake said comfortingly, holding Zoe in her arms while she stroked her hair.

'Oh Lake, that was a horrible dream. The worst one yet,' sobbed Zoe. 'It was so real. Scary too. I was all alone. I couldn't get away from the dangers.'

She relayed the content of her dream to Lake, who wrapped her arms even tighter around Zoe. 'It's okay Zoe. I keep telling you you're safe with us. No one will hurt you here.'

Zoe smiled, but way down inside her the feeling of hopelessness and despair grew stronger. It was a feeling she knew would only be purged when she got back to her family and friends. After the events and dreams of tonight, the thought of living the rest of her life in Lowlands was again starting to weigh her down.

CHAPTER SEVEN

For the next three nights Zoe had similarly disturbing dreams, waking every day in a state of tiredness that bordered on exhaustion. She was finding it hard to summon up enough enthusiasm to lift her melancholic mood, as she became more morose and unhappy with each passing day. Zoe recognised the encroaching signs of depression, even from the little she had learned during her psychology studies. She vowed to fight it if only she could get some proper sleep to help boost her strength. But for the most part she spent the days dreading the forthcoming night time, wondering what terrors her dreams would hold.

On the fourth day Zoe woke early. Her mood was unchanged as her dreams had again been unrelenting and unmerciful. In fact it was the worst night she'd experienced since the sequence began. Her limbs felt heavy and her head ached, as she fought to conjure up some positive thoughts to get her through the day.

Outside, dawn was breaking. Through the gaps in the foliage and thin cloth that served as a covering door for the entrance to Lake's shack, Zoe could see the rosy fingers of early morning sunlight creeping slowly across the last lingering remnants of slate grey night sky. Birds were beginning to test their morning song, tuning up in preparation for the melodic dawn chorus. Already the warmth of the air suggested it was going to be a hot sunny day.

Zoe absentmindedly looked at the watch she still wore on her wrist. It showed the time as four fifty but she had no idea if it was correct. She didn't even know what day or month it was. She knew that it must be summer time. That's if summer time still existed of course. The World had changed so much from the one she'd grown up in and it scared her. In 2015 Zoe had been aware of a huge gap between North and South in terms of wealth, employment, welfare and politics, but in her wildest imaginings she could never have visualised a World in which London and the South were on a separate planet to the rest of Britain. Nor could she have foreseen a situation where such a primitive and hostile lifestyle – bringing extremely limited lifespan for the populace unfortunate enough to be trapped in Lowlands – existed in the country she lived in. *After all,* she thought. *This is still Britain. This is still planet Earth. The original planet Earth. The same one that I grew up on.*

Zoe tried to conjure up a mental image of what the Southern globe might be like. She let her mind dwell on what life might be like up on that man-made satellite hanging in the sky. Then, the craving she had carried inside for so long re-emerged with a vengeance, burning deeply and fiercely within her. She was suddenly filled with desire. She knew she had to get into that alternative World as soon as possible, or her depressive thoughts would take such a hold that she'd be unable to fulfil her ambition to do so. If those negative feelings took over she would quickly lose the will to return home. The outcome of this would be that in all probability she would perish at a young age here on this unrecognisable, desolate planet.

Zoe didn't want to appear ungrateful for the care and hospitality shown to her by Lake and the others, but she needed to be with her own people in familiar surroundings. That hovering sphere in the sky constantly beckoned to her, taunting her every day. Ever since she learned of its existence she had hoped that it might offer her the chance to make her wish come true, if only she could get to it. At the very least, being up there would offer her something different. It might even bring a more permanent relief to her current despondency.

There was no one around as Zoe slipped out of the shack. Lake was fast asleep, whilst the assortment of grunting, snoring noises emanating from the surrounding dwellings suggested that others were sleeping too.

It was still that strange almost ethereal period when day meets night – a sort of half world where light and darkness momentarily intertwine before one yields to the other. Zoe's mood had improved considerably as a result of the renewed passion her thoughts had aroused in her. She found herself enjoying the morning calls of the wild that intermittently broke through the surrounding silence.

The trees at the forest edge rose imperiously in the half-light. Behind them, smaller, older trees seemed to strike a series of almost menacing and threatening poses in their bent, windblown postures. They were now in full foliage, which gave them a mysteriously eerie appearance as the soft morning breeze gently rustled the leaves. It rippled through the lower branches, transforming them into long green fingers that seemed to beckon Zoe to come into the forest.

Remembering her experience with the dog pack, Zoe gave an involuntary shudder as she surveyed this scene, but her brighter mood prevented any thoughts of hesitation. She knew this part of the forest well, so she had no fears as she continued her journey along the path that skirted the woodland. At the border with the river, away from the trees, the first strands of daylight had finally broken through, making it much lighter. A small mixed group of finches, blackbirds, jays and tits – all of which had been drinking and foraging at the water's edge – took to the skies at Zoe's approach, heading for the cover of the trees. The sight of them lifted her mood even more.

At least the birds haven't changed, she thought as she settled on the river bank and began her morning ablutions.

Apart from the birds the river bank was deserted, so Zoe took the opportunity to immerse herself completely in the clear free-flowing river. She languished in the soft cool water that lapped gently around her, enjoying the silence and the beauty of her surroundings. Normally there would be little privacy or peace here, as this place was a hub of activity which usually saw group members bathing, washing, doing laundry or gathering water for cooking or drinking.

It was quite a picturesque spot. The river flowed into

a small sheltered creek that lay at the edge of the forest. To one side of her, the grassy bank dropped away gradually to form a small sand and shingle beach that allowed easy access into the water. The currents in this particular part of the river were not strong, barely more than a ripple or two. This made it an ideal spot for bathing. It was good too for the many forest animals that used the site as a watering hole.

Zoe lay back in the water, closing her eyes as she enjoyed the solitude. The first full rays of sunlight had now broken through the final resistance of night's total darkness. She felt more relaxed than she had done for some time. It felt just like the time when she was a child on family holidays, when she'd floated or swum in the seas, rivers, or lakes of her parents' chosen resort.

Zoe's daydreaming was ended by the sound of a sharp cracking noise that came from the direction of the forest. This was quickly followed by a loud rustling of leaves. Back in the real world she realised she was about to share the river with someone, but who? … or what? She peered into the trees but couldn't see anyone although the leaves and branches were still moving. Holding her breath for a few seconds as her heartbeat quickened, her eyes scanned the bank and forest edge for signs of life or movement.

After a minute or two with no sign of other life forms emerging from the trees, Zoe relaxed again. She let the water wash over her once more as she languished in the cool refreshing liquid, all thoughts of intrusion banished from her head. In a short while it occurred to her that it might be time to leave the river anyway. She needed to get dressed before any of the others arrived to carry out their morning ablutions.

Zoe waded to the small shore, where she clambered up the bank near to where her clothes lay. She quickly began to get dressed. When she had finished she turned to go, and immediately froze with fear. Standing less than five metres away from her was a huge brown bear. Zoe's heart almost stopped in response to the terror she felt. She could only think about the fact she was about to be killed and eaten. She couldn't run, her legs were jelly. Moreover, her brain lacked the will to make them move. In any case, if she had been able to run where could she go? The bear was blocking her way to the camp and the river was behind her. Zoe remembered that bears were much faster at running than humans. She had an idea that they were probably better in the water too. She desperately hoped that someone from the camp would choose this moment to appear. If so, it might distract the bear just enough to provide her with a chance to escape. But despite Zoe's intense willing, no one came.

For what seemed like an eternity – but in truth was no more than a few seconds – Zoe and the bear stood still, staring at each other across a few metres of space on the river bank. It was as if they were boxers or gladiators sizing each other up before a big fight. But Zoe knew that this was a one-sided fight with only one possible winner, and it wouldn't be her! As in her encounter with the wild dog pack, she hoped it would be over quickly. She decided that it would be best if the creature killed her before it devoured her, so she didn't

70

have to suffer too much mental or physical agony. The thought of what was to come brought floods of tears to Zoe's eyes. She flopped to the ground sobbing loudly.

'Don't cry, Zoe. I won't hurt you.'

The words caught Zoe by surprise. She looked about her to see who had spoken. There was nobody in sight.

'Don't worry. You are safe.'

The words seemed to be coming from somewhere near to where the bear was standing. Zoe blinked. She wiped her eyes, trying to see if there was someone beyond the creature, but again there was no one.

What's going on? she thought. *Am I going mad? It seems as if the bear is talking, but bears can't speak. Is this real? Is it my imagination? Is it something that happens when you are facing death? Does your brain conjure up some weird, fantastic, surreal situation, which in my case is a talking bear?*

Before she could come up with an answer to these musings, Zoe received another surprise as the bear faded from view. When she looked up again, Zak Araz stood right in front of her.

'It *must* be my brain,' Zoe muttered. 'It's preparing me for death and is now about to take me backwards through my life events.'

'Hello, Zoe,' said Zak. 'It's me Zak Araz … or Kazzaar if you prefer it, although I wouldn't want to appear as myself at the moment. That would probably cause more distress and panic to anyone who saw me than if I stayed as a bear.'

Zoe couldn't believe her eyes. 'Surely you can't be real?' she asked incredulously.

'Yes, I am real,' replied Zak.

Zoe felt a huge wave of relief sweep over her. This quickly gave way to a sudden surge of anger, as she thought about him leaving her to fend for herself for such a length of time in this dangerous place.

'Where have you been since we came through the time vortex?' she demanded angrily. 'Why did you leave me? Why have you come back? And why now?'

'I've been here all along,' said Zak calmly, 'watching over you. When we were in danger of getting separated in the vortex I changed into moth larva and burrowed down inside the lining of your coat. I've been in and out of there ever since. That's when I've not been an adult moth, a bird, a worm or any number of creatures. I even tried to be a button on your jumper for a while, but that was a step too far for my shape shifting skills. Being an inanimate object is not possible even for a shape shifter like me, so I had to become the larva again. Not that being a moth larva was exactly comfortable. That took an awful lot of doing as well as stretching my shape-changing powers to their utmost limits. As a species, we have the capability to shrink or stretch our internal organs into the shape of the smallest or largest living creatures in any alien World. This helps us to blend in with our surroundings, wherever we are. It's also a survival and safety mechanism to enable us to remain unobtrusive – and hopefully undetected – in the face of potential enemies, or to give us an advantage, should we need to fight or escape. Oh, I forgot to say that I've been a bear before, of course. I became the bear when I needed to protect you, when the dogs came and when the Security Police caught you. It was a good disguise which proved to be perilous for both of them.'

Zak smiled as Zoe's eyes grew wider, her mouth dropping open in surprise. 'Why didn't you show yourself to me before now?' she spluttered. 'I needed you. I needed to know I wasn't alone. Why just stay inside my coat?'

Zoe stopped, thought for a while then frowned. Before Zak could respond to her questions, she let rip with another salvo of words. 'As for you being a moth larva, well that makes me go all goosepimply and shivery. It's not nice. Having moth larva living inside your clothing is bad enough, but when that larva is also an alien being from another planet who is in disguise … that is seriously mind-blowing. You could have been up to anything while you were in my coat … were you?'

'Of course not,' laughed Zak. 'I told you I was…'

He didn't get to finish as the conversation was interrupted by the sound of running footsteps. Zak turned to go.

'I'll talk to you again later,' he said. 'We need to make plans to get out of here.'

'Hey, don't go,' cried Zoe urgently. 'I've still got lots of questions to ask you.'

'I won't be far away,' said Zak. 'I'll reappear when it's safe to do so.'

'Are you going back into my clothes?' asked Zoe screwing up her face in distaste at the thought.

Zak shook his head. He grinned, but before he could reply a voice rang out from the forest edge.

'Zoe … you're here … thank goodness. We were worri … '

It was Lake. Her voice tailed off as she caught sight

of the huge bear that was now padding away from Zoe as it headed towards the furthest trees.

Lake put her hands to her face in alarm. She rushed to Zoe. 'Are you alright?' she gasped. 'What was that bear doing here? More to the point, why didn't it harm you?'

'Not hungry I guess,' said Zoe calmly, although she felt anything but calm inside. She continued. 'Seriously though, it only appeared as you came running through the forest. You must have scared it. Thanks, your timing is impeccable.'

Zoe spent the rest of the morning with Lake, collecting forest fruits and mashing them into a pulp that would later be baked in the fire to form what would be a hot fruit pie but without any pastry.

All day she was on tenterhooks. Her feelings were a mix of excitement and curiosity, with a not inconsiderable amount of fear. Her head was buzzing with a mass of thoughts and questions. She now knew that Kazzaar – alias Zak Araz – was alive and he was here in Lowlands. *But what did he want? Why the urgent need to talk to her? What was he planning? When would he appear again? But the most important question of all was could she trust him?*

Several times during the day Zoe resisted the urge to search through her coat to try to find the so-called larva, telling herself that even if she did find him he'd change into something else to avoid detection. She also resisted the strong desire to tell Lake about her encounter with Zak that morning. Zoe hugged herself mentally, despite her doubts and concerns about him, there was also something that was quite comforting about knowing that she was no longer alone here.

Whether I can trust him or not, she thought, *he probably needs to get back to 2015 as much as I do, so he can try to find some way of getting back to his own planet.*

Zoe paused to think further on this then decided, *but I'll have to watch him very carefully to make sure he doesn't get up to his old tricks.*

CHAPTER EIGHT

It was two days before Kazzaar showed himself again. He was in the guise of Zak Araz rather than the bear, despite the fact that Zoe was on her way to the river again and he risked being seen by one of the villagers.

'This shape is more convenient for me,' he explained when Zoe queried why he'd chosen to be Zak instead of himself or the bear. 'It will also be acceptable to other humans whom we may encounter … my real shape would probably send them running and screaming for help. I guess the bear might too, especially if it was talking. Anyway, Zak has a face that is instantly recognisable to you.' He paused and with a rueful smile added, 'even if not for the best of reasons.'

Zoe inclined her head quizzically. 'What is it you want from me?' she asked.

'I know we have been enemies in the past when you have twice thwarted my plans. As such you have no reason to trust me. But you are an intelligent human being who wants to go back to your own time to be with your people. I too want to get back to your time so I can find my space craft. I need to return to my people too. So you see we have a common goal, something to share. I believe we will be stronger, with a better chance of achieving our aims, if we work together. I can get into places that you can't, whereas there will be times when you can talk to your fellow humans and find things out that maybe I couldn't.'

Zak began to read signs of suspicion and doubt on Zoe's face as he continued his impassioned plea for her help. 'You distrust my motives and doubt my sincerity. I can understand why you might, but I will not let you down. There is no purpose in discussing this now, but if you trust me I will show you in time that we can work together. In your World I was the intruder. Here in this World we are *both* aliens. Neither of us belong here, we are strangers. Individually we are alone and weak in our knowledge of this place and its dangers. Together we have a chance to find a way out.' Zak paused. He pointed to the sphere that was suspended in the sky way above them stating, 'I have been up there.'

Again suspicion registered on Zoe's face.

'Yes, I have,' Zak confirmed. 'Despite your obvious disbelief I *have* been there. Not everywhere, but I have been to the part that is the source of the light beams and also the headquarters of the Security Police. I have seen what goes on in there. I have studied the control room, the CCTV, the security systems, the procedures too. You see Zoe, moth larva can also live on police uniforms. Once I am inside the building I can become anyone because I can change my shape. This means I can go where I like without drawing attention to myself. In doing this I have acquired some knowledge of the planet and its history, although I don't know too much about life in general up there. But I can tell you that the technology I have seen on my visits suggests there is a good chance we might find something that offers us a way back to your time. So … are you with me? It's your choice. If you don't want to join me I can find a way back to your planet alone.'

Zoe thought for a moment – weighing up the possibilities of Zak's proposal – before she spoke.

'Okay,' she said tentatively, in a voice without too much conviction. 'I'm prepared to give it a go, but I can't trust you completely. However, I promise you I'll give my all. I won't let you down, but you'd better not let me down either. If we can find a way back to 2015 we'll do it together which means we both get back, or if it isn't possible then we both stay here. I don't want to find a way back just for *you* to take it and leave me here, so you can go back to carry out your plan to colonise the Earth.'

'I won't,' said Zak. 'Believe me Zoe, whatever has gone before is finished. We are now allies not enemies, so we *must* work together. You must understand though, we are not equal. I have powers that you don't. My ability to change shape and size means I can get into places you can't. This means that sometimes I may have to become similar to people who *are* your enemies. If I do, it is important that you don't betray my cover, even if I appear to be siding with people who want to hurt you. I promise you that whatever happens I will protect you and keep you safe, as I've tried to do so far.'

Zoe made it clear that she understood what he had said. She thought for a moment, then offered her hand in agreement. 'When are we going?' she asked eagerly. 'More importantly, how?'

'We need to wait for a suitable light beam,' replied

Zak, shaking Zoe's outstretched hand. 'Just remember, I am always close by.' He smiled. 'I may even be burrowing down in your clothes again' he added jokingly.

Then adopting a more serious tone he said, 'I will make myself known to you when the time is right, after which you must follow me and do as I say. But you always need to pay close attention to the shape I have chosen so that you can follow the right person or creature. That will be very important Zoe, especially as I may have to change shape more than once … perhaps several times in a matter of seconds.'

Zoe nodded again. 'One thing,' she said. 'Do I call you Kazzaar or Zak?'

'Zak is probably easier,' replied Zak. 'Although my name may change as I take on the shape of different people. That is why you must pay attention at all times … oh by the way Zoe, you mustn't tell anyone about our plans. We can't trust anybody. Only each other.'

'I have to tell Lake,' said Zoe. 'She's been so good to me. I want to say goodbye to her before I leave. I won't tell her about you or about our plans, I'll just say that I might be leaving one day soon and tell her not to go looking for me if I'm gone for a while.'

'Be very careful what you say,' said Zak. 'Our lives – and Lake's for that matter – could depend on it.'

Before Zoe could say anything more, Zak transformed into the bear. The creature gave a soft growl before lumbering off into the forest.

That night Zoe couldn't get to sleep again, but this time it was excitement that kept her awake. Her mind was filled with the conversation she'd had with Zak. The more she thought about what he'd said, the more rigid and restless her body became as it tingled with nervous tension in anticipation of what she hoped was to come. She tossed and turned all night long in her makeshift bed.

'Are you having bad dreams again?' asked Lake in the early hours of the morning. 'I've been listening to you moving about. Is everything okay?'

'Yes,' said Zoe. 'I'm sorry if I've kept you awake. It's not the dreams; I'm just finding it hard to switch off my thoughts.'

There was a lengthy silence before Lake spoke again. 'When are you thinking of leaving us?'

Zoe took a deep breath. 'What do you mean?'

'You've been preoccupied and brooding ever since you first told me you were thinking of going to the South, so I guess it's on your mind most days. You have been very restless tonight, which usually means bad dreams. But you haven't shouted out as you normally do when you have nightmares. In fact you confirmed as much a moment ago, when you also told me you couldn't turn off your thoughts. So, I guess your head is filled with other things, perhaps more pleasant thoughts. If I put all of those facts together it leads me to think the time for you to leave must be pretty close.'

'Yes it is,' said Zoe slowly and deliberately. 'I also need to tell you that I may leave at any time if the chance presents itself, without being able to say goodbye. So don't worry if I go out sometime and don't return. It will mean that I found the opportunity and took it. I *will* miss you, Lake. I want you to know that. I also want you to know that I really appreciate what you and the others have done for me since I came here. You have helped me to survive. So please thank everyone for me if I'm unable to do so myself. I am very grateful. You've looked after me, given me food, shelter and accepted me as one of your family. Whatever happens, I promise you that if I can't find a way back to my time I will come back here to live my life out with all of you. So you may not get rid of me that easily after all. Take care Lake, don't give up. Try to make your World better. If I can find any way to help you while I'm up there on that planet, I will do so.'

Lake didn't speak. In the darkness, Zoe could hear the sound of someone moving about. Suddenly Lake was right next to her, hugging her. Zoe could feel the wetness of Lake's tears against her cheek as they held each other in the dark.

'Good luck,' whispered Lake. 'I'll miss you too. I've enjoyed having you around … I wish you didn't have to go, but I can understand why you must. Please take care.'

Lake gulped loudly, then added. 'From a purely selfish perspective though, I do hope I see you again.'

CHAPTER NINE

Zoe was around for a further five days before her chance to go to the South came. She had just settled into bed for the night at the end of the fifth day, when she heard a voice say, 'It's time Zoe, come on.'

She looked around expecting to see Zak, but there was no one there. Then she became aware of a small dark shape silhouetted against the moonlit sky that was visible at the entrance to the shack. It was an owl. The bird was fluttering its wings as it hovered in waiting. Zoe instinctively knew it was him. She got up.

'Are you going now?' Lake's voice, cracking with emotion, came from the other side of the room.

'Yes,' hissed Zoe. 'I have to. Goodbye. Thank you for looking after me.'

'Goodbye,' Lake croaked, her voice revealing her tears. 'Good luck.'

Once outside Zoe looked for the owl. It was flying slowly above the path that led into the forest. She followed, running to catch up. It wasn't as dark as she thought it would be. There was a full moon and the lights from the Southern sphere added to the brightness, so visibility was good.

In the distance Zoe could see two long slender shafts of light. They criss-crossed in the sky like the wartime searchlights she'd seen on mocked up film posters in art lessons at school. Together they formed an illuminated path between the South and Lowlands, joining the separated parts of Britain as if the two locations were now held together with two pieces of yellow string.

At the forest edge the owl disappeared. It was replaced by the bear. The animal padded over to Zoe where it knelt before her, in a gesture indicating that she should climb aboard. Zoe clambered onto the creature's back, holding tightly to the thick rough fur at its neck. When she was settled, the bear walked around for a few minutes – as Zak made sure that she was comfortable and wouldn't fall off – before beginning its charge through the forest in the direction of the twin streaks of light.

As the beast gathered speed Zoe flattened herself along its spine, trying to avoid the flailing branches that were swept back and forth by the impetus of the ursine body as it raced past at a high rate of knots. Once or twice Zoe *did* almost fall off, grabbing the bear's neck scruff in an even tighter grip as she tried to stay on board while her legs slid down alongside its galloping torso. She somehow managed to hold firm on both occasions, panting loudly as the breath was forced from her bouncing frame by the momentum of this unconventional ride. It was also an uncomfortable ride, but Zoe clung on.

The ride came to a halt, with the bear performing its own version of an emergency stop, in an attempt to avoid detection by bursting beyond the cover of the trees where the pair would have been visible to anyone. The impact of the bear's sudden action caused Zoe to shoot over the animal's head. She grabbed at the nearest thing to hand as she sought to save herself from falling. Unfortunately for Zak, her fingers clamped firmly onto the creature's ears. It let out a sharp yelp, followed by a long growl which suggested that having its ears pulled wasn't something that the beast was comfortable with.

Zoe dismounted awkwardly. She stood on the rough wet grass, stretching herself whilst simultaneously giving a vigorous massage to her legs and backside which had both grown numb from her rumbustious ride. She could see a large circle of light in the glade ahead of them. The bear had brought her to the meeting point of the two beams. In the shadow of the trees, the creature briefly became Zak Araz. He spoke quietly to Zoe.

'Stay here!' Zak said. 'Watch closely! Be silent! I will return soon. You need to be ready to follow me when I do.'

Before Zoe could respond, the bear was back. She stood behind a tree as the animal ambled off. She kept watching as instructed, despite being uncertain about what it was that she was supposed to observe. Then her gaze caught a movement near the edge of the well-lit circle. It was a man.

Zoe saw that the man was wearing a security police uniform. She looked around for a second man as she knew the security police always worked in pairs. It wasn't long before another movement – this time by the trees on the far side of the clearing – caught her attention. It was him, the other policeman. He appeared to be running towards the first man, waving his arms wildly as he ran. His colleague responded in similar fashion. The two men ran towards each other across the clearing. Zoe could hear the second man shouting. She strained her ears to try and catch the words.

'Look out … run … bear!'

The urgent warning exploded through the stillness of the night, echoing back and forth through the trees. Zoe saw the two policemen come to a standstill as they met on the fringe of the large halo of light. The first man, still close to the edge of the forest, turned his head to look in the direction his fellow officer was pointing. Zoe saw a blur of motion in the trees behind him. She heard the man scream. Then he disappeared beneath a large brown body. Meanwhile, the second man had decided to make a run for the nearest shaft of light. He was speaking hurriedly into what appeared to be some sort of communicator as he ran. One of the light beams was immediately extinguished. The bear had spotted his run though. It turned, heading towards the policeman, who was by now almost at the base of the beam. The running man stretched out his arms, in a last ditch effort to reach his identified source of escape. It seemed almost as if he was trying to pull it closer to him. His face bore the pained expression of someone whose lungs were close to bursting. The light touched his hand. From where she stood, Zoe saw the relief begin to show on his face as he prepared to climb inside. Then the bear arrived. Having easily disposed of his companion, the creature now administered the same treatment to him.

Within a few minutes, Zak Araz stood next to the

two bodies that lay prone and unmoving on the ground. He beckoned to Zoe to join him. By the time she got there, he had stripped the uniforms from the men.

'Here, try these on,' he said, thrusting the uniforms at Zoe. 'See which one fits you best. But you need to be quick. The policeman radioed that there was a bear. He asked for one light to be turned off. Luckily I got to him before he could tell his control officer that his colleague had been hurt. We need the people up there to believe that both men are returning.'

'Are they dead?' asked Zoe.

Zak shook his head. 'No, I was very careful. But they will be unconscious for a while, and when they do come round we'll be up in the South in their place.'

'So why do we need to rush?' Zoe queried.

'The beam will be switched off if they aren't back within a short time. The operators up in the South headquarters will assume that the bear has killed them both,' said Zak.

He picked up the radio communicator from where it had fallen. Then tossed a second one to Zoe. 'I took that from the other man,' Zak said. 'You'd better hold onto it, as we may need to hand them in when we get up there.'

Zoe deftly caught the object. She tried on the uniforms. Neither of them was perfect for her size, but she selected the one that at least looked as if it might be a reasonable off the peg fit. She offered the other one to Zak. He shook his head. Zoe looked puzzled.

'I don't need it,' he said. 'Look.'

His shape changed until he became an exact copy of

one of the two security policemen he'd just incapacitated. Zoe looked from Zak to the figure lying on the ground. They were identical, except that Zak had a uniform and the policeman didn't.

'I can become any living thing. I don't need the uniform. My shape-changing capabilities allow me to absorb and take on every detail of whatever I am replicating. My body automatically duplicates skin texture, DNA, hair and eye colouring, even clothing.'

'I forgot,' smiled Zoe.

'I'll take his identity disc though,' said Zak, rifling through the uniform pockets. 'You'd better take the other one even though you look nothing like him. It might get you into the base, or even beyond if you wear the helmet all of the time.'

'And if it doesn't?' asked a worried looking Zoe.

'We'll deal with that if it happens,' said Zak. 'So come on, let's see eh?'

He handed the disc to Zoe, who donned the police helmet so that the darkened visor immediately obliterated her facial details.

'What will happen to them?' asked Zoe, mumbling through the small mouth grille on her helmet. She pointed towards the two prone bodies.

'They'll probably wander around down here for a while, or maybe they'll look for one of the transporter stations. I doubt they will find one though, as these two look as if they are on the searchlight patrol rather than the transporter group, which means they won't necessarily know the locations of the stations. The searchlight patrol personnel operate during the night, whereas the transporter team are on daytime vigil. The transporter stations are very well camouflaged to minimise the risk of detection which might lead to an attack – on policemen or the station – from Lowlanders. Anyway, training is different for both police forces, so I doubt if the transporter team have knowledge of how to use the light beams or if the night patrol are aware of where the stations are sited.

'Besides, these two have no formal ID or any way of communicating with their HQ. Even if they did, we will be long gone by the time all of the checks have been done. Of course, someone down here might help them … or possibly whoever finds them will imprison them. I'm sure there will be some who would be happy to take their revenge for those that have been taken before. On the other hand they might both fall foul of the wild animals that live around here. Either way it doesn't matter. They are killers. They would quite happily take people from down here back to their space station to be tortured and killed. They would certainly have had no worries about killing us.'

Zoe wasn't entirely comfortable with this, but she shrugged and nodded in response.

'Come on,' said Zak. 'We're going south.'

He led the way to the foot of the light beam. Zoe followed. When they got there she looked up inside the beam. There was nothing there but light.

'There are no stairs,' she said. 'Is there a lift?'

'Sort of,' replied Zak. 'It's hard to explain. Basically, the light beam is similar to a torch beam. Well, it's an intense laser beam actually. The beams have been perfected over the centuries to the point where it is now possible for people to walk inside them. They usually have two beams so that the policemen can use one each. This enables a speedier, and therefore more efficient method of transport.'

'That's all well and good,' said a puzzled Zoe. 'But we've only got one beam and we've not been practising for centuries, nor have we received any training. So how do *we* get up it?'

'We walk,' was Zak's reply.

'Walk?' queried Zoe. 'Even if we knew how to walk inside the beam, that planet is miles above Earth. It would take us several days – perhaps weeks or months – to walk that far on a level road. How are we going to walk upwards inside a beam of light, before either the sun rises or the beam is switched off when they realise their patrol is not returning?'

'I'll show you,' Zak replied. 'It's not really like walking that distance. This beam is a bit like a supersonic lift. But instead of just standing there while the lift takes you upwards, you have to use footholds inside the light in order to help it raise you up. The elevation is provided by energy inside the beam. It carries you upwards as you walk. Each foothold activates the energy to lift you to the next foothold when someone steps into it. We'll be up there in no time, as long as you follow me carefully and tread where I tread.

'Now come on! We have to be quick, or they may think that the bear has killed both of the officers. If that happens they'll definitely turn off the light. I'll lead, you follow. But you have to pay attention. I know where the footholds are, but you won't see them. They are indented into the light in regular stages like rungs on a ladder, but unless you know exactly where they are placed you can easily miss one. It's important that you tread where I tread and walk at my pace. There are no handrails, but if you watch me carefully and walk in my footsteps we'll get there. It's quite easy once you get the hang of it. Since the initial Higgs-Bosun experiments on your planet there have been many others, exploring different fields. It is now possible for humans to travel through light, when inside light beams that are equipped with this lift technology. Although it is not common knowledge, in the South this skill is used exclusively in matters of national security or regular Lowland patrols. So Security Police, along with a few other special Government agents, are the only ones to have received training.

'We are also going to walk inside these shafts of light. But beware, if you slow down or miss a foothold you will fall to the bottom. Trust me Zoe, you can do it. I've been up inside one of these several times before. Not exactly walking though, as I've always been in someone's uniform. But I've watched them closely. I know how it's done and where to put my feet. We've been using this technology for some years on my planet, so I do have some experience of how it works. Once we get going you'll soon get used to it. If you do get stuck, don't panic. Hold onto me and I'll guide you. The secret is to keep moving. Try to take regular deep breaths so that your steps become swift and light, similar to a stone that is skimming across water when thrown.' Zak grinned as he concluded. 'Going down is much simpler.

You float on the energy burst rather like having a jet pack. You won't find out what that's like though, as we will hopefully find a way back to your time, so we won't need to come back down.'

Zak stepped inside the beam. Zoe took a long deep breath then went in after him. It was very bright inside the light shaft, and it took a few seconds for Zoe's eyes to acclimatise. By this time Zak was way ahead of her.

Heart beating quickly and anxious not to make a mistake, Zoe took her first steps inside the light. She was scared, afraid of what might lie ahead – but also terrified of getting it wrong. She hadn't seen Zak start his ascent so she wasn't sure where to put her feet. She didn't want to call out to him in case there were microphones hidden inside the beam, or the communication devices they had taken from the policemen picked up the sound.

After just two steps, Zoe found she wasn't moving. She tried again but still remained in the same place. The light around her seemed to be alive. It was twisting, spiralling and swirling like a thick fog, yet instead of murk and gloom there was brilliant bright illumination all around her.

Zoe was about to make her third attempt at climbing upwards when something grabbed her hand, gripping it tightly. Zoe's heart shot into her mouth. She thought for a moment that one of the policemen had regained consciousness and come after her. Then she saw it was Zak. He had climbed back down to help her. He mouthed 'follow me,' before giving her hand a sharp tug. Zoe suddenly found herself moving very quickly, propelled forward and upward as Zak held on tightly to her hand. He turned his face to her. He was grinning broadly as he lifted the thumb of his free hand. Zoe smiled back as she gave him her own thumbs up in return.

It was very strange inside the tube of light. Zak had been right, there were no handrails, but Zoe quickly got accustomed to placing her feet in the footholds that were evenly spaced out. She then got her feet and her breathing into a synchronised rhythm. After this she found progress to be easy. Having Zak to help her was a benefit, yet she felt confident enough now to believe she could do it alone if she had to. She had decided the experience was more akin to being on a futuristic escalator rather than a lift.

Zoe was curious to find out if she could touch the light. She wondered what it felt like. *Is it cold and wet, just as it is when I touch fog, or does it feel solid?* She reached out her free hand as she climbed. To her surprise it went straight through the outer edge of the light beam. She quickly pulled it back as she didn't want it to be seen by whoever might be monitoring from above. Zoe found it hard to believe that she was running inside what was effectively a torch beam. It was unreal. She felt as if she were in a dream.

'Are we walking at the speed of light?' she asked, trying hard to keep her voice at a low level.

Zak frowned and placed a finger on his lips. Then, putting his mouth close to Zoe's ear he replied. 'You can call it that if you want, but technically we are not walking, we are being driven and carried to the top. It works on the principle of what was often referred to as a tractor beam in your science fiction films on Earth. It has now become a reality. We are being carried along by sound waves, which provide the energy lift I was talking about. We are not moving at the speed of light either, although we are going much faster than humans would normally travel.'

Zoe preferred to think that they were actually walking inside the beam. She thought back to her schooldays.

I can't believe I'm moving as fast as the speed of light, she thought. *What would my old PE teacher make of this? She was always telling me I was slow and useless at athletics. Now I can honestly say I'm running faster than Olympic gold medallists.*

Zoe's thoughts were interrupted by a double tug on her hand. She looked up. Zak was making wild signals with his free hand. She correctly interpreted his sign language to mean they were close to the top. She couldn't see beyond the light, so had no idea of what to expect on arrival. However, Zak seemed quite at ease and he had claimed to be familiar with the layout, so she decided she'd just follow his lead.

They came to a sudden halt at the top. Zoe almost ran into Zak. He motioned her to stay silent, miming that she should leave any talking to him, He also indicated that she should communicate only by nodding or shaking her head.

As they stepped out of the light beam, Zoe saw that they were in a medium sized room. It was a soulless place with grey walls. She looked up at the ceiling, in which were embedded a series of small circular single bulb lights. These cast sufficient light for the whole room, but paled in comparison to the brilliance of the illumination they had just travelled inside. The equally dull floor was constructed of a synthetic material that Zoe thought resembled bare concrete.

Zak let go Zoe's hand. He jerked his head sharply, then walked diagonally across the room to a single door set in the far wall. Zoe followed closely behind him. Glancing about her as she walked, she noticed the sensors in each corner of the room. She guessed they might also double as cameras, so she pulled herself up to her full height to look as much like the stranded policeman as was possible. The sensors swivelled from side to side on their mountings, blinking frequently as they surveyed every movement made by her and Zak.

When they got to the door, Zoe saw a small machine mounted on the wall. It had a square screen, next to which was a slot with a painted arrow. She correctly guessed that this contraption controlled the entrances and exits. Zak whipped out the ID disc he'd removed from the policeman. He nodded slightly toward Zoe, who quickly fished hers from her uniform pocket. Zak inserted his disc into the slot on the machine and waited as it was scanned. A message appeared on the screen: ID DISC VALID. PLEASE INSERT DISC OF ACCOMPANYING OFFICER TO GAIN ENTRY. Zoe, holding her breath, pushed her disc into the slot. After a few seconds the machine flashed another message, SECOND DISC VALID – LIGHT BEAM NOW EXTINGUISHED – ENTRY AUTHORISED.

Zak and Zoe put the discs back into their pockets.

The door slid open with a barely audible whisper. The pair passed through it. A backward glance from Zoe confirmed that the transmitter beam was switched off. She was now in the South, where she'd yearned to be for so long. Her heartbeat had quickened slightly, and she was aware of a tingling sensation coursing through her veins. There was no going back now. She quietly urged herself to stay calm, even though her mind was racing. The two policemen who were stranded back on Lowlands had no way of getting back here, at least for tonight. Zoe hoped that Zak hadn't overlooked anything. She also hoped that the policemen didn't have other transmitters that allowed them to talk to people in police headquarters; otherwise she and Zak were in trouble.

As the door glided shut behind them, Zoe saw that they had emerged into what looked to be a busy office. Several people walked back and forth, carrying metal discs and boxes. She recognised the computer screens as being similar to the ones from 2015, but not much else was familiar. There were no computer towers or laptops visible and Zoe wondered where the hard drive and other components were housed, if indeed they still existed. Every screen on the multi-layered banks of television screens that filled each wall in the room was active. Some displayed data, others showed images of the interior or exterior of a variety of buildings and streets. Zoe presumed these were pictures of various places around the city that lay beyond the exit to this building. There was a lot of noise in the office. It came from people talking, but they all seemed to be talking to themselves. Zoe pondered on this for a few seconds before deducing that maybe this was perhaps the latest form of telecommunications. She couldn't see any obvious earphones or microphones anywhere. However, people appeared to be pressing buttons on their clothing as they talked. Zoe guessed there may be minute inter-personal devices attached to each person's uniform, or even to their body. Whatever, it seemed as if every aspect of office conversation in 3015 was fully automated.

She followed Zak across the office. He went through another door, then walked along a corridor that had walls seemingly made of glass, allowing an uninterrupted view of every other office in that part of the building. Zak seemed to know what he was doing and where he was going. Zoe trailed in his wake, trying to look self-assured, despite the thudding of her heart beneath the tight uniform and the sweating skin on her face. She was grateful for the cover provided by her helmet.

At the end of the corridor Zak opened one of three doors, walking confidently inside. Zoe slipped into the room behind him. He was already making his way across to a long counter that ran the length of the room. Behind the counter were a number of people in uniform.

At the counter Zak flashed his ID disc. He was given a smaller metal disc by one of the men, who nodded a greeting. Zoe followed suit, almost dropping her own disc in her nervousness. She quickly recovered from her fumble, skilfully catching the object before it hit the floor. Zak ushered her away, leading her into a side room to the left of the counter. Once inside Zak checked that no one else was around. When he was certain they were alone he pointed to the swivelling, blinking device in the corner then whispered, 'We've got to complete our logs for the visit to Lowlands. Then we can go off duty.'

Zak sat at a small desk in the centre of the room. Inserting his new disc into the small opening on the front facia of the machine that sat on the desktop, he said loudly in a voice that was unlike his own, 'C2217 reporting back from Lowland duty. It was a generally quiet night. We had no sighting of any Lowland inhabitants, nor did we witness any disturbances. But as previously communicated to you, we did see a bear. It came after us, meaning we had to retreat quickly. We tried to use our guns on the creature but they were ineffective. It was a very dangerous situation for both of us, so I asked for one of the beams to be extinguished in order that we could cover each other's back. This action is much easier to carry out if there is just one exit. We had to get away from danger quickly, that's why we're back a little earlier than scheduled. If nothing else, the bear will help with keeping the Lowlanders in check. There is nothing further to report, C2217 signing off duty now.'

When Zak had finished he motioned to Zoe to sit at the desk but to be silent. With trembling fingers she placed her disc in the machine. Zak – with his back to the winking eye in the corner and using yet another different voice – introduced himself as D1104, before giving a corresponding account to his previous one, albeit with slightly different vocabulary. Zoe looked on incredulously. She was impressed by his performance.

After completing the duty reports, Zoe and Zak went back into the main room, Zoe still wearing her helmet. They handed their discs to one of the people behind the counter. No one paid any heed to the couple as they exited the room through yet another door. In the corridor beyond, Zak summoned the lift that took them to the ground floor. The lift doors opened to reveal the main exit that led to the street outside.

The process of climbing up the beam, filing reports, and logging off duty had taken longer than Zoe thought. When they finally emerged from the building she was surprised to see that dawn had broken. It was now daylight as they stood on the street in front of the police headquarters building.

CHAPTER TEN

'Welcome to London,' said Zak, extending an arm, which he waved around him in a sweeping arc.

Zoe opened the visor in her helmet so she could look about her. This place was nothing like she'd expected, nor anything like the London she remembered. There was very little traffic, and what there was seemed somehow to be fixed to the road. She saw a few cars as well as a small number of conveyances that appeared to be a cross between a single deck bus and a people carrier. Zoe noticed that none of these vehicles moved independently. It was the road that was moving. The pavements moved too. Pedestrians simply stood on the footpath, letting it take them along to their destination. A few people ran along the pavement. Some also ran across the street, dodging between the vehicles as they battled against the motion of the moving road. But the majority were happy to be static commuters.

Zoe shook her head at the running pedestrians. 'Some things never change,' she said. 'Those people are just like the ones who ran up and down moving escalators back in my time. What's the point of running when the thing you are standing on is moving in the direction you want to go? I wonder why everyone is in so much of a hurry that whatever is invented to bring more comfort to their lives, they don't have time to appreciate it.'

Zak looked at her and smiled. 'You've only just got here and already you're complaining,' he said.

'Where to now?' Zoe asked, choosing to ignore Zak's comment.

'Let's go sightseeing,' he replied, stepping onto the moving pavement. He reached out, pulling Zoe along behind him.

They rode along on the pavement for a while, taking in the surrounding scenery. Zoe's head turned this way and that. Her eyes darted from side to side as she stared at every building, every person, and every object they passed. She found the experience of just standing on the footpath watching everything go by to be a little disturbing. It was a weird feeling. Even though they were travelling quite slowly, Zoe found that her body was struggling to cope. She was finding some difficulty in keeping her balance as she turned her head backwards, forwards, upwards, and downwards in rapid succession, while trying to take in her surroundings. The bizarre experience of climbing through the light beam hadn't helped either. A slight nausea crept up inside Zoe's body, causing her to swallow hard. She screwed up her face as she caught a definite taste of bile in her throat.

As they passed through the long shadows cast by tall buildings, Zoe noticed a slight tinge of colour on the pavement and the road. She pointed this out to Zak.

'Those are ultraviolet particles that are embedded in the surface. They absorb light during daytime then give off a glow in the dark,' he said. 'It's usually blue, but can be other colours too. Part of the night time luminescence from this planet that can be seen in Lowlands is formed by the light from those particles. It saves on the cost of street lamps too.'

Zoe stared in awe as she took in the information.

The buildings in this part of London were all of a similar shape and size. They were tall, with each one towering upwards to form a landscape that was even, imposing but unexciting. Each building had a mainframe structure that had the appearance of steel. However, the substance felt considerably softer with a lot more flexibility than any metal, when Zoe pressed her hand against a wall as they passed. The outer skeleton of each edifice was sheathed in what looked at first glance to be glass, but the dark coloured material seemed considerably more pliable when she pushed powerfully against it to test its firmness. Zoe guessed that despite this flexibility it would be quite difficult to break.

'It looks like thick plastic or PVC,' said Zak, noticing the puzzled look on Zoe's face. 'At a guess I would say that both substances are combined in a more advanced form than you recognise from your time. Human technology and knowledge has developed substantially since the twenty-first century. These modern materials are extremely durable. They are much stronger than glass and steel. They are also cheaper and easier to put together, so when you buy in bulk you get what amounts to a supply of almost instant buildings. It's very cost effective when you are constructing a large city such as this one. Another advantage is that visibility is controlled internally, so people are able to see out but no one can see in unless you want them to.'

Zoe looked amazed. 'How do you know this?' she asked.

'We used similar materials for our buildings on Zaarl,' Zak said, 'until we got more advanced and found something better.'

'What do you think *they* are?' Zoe enquired, pointing to one of many rectangular shaped booths that were situated on most of the street corners they passed by. The booths were similar in shape to the old style telephone boxes she'd seen on Earth when she was a little girl, except they weren't red. These booths were green. They were larger than the old red phone boxes too.

Zoe had noticed a number of people going into each of the street corner booths. She also observed groups of other people coming out. She was curious about what they did in there.

'They're teleports,' Zak replied.

'What do they do?' Zoe asked.

'They transport people to different parts of this globe,' said Zak. 'I know that because when I've been up here before I once took a little trip out – in disguise of course – so I did get a chance to study them. They are like the teleports between here and Lowlands, but these are programmed to transport people internally in the South only. There are lots of these booths – or teleport stations as they're called – all over this planet. Inside each one is a list of places you can go to from that booth. If you want to go somewhere that is not on the same teleport circuit as the booth, you change ports along the way. The only places civilians can't get to from the teleport are Lowlands or other man-made planets.'

'Oh,' said Zoe, 'It sounds a bit like our underground and mainline train systems, but without the trains and stations.'

She guessed that when they constructed the substitute planet it wouldn't have been possible, or practical, to reconstruct the tube system or any rail networks. The more she thought about it the more sense it made, especially as there was no longer any call for long northbound journeys. Zoe remembered what Lake had said about the South being London and the old Home Counties. Everywhere else that still remained of the once United Kingdom, was in Lowlands.

It was at this point that Zoe caught a glimpse of Lowlands on the horizon. The view appeared through a large gap between two buildings. In fact it was more than Lowlands. She could see planet Earth. At least, she could see the part that contained the remnants of the British Isles and the neighbouring coastline of France. The English Channel appeared to be far wider than when she last travelled across it. In fact the gap between England and France was now massive.

Zoe couldn't believe that Earth was so far below her. It looked so close. In fact it looked huge. She stopped, walking on the spot as she took time to observe the stricken planet. It was extremely beautiful. The sight took her breath away. The view she had wasn't an expansive panorama but it provided a vista which was far superior to anything she had ever seen from an aeroplane. The part of Earth that was visible to her looked very different from how she remembered it on maps she'd seen in her childhood. She could still make out some of the familiar contours of land masses, but all around the British Isles there was a lot more sea than she could recollect from the books and globes of her school days. Zoe couldn't help thinking that at least this part of the blue planet was most definitely bluer now than it had been back in her time.

Another thought struck Zoe. She immediately raised it with Zak. 'If the Earth is still rotating around the sun, how can the Security Police be sure of landing in Lowlands when they cast their beams at night? Surely Lowlands wouldn't always be directly below here. Its position would vary according to Earth's movement around the sun. The planet South is man-made, so it must either be static or orbiting the Earth?'

Zak scratched his head in thought before answering her. 'I would guess that the new planet must have been made with a magnetic force that locks it into Lowlands,' he said. 'Which means that this globe rotates at the same speed as the planet Earth, hence the South is always in line with Lowlands. The smaller globe up there must also be aligned to the South, so that will form an alliance with Lowlands too. If you think about it this planet does not orbit the sun and unlike your moon – which orbits the Earth – it remains at a particular fixed point above the original planet. The replica planets are held rigidly in line by a self-generated gravitational field that locks onto a specific point on Earth, so that each artificial planet is always maintained in the same place. Hence, every one of these man-made structures is aligned to the geographical location of its original country. As planet Earth revolves, so it pulls each new planet along with it. That's just an educated guess from what I've experienced on my own planet. I can't say for certain that the same principles apply to this one, as I have no official information about its origin.'

Zoe took in this explanation, but wasn't altogether convinced of its accuracy. It was too much for her to get her head around at this point, given what she'd recently gone through. However, Zak was an alien from a planet far more advanced in science than the Earth she knew, so who was she to argue with his theory. Certainly not having just accompanied him on a climb up inside a light beam. Whatever the explanation, she was fascinated by the impressive sight of the large planet that hung alongside this comparatively tiny orb.

The pair continued their journey in silence for a while. Zoe's brain was energised and animated by everything she saw, sometimes even by what she didn't see.

She had not seen or heard any aeroplanes. She remembered when she'd visited London with her school and with her family, there would always be an aeroplane in the sky. She wondered if planes still existed, or if teleports had rendered them redundant. *If that was the case, how did people travel the world?*

Her brain was still pondering this as Zak suddenly grabbed her arm, dragging her from the pavement. He pulled her into the doorway of a nearby building.

'What's up?' Zoe asked, alarm registering on her face.

'People are staring at us,' Zak replied. 'We need to

get out of these uniforms. They make us noticeable to passers-by. Believe me that's not good, given that we're intruders into this world. It's probably not that unusual for residents to see police in uniform, but a number of people are staring. They probably do that all the time, but given that we don't want to be noticed, it's best if we can find some other clothes. If we stay in these, we could get stopped and asked some very awkward questions. That is something we don't want, especially when the two Security Policemen – who have just registered a report before signing off from duty – don't turn up for their next shift. When that happens the authorities will launch an investigation, which won't be good for us if there are witnesses who can testify to seeing us around here. There's also the fact that we are being monitored by the security devices that are on these buildings.'

'You're right,' agreed Zoe. 'I'd forgotten we were still wearing the police uniforms … but where will we get different clothes? And what do we use for money?'

'Leave it to me,' said Zak. 'You wait here and keep out of sight. I'll be back soon.'

Zak swiftly transmuted into the body of a bird. He then flew off into the distance. Zoe watched him go, flattening herself against the side of the building in a considered bid to avoid detection. She stayed in the doorway, cowering as she awaited his return. She suddenly felt rather conspicuous since Zak had reminded her that they were still wearing the clothes of men who might well be dead by now. Zoe shuddered at the thoughts that immediately entered her head. *If the policemen were dead and their bodies were recovered, what then? Or what if they survived, and were somehow able to get back to their headquarters?*

Zoe had gone from excitement and curiosity to apprehension in just a few minutes. She was once more alone as she waited for Zak to come back. Her mind was beginning to let fear influence her ideas. *We could be executed,* she thought, shivering nervously at the prospect.

CHAPTER ELEVEN

Zoe waited patiently but Zak didn't return. Her eyes continually searched the skies for sight of a bird, but there were no birds to be seen. Zoe's concerns began to mount. She didn't know exactly how long Zak had been gone, but guessed it must at least be a couple of hours by now.

What if he doesn't come back? What if he's been killed? Or discovered. Will he tell on me? Will the police come for me? What if he's been working with the authorities all along, and he's tricked me into coming here so they can arrest me in exchange for his safe passage back to 2015 to find his own people? That's a possibility I guess, as he's been here before. Maybe they can even teleport him directly back to his own planet? Why, oh why did I let him bring me here? I knew I shouldn't have trusted him.

As all of these thoughts ran wild and unchallenged through her head, Zoe convinced herself that Zak *had* been collaborating with the security police, and it wouldn't be long before they came for her. She decided she ought to try to make her escape before the police arrived, so she stepped out of the doorway.

Zoe's feet had barely touched the moving pavement when someone tapped her on the shoulder. She flinched and her body quivered slightly. Convinced she was about to be arrested she turned around. A man stood there. He was a complete stranger to Zoe, but she was somewhat relieved to see that he wasn't wearing a police uniform. The man was smartly dressed. He wore a close fitting dark grey suit, a light blue shirt and a check patterned tie. The style looked very modern for the period. It was certainly fashionable, as far as Zoe could tell from what she'd seen other people wearing in the short time she'd been on this globe. In his hands he held a number of parcels that were wrapped in a sort of membrane and held together with a thin metallic twine. The man struggled to balance them against his chest as he reached out his right arm in her direction.

Alarm shot through Zoe as he moved towards her. She tried to step back into the doorway she had just left, but his hand clamped firmly onto her shoulder. She grabbed his fingers bending them backwards, struggling to break his grip so she could get a chance to run away.

Then the man spoke. 'Zoe, it's me Zak,' he hissed. 'Come, I have clothes for you. Change into them quickly before you are discovered.'

He hauled Zoe inside the building, handing her the parcels as he drew her attention to a sign indicating the whereabouts of nearby toilets.

'Go in there and change,' he said. 'When you're done, pack the uniform inside the discarded wrapping, then bring it out here.'

Zoe did as she was told. It wasn't long before she emerged. She was clad in a modern black trouser suit, complemented by a cream silky blouse. This was topped by a cream coloured scarf that had a two-toned black floral pattern running lengthwise along the edge. On her feet she wore flat black shoes. She looked every inch a business woman.

Zak was now back as himself. He smiled as he looked her up and down. 'An excellent match and a perfect fit if I may say so,' he said, taking the parcelled up uniform from Zoe.

'How did you know what sizes to get?' Zoe asked.

'A combination of guesswork and mental calculation,' Zak replied. Then he grinned and said, 'plus a bit of inside knowledge from being a moth larva.'

Zoe pulled a face. She glared at him, shaking her head in disapproval. Zak – still grinning broadly – walked across the lobby to the far wall, where he opened a door that had a crude drawing of flames embossed onto its surface. He took the bundled up uniform from Zoe, then dropped it down the open shaft inside.

'Incinerator,' he explained. 'That should leave no trace, except for a few ashes and no-one will be suspicious of those.'

'Why were you so long? Where did you go? More to the point why did you return as a stranger?' The questions tumbled from Zoe's mouth.

'Slow down,' said Zak calmly, 'Let me answer your questions. Firstly, it took a lot longer than I thought to get these clothes, partly because I had to make sure I got something that fitted you better than that uniform.'

He smiled. 'Secondly, I got them from a high class supplier, where I also managed to get us both what you used to call credit cards. These are now today's equivalent of money. They are linked to mobile communicators, which are similar to the mobile phones of your time but are now much smarter and far more advanced. They are mini computers that are automatically connected to everything that you buy. Your travel costs, rent, general living expenses. In fact, everything you purchase is instantly deducted from your overall credit, which you pay in advance rather than in arrears. If your credit runs out, you can't buy anything until you pay in again.

'These cards – which are actually mini discs – also serve as identity cards. All of your personal details are included. So is your photographic image and DNA base, which incidentally you need to register. This information is linked directly to a national database, which means that the Government know all there is to know about you and your movements. Everything you do on this planet is monitored, with every detail openly accessible to police and Government officials.'

'How did you get hold of those?' asked Zoe. 'What information did you put on them? And how did you manage to get us credit?'

'Better not to ask,' said Zak.

'Is it legal?' asked Zoe.

'Probably not,' replied Zak smiling. 'But it's almost undetectable. I used my technical knowledge to hack into the database – where I made a few adjustments to increase the number of citizens in London by two, including our names, false dates of birth, our addresses, and bank details. I opened bank accounts in both our names, taking the liberty of investing funds from some existing business accounts into them. There is so much money in those business accounts that the amounts I have transferred won't even be missed. And before you ask, no, they won't find out.

'There's now enough in our accounts for us to live comfortably even if we have to stay here for life, which incidentally makes us rather special citizens. Oh by the way, I didn't know your full name. I only know you as Zoe so I registered you as Victoria Boswell. That's the name you used when you came to my factory.'

Zoe shuddered as she thought about that visit and what it had led to. 'I'll try to remember that when I need to give my name. What about your appearance as a stranger. How did that come about?'

'Long story,' said Zak. 'But the short version is that I had to change quickly from being a bird as there are no birds, or animals, any more. It seems that all wildlife has been banished from this planet. It only exists in Lowlands as people up here don't want the inconvenience or the mess. In the short time I was flying I discovered the planet has a transparent roof. Well, it's more like a skin which is inflated to varying heights according to what's required. The distended skin forms an air bubble around the planet. This is what gives the planet its globular appearance. The skin is made from a material that enables sunshine and other light to filter through whilst keeping out rain, snow and foreign bodies that might potentially cause harm to inhabitants. The bubble also internally percolates oxygen into the atmosphere of the planet, as well as operating an air conditioning system that maintains an even temperature throughout. There are special panels built into the skin that can be temporarily retracted when needed. These allow authorised space flights to leave or enter, without interfering with the day to day functions of the equipment within the bubble. On the outer membrane of the planet are a number of nodules, which are designed to generate the gravity force that helps keep the planet in position.

'But to get back to why I changed my appearance, it was because as I was flying across the city I got pointed at by people below. Someone also shot at me. Fortunately, they missed. But I had to evade several attempts to capture me, before I managed to find somewhere that was both safe and isolated enough to allow me to land so I could change my shape. Even then there were lots of people still looking for the bird as I made my escape. I didn't want anyone seeing me in that situation, either as Zak – or as a Security Policeman – in case someone remembered me being around and told the authorities. So when I eventually got the chance to safely alter my appearance I became someone in the crowd. When the crowd dispersed I stayed as the person I had become until I came back here. Any more questions?'

It was Zoe's turn to smile. 'No,' was all she said.

Zak handed Zoe a tiny disc shaped object that appeared to be an extremely miniature version of the smart phone she remembered from 2015.

'This is your identity and credit link,' he said. 'Now switch it to camera to take a picture of yourself. After that, rub your finger along the red line at the top of the screen, press register, and then transmit. Your photo and your DNA database will be automatically recorded and registered.'

Zoe did as Zak ordered. Afterwards she looked at him with eyebrows raised.

'You are now officially a citizen of the South. You exist in this World as Victoria Boswell,' he said.

The two of them emerged onto the street wearing their new clothes. Zoe began to pay close attention to the moving road. She noticed that some of the vehicles were empty, whereas others had people sitting in them yet no one seemed to be driving. She screwed up her eyes as she stared into the vehicles in a bid to see what was happening inside. Zak, not for the first time, seemed to read her thoughts.

'Remote control,' he said. 'All vehicles are privately owned by business people. Individual citizens are not allowed to have them. If you want to use one you climb aboard either an empty one, or one already occupied if you prefer. Once inside, you pay by using your mobile ID disc. Once payment is confirmed the vehicle moves off. If you don't pay the vehicle doesn't move. Then the doors automatically lock so nobody can leave. Any other passengers inside the vehicle will put pressure on you to pay, or they will summon the Transport Police. If you are alone, you will be held prisoner inside the vehicle until either you pay or the police arrive. The cars go where the streets go. They are programmed to turn at corners, but are in a fixed position so they cannot overtake or be overtaken.'

'Can we go in one?' said Zoe, excitedly. 'You know, on our sightseeing tour.'

Zak smiled. 'Come on then,' he said, stepping into the road and opening the door of a passing empty car.

Zoe climbed in beside him as he took a seat in the back, placed his ID disc in the meter slot, motioning for Zoe to do the same. She did as bidden, then sat back to enjoy the ride.

'It's a fixed rate,' explained Zak. 'The route is circular so you can get off anywhere. But wherever you go it costs the same amount, so I guess there's a good profit margin.'

'I guess it's a bit like a taxi service but with no driver,' said Zoe, 'I wonder if they still pay road tax?'

She saw the puzzled look on Zak's face. 'That's the tax that drivers pay to use the roads in my time, supposedly to help subsidise road maintenance. Although according to my dad it never was.' Then, attempting to answer her own question she said 'It's probably included in the charge for the journey. I guess it's like the toll roads in my day, whereby drivers paid money to use certain roads. Perhaps this is the modern equivalent. But why no driver, and why make the roads move?'

'No petrol costs, repair bills or wages, and no air pollution.' Zak replied. 'Besides, taxi driving or bus driving is hardly a job that fits in with the image of the ultra-modern business world that this planet tries to project.'

Zoe was still staring in wholehearted fascination at buildings, street corners, kiosks, and everything they passed by. She was like a young child on an outing to somewhere new, finding it both exciting and strange at the same time, especially being in the self-propelled car. Zoe's elation was soon tempered with the realisation that each building and every street was very similar in design. It was as if they were sitting in a cinema with the same film footage continually played on a loop. She found it weird. It was a little unsettling too. Zoe gave a small shudder as she thought how secluded, sanitized, and unfriendly this place was in comparison to her life in Cristelee.

She suddenly realised something was missing from the landscape. 'I've not seen any shops,' she said.

'There are no shops,' Zak replied. 'All goods are bought directly from manufacturers by computer. You order what you want and it is sent to you directly through a modern 3D printer. Everything on this and every one of the other new planets is owned by just one company. It's called Mofanza Holdings. It does have smaller subsidiaries spread about the various planets but they all belong to the parent company, which incidentally has the President of the South among its board of directors.'

'So how did you get our clothes then?' Zoe asked. 'You said you got them from a high class supplier. You didn't have access to any printer and you couldn't possibly have got them delivered so quickly. So, where did they come from?'

'I told you it was better not to ask questions,' said Zak, turning his face away. 'Just accept that we've got everything we need for now.'

'You said the President of the South,' exclaimed Zoe, remembering Zak's earlier words. 'Isn't there a King or Queen now?'

'The Royal Family no longer exist,' Zak replied. 'Haven't done so for centuries.'

'How do you know all this?' Zoe's suspicions were aroused.

'Well,' said Zak, patiently, 'when you hack into databases it's surprising what you can find out.'

They rode on in silence for a while, with Zoe wondering what Zak *had* done to get their clothes, credit, and mobile ID discs. She hoped that whatever it was it wouldn't land them in trouble with the police, but she had a nagging feeling that it just might.

Zoe's thoughts were interrupted as she caught sight of a large illuminated object at the roadside. 'Let's get out here,' she shouted, grabbing at the door handle.

'Why here?' asked Zak.

'There's something I want to see,' Zoe exclaimed. She had yanked the door wide open and was halfway out of the slow moving vehicle before Zak could move. He quickly followed behind as she crossed the road. Zoe stopped in front of the display unit she'd espied from the car.

It was a map of London, showing streets and places of interest. Zoe read it with a shiver of excitement running through her as she saw a cluster of names that she recognised instantly. Among them were Big Ben, Houses of Parliament, St Paul's Cathedral, Buckingham Palace, Westminster Abbey, Nelson's Column, the Tower of London, and various museums and art galleries, including the British and National.

'They can't be the original buildings, surely?' Zoe queried. 'Maybe they're holograms, or pictures? Can we go and see what they've replaced them with, please?'

Zak shrugged his shoulders, as he nodded his consent. Zoe, having made a mental note of the direction they needed to travel in, stepped into the road to hijack another vehicle. She was pulled back by Zak, who jerked his head in the direction of one of the corner booths.

'Let's go by teleport,' he said.

Zoe looked scared. 'Are you sure we'll be okay?' she asked nervously.

'Of course we will,' said Zak. 'We do this all of the time on my planet. People who live here do likewise and they seem fine.'

He pushed Zoe into the nearest kiosk then stepped in behind her. Zoe looked around the inside of the booth. It was roomy enough to have held another four or five people. She found a meter similar to the one in the car they'd just vacated, but this one had a small narrow display screen next to the credit disc slot. Illuminated letters moved horizontally across the screen. It took Zoe a few minutes to realise that they were the names of destinations available from this booth. Seeing the words *"St Paul's Cathedral"* pass by she punched the button. The display unit ceased its movement and a green light flashed on the meter, accompanied by a message which read, *"Please insert credit disc."*

They pushed their discs into the slot separately, pressed the button on the identified destination then awaited further instructions. Nothing appeared on the screen, but there was a humming sound. Zoe suddenly experienced a vague feeling of dizziness that lasted a few seconds. Next thing she knew they were stepping out at St Paul's.

'That was amazing,' said Zoe. 'It was a bit like travelling ...'

She had been about to say "through the computer when I came into your spacecraft," but thinking that would be undiplomatic in the circumstances she let her sentence tail off, finishing it with 'in a lift.'

'I told you it would be alright,' smiled Zak.

They approached the cathedral which stood ahead of them in all of its stately splendour. Zoe couldn't believe what she was seeing. 'It looks just like the original' she gasped.

'Maybe it is,' said Zak.

'How did they get it here then?' asked Zoe.

'The same way that we came?' suggested Zak.

As they walked further, Zoe caught her breath. 'Look at that,' she breathed, 'I can't believe this.'

Alongside the cathedral stood Westminster Abbey, to the left Big Ben looked down on the Houses of Parliament, right ahead was the Tower of London. To the right of this Nelson stood atop his famous column surveying all below, with the National Gallery and British Museum as neighbours. Other galleries and museums completed a four-sided rectangle of wide streets that were currently crowded with sightseers. The centre-piece of the whole extravaganza was Buckingham Palace. All of the buildings looked exactly the same as Zoe remembered from the trips she had taken to London as a little girl.

'I can't believe it,' she repeated. 'They all look so real, but they can't be.'

Zak nudged her. He pointed to a sign on a small screen set in a nearby wall. The wording read *Take a walk through history. See these buildings in their*

historic glory and marvel at the technology that brought
them here. Tutorial about to start in the Historical
Department building in ten minutes.

The two of them easily found the department building and went inside. An hour later they emerged after a wistful, nostalgic Zoe had relived some of her history and her childhood. She learned that the historic buildings she could see before her were indeed the real deal. They had been transported brick by brick before being reassembled with help from computer technology in their present environment, along with original artefacts, furniture, exhibits and paintings. None of the buildings were used nowadays, other than as historical museum pieces and visitor attractions.

After spending the rest of the day viewing the old relics, they walked back towards the transportation booth. Zoe asked Zak where they were going to stay while in the South.

'You said you had entered false addresses on our identity details. Does that mean we are staying in a hotel?' she asked.

He shook his head, producing two small solid triangles from his pocket. Zak handed one to Zoe saying, 'No, we have our own apartments in one of the tower blocks. These are the addresses I recorded on the database. They are false only in the sense that we don't usually reside on this planet.'

Zoe took the triangle. She examined it closely, turning it over and over in her hand before pressing, prodding and shaking the object. As far as she could make out, the disc was made from a hard substance. She guessed it was some kind of metal, but not one that she recognised. There was a code number embossed into the surface on the rear, but apart from that it was blank on both sides.

'It's a key,' said Zak. 'A key to your fully furnished apartment, which is in the same block as mine but one floor below.'

'How did you get those?' asked Zoe.

'I told you not to ask,' replied Zak. 'So don't, then you won't get into any trouble.'

'Whereabouts are the apartments?' Zoe asked, feeling suddenly excited at the prospect of having her own place to live, wondering what it would look like.

'I'll take you there now,' said Zak. 'It will be a secret until then.' He opened the door to the booth, bending slightly as he summoned up their destination on the screen. He stood up, shielding the screen message with his body to maintain the surprise as Zoe entered, pressing the transit button when she was inside. But just as he did Zoe let out a yell.

'I've left my ID credit disc in the art gallery!!'

She dashed out of the booth as the doors were closing. Before Zak could follow her the transportation process kicked in, dispatching his body into the ether.

Zoe ran back to the gallery, where she was lucky enough to find her disc, lying where she'd left it when she'd absentmindedly put it down to examine one of the exhibits more closely. She picked up the disc, put it in her pocket then headed for the exit. There was no one else around as she left the building. She looked around for Zak, unaware that the transportation booth had

121

completed its job by sending him to his chosen destination. When Zoe saw that he wasn't there, she cursed.

'He's gone and left me here. So now I've got a key to an apartment but I don't know where it is. Why didn't he wait for me?' she growled. Then she thought, *He'll come back for me so I'll just wait.*

Zoe wandered over to the booth but found she couldn't wait inside as it interfered with the transportation process unless she was actually travelling. She couldn't wait outside either, as the pavements were moving. Eventually she settled for the doorway of a nearby office block from where she could see the booth.

Zoe hadn't been there long when she heard a deep voice from behind her say, 'Don't move or make a sound, just hand over your credit disc and you won't get hurt.'

Zoe felt the blade of a knife, or some other weapon, pushing against the small of her back. She tried to turn round but an arm snaked across her throat.

'I said don't move,' the voice repeated.

Zoe wondered what use her credit disc was to a thief. The identity and information encrypted into it was hers so unless the thief knew of a way to change *that* it was useless to him.

'What's the point of me giving my disc to you?' she asked, trying to keep her voice calm and normal. 'It's a registration of me. You can't use it.'

'I'm not interested in your personal details,' said the voice. 'I can still spend your credit. So hand it over.'

Zoe wished Zak was here. She wouldn't be in this

mess if he was. She didn't want to get stabbed, maybe killed, so she decided that the best thing to do in the circumstances would be to hand over the disc. Even then she thought that the thief might still use the knife on her if he so wished. She felt helpless. Reaching into her pocket, Zoe slowly withdrew the disc. A young man quickly appeared in front of her, his hand outstretched palm upwards. She could still feel the blade in her back so she guessed that there were at least two of them.

Zoe was about to put the disc into the young man's hand when another voice rang out. It came from the direction of a booth to her left.

'Stay where you are, you are under arrest. Do not attempt to run away or you will be shot. We are the Street Police. You are breaking the law, therefore we are taking you into custody on charges of aggravated burglary, carrying a weapon, and possibly, attempted murder.'

Almost before the voice had delivered its full message, six people in blue uniforms had rushed from the cover of the building. They quickly overpowered Zoe's assailants.

One of the policemen stood in front of Zoe. 'Are you alright Miss?' he asked.

Zoe nodded, relieved to see them. She was grateful for her reprieve.

'I'm afraid you will have to come with us to the police station too,' said the officer. 'We will need your statement as evidence. You are not under arrest'.

Zoe was escorted to another booth that was on the corner of the street, close to the one that she had been watching from the doorway. The booth was similar to the one she and Zak had travelled in, except it was light blue in colour. She found she was sharing the kiosk with all of the police officers as well as both would be robbers. It was rather crowded on the ethereal journey to police headquarters.

As the door of the police teleport booth closed on the group, the door to the public booth flew open and Zak stepped out. He headed for the art gallery, calling out Zoe's name as he went.

CHAPTER TWELVE

Zoe stepped out of the transporter to find herself inside the police station. She noticed that although it was not the same station used by the security police, the layout was quite similar. She was taken to a plain undecorated room that was bare except for a desk and two chairs. A uniformed officer sat at the desk. He pointed to the empty chair, motioning Zoe to sit down.

'What's your name?' he asked abruptly.

'Zoe Marshall,' was the reply.

'Well Miss Marshall,' the officer continued. 'Tell me what happened out there at the historic site.'

Zoe narrated her story about the attempted robbery. She didn't mention Zak or her mislaid credit disc, as she didn't want the officer asking her questions she might not be able to answer. The policeman didn't write anything down, but Zoe had the feeling that her statement was being recorded anyway. When she had finished he said 'Thank you for that Miss Marshall. You've been very helpful.'

Zoe stood up to go. The policeman motioned her to sit down again. She did so. A warning bell rang somewhere in her head. Something was wrong. The officer spoke again.

'You said your name is Zoe Marshall.' He said

sternly. 'We have no record of any Zoe Marshall living in the South. Also, the credit details on what you claim to be *your* identity disc, are in the name of Victoria Boswell. Would you like to explain?'

Zoe's first reaction was to experience a rapidly rising sense of panic. This was followed by a vision in which she saw everything unravelling as she and Zak were arrested. She tried to calm herself by taking several deep breaths. The exercise brought about a more composed state of mind, in which she was struck by the realisation that she'd committed a massive faux pas in giving her real name.

In the confusion caused by the attempted theft and being brought to the police station, Zoe had forgotten that Zak had registered her as Victoria. Now she had to try to redeem her error somehow. She considered asking them to body scan her, which would prove that she was Victoria Boswell, but then thought, *What if their check somehow revealed that Zak has manipulated their computer systems in order to falsify credit and identity for both of us. We'll both definitely be arrested then. We could end up in prison for a long time.*

Zoe decided she would try to bluff her way out of this situation without arousing suspicion. She looked up at the policeman. 'I'm sorry,' she said, shaking her head as if in annoyance with herself. 'When I said I was Zoe Marshall I wasn't really thinking straight … shock you see … from the attempted assault and robbery. I am Victoria Boswell. Zoe Marshall was someone I knew a long time ago. I was thinking about her in my panic when I believed the robbers were going to kill me. I *am*

Victoria Boswell. You can see that from my identity disc. How else would I have that disc?'

The policeman stared unblinkingly at Zoe. 'I'm sorry Miss,' he said, shaking his head. 'I'm not convinced by your story. I'm going to have to make further enquiries. You could have stolen that disc from Victoria Boswell, for all I know. You'll be put in a holding cell overnight while we carry out further investigations to try to ascertain the full facts.'

Zoe's heart sank. She slumped back in her seat. The policeman took her by the arm. He led her from the interview room into one of the rooms that served as a holding cell. It housed two small beds and a toilet. As the door slammed shut behind her, she wondered how on earth she was going to get out of this situation. She sat down heavily on a bunk, aware that she couldn't even call on Zak to help her. Zoe didn't know where he was, but what mostly filled her with alarm was the thought that he didn't know she was in this mess.

She knew she was in a mess brought about by her own stupidity. Her feelings fluctuated between panic and despair. Then, a sudden idea sparked in her head. The notion became more feasible the more Zoe thought about it. At the very least it offered a small glimmer of hope in her current desperate situation. Perhaps she had been a little hasty after all in dismissing Zak's inability to help. Her thoughts were now considerably more positive. *Maybe he did come back for me. He could have seen the police taking me away? If so he wouldn't want them to see him so he could well be plotting to get me out of here.*

She remembered Zak's words to her when he'd

revealed himself as the bear. *He'd said "I may have to become like people who are your enemies" In that case, he may even be here now as a policeman* Zoe thought.

She perked up a little more at this thought. She was filled with even more optimism when she recalled Zak's later statement to her on that occasion "*Just remember I am always close by. I may even be burrowing down in your clothes again.*"

Zoe quickly took off her jacket. She held it up in front of her face and asked, 'Are you in there?'

There was no response. Zoe moved her face closer to the coat so that her nose was almost inside one of the pockets.

'Zak … Zak … are you in my lining? … Come on Zak. If you are there please come out … I need you!'

Again there was no response. Zoe grabbed the coat by the sleeves and began shaking it wildly as she yelled. 'Come on … don't mess me about. If you are there show yourself.'

'Hallo.'

A woman's voice interrupted Zoe's frenzied efforts. She stopped what she was doing and half-turned. It was only then she saw that there was another person in the cell with her. She had obviously been there when Zoe was brought in, but Zoe had been too preoccupied with her thoughts to notice. The woman was smartly dressed. She looked to be in her late thirties.

Zoe swiftly put her jacket on again. She could feel her face rapidly reddening. Approaching her newly discovered cell mate she said 'I'm sorry about that. I do funny things when I get into a flap.'

The woman smiled, nodding sympathetically. 'I'm Jane Marston,' she said, extending an arm to shake hands with Zoe.

'Zo ... um, Victoria Boswell,' said Zoe taking the proffered hand and shaking it loosely.

'What are *you* in here for?' asked Jane.

Zoe was about to tell her when she had second thoughts. She was reluctant to give information about her background to this woman, whom she didn't know, in case it came back to haunt her.

She could be a spy, Zoe thought. *Someone the police have put in here in the hope that I talk to her and incriminate myself. Even if she's not a spy, then if I tell her I'm from a different time she could use that information to buy her freedom. Where would that leave me? I might be seen as a Government enemy then possibly killed, tortured, or even put in a museum to talk to visitors about the past.* Zoe grinned wryly at this latter thought. Then the serious thoughts returned as she plotted her future actions. *At the moment the police have nothing on me, so they might let me go. Although, I guess they could send me back to Lowlands, though I doubt that would happen. Still, if they did, it would at least mean I have another chance to get back up here at some time in the future.*

I can't ignore Jane though, if we are going to be together all night, so I have to say something. Even then I need to be careful, as there are probably hidden cameras or microphones in the cell.

After this prolonged period of thought, Zoe decided there would be no harm in relaying her encounter with the thieves that had led to her being in the police station.

She could also reiterate her story about a slip of the tongue raising suspicion, after all if anyone was listening in to the conversation they would know that already.

After finishing the brief account of her presence in the cell, Zoe asked Jane about herself. Jane, unlike Zoe, displayed no reluctance to tell her story.

'I'm a student of history,' she began. 'I spend my time at the only university on this globe, the University of Historical Learning and Acknowledgement; I've been there for most of my adult life.'

'How come you are here in this prison cell?' asked Zoe.

'Because of what I did and what I know,' Jane replied.

'What you know?' echoed Zoe. 'How does that work then? Surely if you are a student you're *supposed* to know things?'

'It's a long story,' said Jane.

'We've got all night,' said Zoe, quickly warming to this woman. Then lowering her voice to a whisper she added, 'But be careful, they might be monitoring us and our conversations.'

Zoe waved her hand around in a circular motion, in a gesture indicating there might be hidden surveillance equipment in the cell.

Jane shook her head. 'It doesn't work like that,' she said in her normal voice, ignoring Zoe's perceived need to whisper. 'They don't need to eavesdrop.'

A puzzled look came over Zoe's face.

'Microchips,' said Jane.

Zoe looked even more confused.

'Babies and education,' said Jane, her tone becoming louder and more emphatic. 'You must know about that?'

Zoe wasn't sure what Jane meant, so she decided her safest bet was to continue to feign ignorance. She shook her head, then seeing a look of suspicion appear on Jane's face she decided to come clean. Well, at least she would tell half of the truth about how she arrived in the South. Hopefully this would allay Jane's suspicions and encourage her to talk. She wanted to find out about this planet, and who better than a history student to tell her? Whatever it took, she needed to keep this conversation going.

'Actually I'm from Lowlands.' Zoe said, keeping her voice to a whisper 'I came here illegally a few days ago. Now I'm probably going to get sent back there, so I know very little about your World.'

Zoe didn't really expect to be sent back to Lowlands, but she decided there was no harm in letting Jane believe that she was.

'I doubt I'll get the chance to come back again, so please tell me all about the South and its history,' she added.

'Where do you want me to start?' asked Jane, her doubt subsiding as she too warmed to Zoe's plight and the intensity of her pleas.

'Tell me about the split. Why does the South have its own planet?' Zoe asked.

'Personally I think the concept is more akin to what you might find with a space station,' corrected Jane, 'but I guess the scientists who created it said it was a planet and as that was what they initially set out to construct,

131

then – according to them at least – it's a planet. So that's what everyone refers to it as, and I have to admit it does *look* like a planet. Whatever it is, it is man-made like the ones used by other countries. Each planet is programmed to rotate in line with the real planet Earth as it revolves around the sun, hence a year up here is the same as a year in Lowlands.

'The split happened about two hundred years ago. History shows there were a lot of wars between different countries in the previous eight hundred years. There was a lot of terrorist activity too, with online communications being used to organise and co-ordinate attacks as well as for recruitment. When it became clear that military action was having no effect on terrorism, the richest, most powerful countries combined to close down the internet. This resulted in various terrorist groups joining forces and declaring war on the rest of the World. To combat this, the most powerful Governments developed genetically modified – part robot – soldiers to help them fight. It got to the point where no one knew who was fighting whom, so different Governments fell out with each other, declaring war on everyone. In the ensuing conflict – which every Government wanted to win – human soldiers became an extremely rare commodity, due to an excessive number of deaths and a huge quantity of deserters. As a result, robot production increased rapidly to cover military need. This time they were pure robots. At first these androids fought alongside the remaining regular and volunteer soldiers as part of each country's army. But these machines weren't capable of independent thought. The robots were programmed to kill, so that's what they did. However, they couldn't tell the difference between allies or enemies, so they killed anything and anyone. The World's population was almost wiped out until representatives from every country agreed to come together for peace talks, which eventually led to the robots being decommissioned and abandoned.

'Alongside this, the effects of global warming – mostly caused by mankind's greed coupled with an unwillingness to accept that the planet was being damaged – created massive problems too. Earth suffered severe and extreme weather patterns. There was a subsequent increase in disease, food shortages, flooding, along with devastation of forests and destruction of urban developments. These cataclysmic events brought the human race to the brink of extinction. The ultimate scenario of a dying planet caused further friction between nations, who then fought over dwindling resources. Every country was anxious to preserve its own resources. All borders were closed as Governments – who would rather spend money on wars that kill millions of people than on saving the planet and saving lives – collectively turned their back on the increasing numbers of refugees who had lost their homes, their livelihoods, even their country of birth. Earth was not only in a state of major conflict, it was in absolute chaos.

'The richer countries decided the human race needed a different environment in which to live, as the Earth could no longer sustain the quality of life that they wanted. As a result, their respective Governments increased financial help to scientists – who had been working on creating a planet capable of supporting human life since the Hadron Collider experiments in 2012. It took a long time though. At first every country worked together, but as each nation's economy and population declined, they all took unilateral action. The upshot is that all of the richest countries now have their own planets. These are the ones that stretch beyond the South. You can see them all strung out in the night sky, like a row of pearls. There's Germany, France, Russia, China, The Union of Europe, and one or two others, although the USA has the biggest. They have the most too, as they have four. The USA rule the skies with their Space Patrol Force. They also have force fields around all of their planets to ensure that they are isolated from the rest of the countries. Any inward bound shuttle flight needs advance permission and appropriate permits before being allowed to land on US property. The USA also has major financial interests in every other country – effectively owning them as well as their politicians – because all of the multinational industries have merged into one big company called Mofanza, which has its roots in the USA. There is no meaningful contact between the Governments of any country anymore, apart from settling financial matters. Each country goes its own way. There is no dialogue, no aid. Every country looks after its own interests.'

'What about the UK?' Zoe enquired.

'It's basically this planet and Lowlands,' said Jane. 'But it's no longer the UK. Lowlands isn't officially recognised as a country nor is it seen as connected to the South, or anywhere to be honest. Scotland has its own planet. It broke away from the rest of the UK a long time ago. Most of the glens and towns are now underwater, so the Scottish Government hired international scientists to help them produce their own space station.

'The area that used to be Wales has no towns or cities. Most of the mountains are still visible … at least partly. Nobody lives in Wales since Cardiff and Swansea were submerged into the sea. Ireland does have people living in it, but has shrunk so much that most of the inhabitants have left to live or work on other countries space stations. As a matter of fact there is no England either, as the South is not recognised as a country in its own right. It is technically owned by American businessmen, so as such it is seen as a state of the USA, even though our Government would never admit to this publicly.

'The original planet Earth now only supports people who live in poverty. These are people whom the rich blame for their decline in wealth. People whom they see as having no role or purpose in shaping the future, so they are doomed to remain on Earth. Not that there is much of the original planet left. Climate change has resulted in more than 90% of it now being water. With no resources to arrest the decline or to improve the situation, the world has become wild and unpredictable. The human race is dying out down there. It will soon be a world where only feral animals and plant life exists, if the sea doesn't swallow it up first.'

Jane paused as she reflected – with sadness etched on her face – on the fatally injured planet that was slowly expiring way below her. Deep down inside she knew that very soon she could well be a part of it.

'Up here it's very different, but no less alarming if you are not one of the very rich. You only work until you outlive your usefulness. People usually travel by transporter beam. But if you travel to another country – which is very rare these days – you go by spacecraft. There are no aeroplanes any more. There used to be small flying machines called drones that were used by individual travellers, but these were banned when the Government decided their use was interfering with the journeys of politicians and business people. Road vehicle profits were also affected by the use of drones. Now everyone has to rely on the moving cars or transporter booths. There are some bigger spacecraft, but these are only used to travel to the colonies on the Moon or to the settlements and space station laboratories on Mars. Only scientists get to use those flights though, as they all depart from the third planet where non-specific citizens are not allowed.'

'Third planet?' asked Zoe.

'The South Government decided to separate what they called the workrich from the superior classes so they created a third, smaller, planet exclusively for ultra-rich people, scientists, bankers, businessmen and of course politicians. The South is used just for working people who can pay their own way, but if you fall below the poverty line you are sent to Lowlands or terminated,' Jane replied.

'Terminated?' queried Zoe.

'I'll come to that in a minute,' said Jane.

Zoe nodded. 'What about elections?' she asked. 'Why didn't people vote the Government out?'

'Elections disappeared a long time ago,' explained Jane, echoing what Lake had said about there being no elections in Lowlands. 'Over the years, less and less people bothered to vote. The population rapidly decreased too, so the same Government got in every time. Without opposition they regularly changed boundaries and altered rules until elections were eventually abolished. There has only been one political party for many years now. This planet has a small population. People only keep their jobs and homes if the Government say so.'

'What about schools and hospitals?' asked Zoe. 'Surely education helps young people realise what is happening, and offers them ways to consider alternatives?'

'There are no schools or hospitals,' replied Jane. 'Education is provided centrally through a national programme transmitted directly through Wi-Fi. Exams are taken through secure Government web sites. Young people are then categorised as normal or higher intelligence. If you are classed as higher, you are earmarked to work on the small planet with the chance to get really rich. Normal classification means your life will be lived in the South. Like many adults, children have no social contact with other people outside of their home, except through the computerised education programmes which are strictly controlled by the Government to ensure consistency in both input and output.

'Hospitals aren't needed, as no one gets ill. All known illnesses have been wiped out and regular insurance payments to Mofanza ensure that you will never get any of the new diseases that may arise. In fact people should be immune to any illness, as our entire reproduction system is based on controlled parthenogenesis. The system is known as The Uniprogenetation Programme, to give it the full scientific title.'

'What's Uniprogenetation?' asked Zoe.

'It's the creation of life from a single cell,' snapped Jane, annoyed at the interruption. 'To get back to what I was telling you. The only risk to health is when the Security Police bring people in from Lowlands, but if they aren't killed immediately they are put into quarantine for six months to control or destroy any diseases they may bring. Of course with our extremely safe transport systems, our fully automated homes and the absence of social contact or gatherings, accidents are rare. So is personal injury from criminal activity.'

Zoe reflected on how unlucky she must have been to encounter robbers. Or perhaps criminal activities were not as rare as Jane believed.

Meanwhile, Jane continued her monologue. 'There *are some* doctors in the South, who can be called on if someone does get injured, but such cases are treated at home. Even food intake is regulated. Everyone gets food capsules which contain all of the vitamins needed to stay healthy, so there is no risk of food-related illness. Like many things, obesity is a thing of the past.'

'You said that your reproduction system is based on parthenogenesis,' stated Zoe, harking back to an earlier comment Jane had made. 'Tell me about that.'

'All babies are artificially created from single gene

cells. This produces a clone which is then genetically modified before being classified as a child. The babies' immune systems are programmed to withstand any disease, virus, germ or bacteria, including new or unknown diseases that may arise in the future. The authorities do this by an automatic gene-regulating programme, which remotely updates all babies' immune systems as soon as scientific evidence identifies a new uncategorised disease. Only people who have been licensed and approved are allowed to parent children. Once authorised, parents can select – from a catalogue – the required body dimensions, as well as eye, hair and skin colour of their chosen child.'

Zoe's jaw dropped wide open. 'What do you mean, licensed and approved?' she gasped.

'No one can bring up a child unless approved by the Social Police,' said Jane. 'All babies are sterile, so they can't reproduce as adults. Babies are manufactured to order before being allocated to parents. Potential parents have to attend courses and pass exams before they can be approved. Afterwards they are tested regularly, to ensure their financial and practical ability to meet the required standards remains unchanged. Homes are inspected every three months. A maximum of two children are allowed for each family.'

'Who are the Social Police?' asked Zoe.

'Historically they were Social Services and then Social Care. However, they had long ceased to provide proper help, care or protection, due to a combination of dwindling resources and continuing incompetence. Additionally, their ethos had evolved into a regime of accusation, punishment and mistrust, so it was apt that the Government rebranded them as Social Police. Their role now is to monitor all aspects of family life for signs of change or illegality.'

Zoe listened intently. A lot of what she'd heard merely confirmed what Lake and Zak had previously told her, but Zoe wanted to encourage Jane to keep on talking so she could find out as much about the South as possible. She probably wouldn't get a better opportunity to do so.

'If as you say all education is broadcast and there are no schools, how can *you* be a student at a university?' enquired Zoe, deliberately changing course, in order to broaden the scope.

'It's a closed shop university,' Jane explained. 'The only university we have. That's because only specialised scientists, people in politics or those employed by the Government, are allowed access so they can study history and learn from past mistakes.' She cynically added, 'Or manipulate the past to suit their own ends if they wish. Of course, I was at the university before this rule came in. I managed to stay there until now because of my past experience, which constituted special circumstances.'

'How do you study?' asked Zoe. 'If education is universal and is transmitted by Wi-Fi, what is different about the university? Do you have books?'

Jane shook her head. 'We learn by direct experience,' she said.

'What's that?' enquired Zoe.

'There's a special machine in a room known as the

Time Gallery,' answered Jane. 'It's the only one of its kind in existence – outside of official Government Headquarters – and it is absolutely top secret. Access is severely restricted. In fact only four people on the planet have been cleared to use it.'

'What does it do?' asked Zoe, her curiosity now well aroused.

Jane's answer was delivered in a matter of fact voice. 'It takes you back in time.'

CHAPTER THIRTEEN

Jane's last sentence lit a burning fuse inside Zoe. A feeling of wild excitement shot through her like a bolt of lightning. *A time machine! Could this really be what she hoped it was? Could this be the machine that would take her back home?*

'Go on,' she urged.

Jane continued her story. 'It's really an old prototype that we use to explore specific times in history. Whoever uses it can travel back in time and collect data about that era. This information can be obtained by collecting books, papers, and plant or soil samples. These can be picked up during any visit to a different time period. Sometimes it is possible to make contact and conversation with some of the people who were alive at that time. There are lots of things we can access. We also take photographs.'

'How does the machine work?' asked Zoe, keeping her voice calm despite the exhilaration she felt inside.

'Whoever uses it obviously needs official authorisation to pursue their project. Once that's given, they are okay to go. There's not much room inside, but a minimum of two people have to travel on each expedition. The limited interior space is to minimise the risk of stowaways on any leg of the journey as well as for safety reasons, although we do sometimes get the odd person from the past who manages to hitch a ride. If that happens, they are usually imprisoned or put into a historical human zoo so the public can pay to see them.

'Before you start your journey, you set the date for whichever year you want to visit, then the machine takes you there once the start button is pushed. The machine operates on a fixed point level. Both Lowlands and the South are in constant motion as planets, so – although they are aligned with each other – there is often a slight differential, which means the fixed points can sometimes vary. The time machine can in fact surface anywhere within a twenty mile radius. That's okay though, as this can offer a variety of perspectives on any given year.'

'From what you said about collecting information, I take it you can get out when you get to a different time zone?' asked Zoe, who by now was struggling to contain the joy she was feeling inside. She may have been appalled by the horror of what the World had become, but her disgust – along with her sympathy for the people – was now far outweighed by her desire to find this machine and use it to get home.

'You *can*,' said Jane. 'But you have to be quick, otherwise the machine will return to the present day without you. You are only allowed a maximum of half an hour for each trip, unless you get extended clearance discs to cover the extra length of your stay. These discs provide for you to get up to twenty-four hours on any field trip. This gives you sufficient time to get out, look around, take photographs, talk to people and take samples, collect artefacts, or do anything else you need to do. You can go to more than one time period on any visit by resetting the dial for up to two more time zones after you arrive at your first port of call. This is only really effective if you have extended stay discs. The half hour period offers enough time to take photographs and get a few artefacts, but the machine will automatically return to base when your time is up. If you are not inside, it will return without you. With an extended stay disc, the timer is set for the length of stay on a separate time clock inside the machine. If you exceed your time you are stranded. Generally, one of the party will stay aboard to keep an eye on the time and call you back before the limit. Extended stay discs start at one hour and increase by hourly periods to twenty-four. The timer determines the length of stay from the disc. If time is wasted, you run the risk of having your authorisation cancelled.'

'Only four people allowed access, you said?' Zoe, was tentatively weighing up her options.

Jane nodded. 'There used to be six,' she answered, 'but we lost one to the dinosaurs and another absconded to live in the 1960s. The authorities say they will close the project down if anyone else is lost.'

'How does it travel through time?' Zoe asked.

'I'm not sure I fully understand it myself,' replied Jane. 'I'm no scientist. I only know what I've been told, but I think it's based on the principle that works a drill.'

'A drill?' echoed Zoe, puzzled by this description. 'What do you mean, a drill?'

'Well as I told you before, the time machine is situated on a fixed point,' said Jane, pleased that her temporary cell mate was paying her such attention and was obviously interested in the knowledge she was demonstrating.

'Time particles are variable. They don't follow a set pattern. I guess it's a bit like having layers of time piled on top of each other, and moving all around you. During travel you virtually stay on the same spot, while the machine moves you through time. Some people say it works a bit like a sophisticated elevator, but instead of taking you up or down it takes you sideways, on a journey through the fourth dimension. I prefer to liken it to a drill burrowing into the past.

'When a date is set on the control panel, the machine bores its way through time, creating a makeshift door. I think the scientists call it a wormhole – or a time portal – between two separate time zones. This means that for a short time the two zones are able to co-exist alongside each other, allowing someone to step from one zone into another. However, it takes a tremendous amount of energy to do this. So, if the wormhole were to continue for longer than the maximum twenty-four hours, then both worlds would probably burn up or explode. As you can imagine that would drastically change not only our history but our Universe too. All life on our planets would definitely cease – as would the planets themselves – I guess.

'As our machine is one of the original prototypes, it can only travel backwards in time. Our Government – and no doubt the United States and some other Governments too – have time travel equipment that can travel into the future as well as back in time, but that's supposed to be an official secret. Access to the time travel programme is severely restricted, to a very small number of people who have been specially cleared to take part.

'We were very fortunate to get our machine. It was only because of the historical work we do, that we were given one that would otherwise have been scrapped. This was meant to help with our experiments. Even so, we have to keep the Government fully informed of all of our research programmes and experiments well in advance of any visits we make. Every trip back in time needs official Government endorsement, at least a month before they are carried out.'

Zoe was impressed by Jane's knowledge. She admired too the technology involved in such a process. However, her elation subsided a little as she contemplated the complications involved in getting access to the time machine, as well as the dire consequences that could be brought about if she ever did get to use it and got her timings wrong.

'You say it's a fixed point,' said Zoe, as another thought struck her. 'But here, in the South, well it's a new man-made planet which is suspended some distance above the real planet Earth. Surely if the time machine travels back on a fixed point, then if you travelled back to a time before the new planet was made, the wormhole would just hang in the sky above the Earth? How can people get to the ground from there? Or do you just float in space while you take your pictures?'

Jane laughed. 'That sounds funny. But it's nothing like that,' she said. 'The machine locks onto the nearest land-based point on the Earth's surface. It could be anything really, a building, a tree, even an open field.'

'What about water?' asked Zoe, trying to foresee any possible dangers. 'Could it land in a river, or the sea?'

Jane laughed again. 'No,' she replied. 'It has to be a land-based point.'

'Have you been in it?' asked Zoe, changing tack slightly.

'A few times,' nodded Jane. 'I'm one of the four who are allowed to use the machine, because of my work. I've got a special pass I can use.'

Zoe's eyes lit up at this information. 'Really?' she enthused.

'Yes,' said Jane. 'But I would think it's probably been cancelled now.'

Zoe's heart dropped into her shoes. 'How come?' she asked, disappointment suddenly washing over her.

'I had a position of trust where I was able to come and go as I liked at the university,' Jane said. 'But I'm not the same as everyone else. I have lived a lie for the past ten years. After a while I got used to that lie but then I got found out.'

'What do you mean, you are not the same as everyone else?' queried Zoe, intrigued by this statement.

'I didn't know I was different,' Jane said, 'not until I was aged twenty-eight, when I had an accident.'

'Tell me about it,' urged Zoe. 'Was it serious?'

'Serious enough,' replied Jane. 'I banged my head quite severely. I was knocked unconscious for a while. There was no one else around at the time, so when I recovered I gave myself a quick once over then went home to rest for a while.

'A few days later I began to feel different. My mind

seemed to be working in an unfamiliar way. My thinking was somehow clearer and sharper. I was suddenly analysing everything. My creative juices were flowing. I was hypercritical of things I disapproved of. It was as if my brain had become alive. Like it was switched on and I couldn't shut it off.

'I began to see my work and studies at the university in a new light. I was more cynical and sceptical, always challenging what was said or what I read in official documents, looking at things in more depth than I'd done before, particularly history and genetics. It was then that I made a shocking discovery. I found out that not only were children genetically engineered, but each child had a microchip inserted into their brain before being given to their prospective parents.

'I researched a bit more, discovering that these microchips enable the State to control and monitor everyone's thinking processes. All behaviour and activities are controlled too. The microchip also feeds back information on each child's development and progress right through childhood, adolescence, adulthood into old age. Everyone is kept under observation. Every building, every vehicle – even people's own homes – are equipped with monitoring devices that are logged into the microchips, so they can follow every person's movements throughout their life. Any criminal act or transgression of any law brings police to the scene instantly. Minor offences result in deportation to Lowlands, whilst more serious offences carry the death penalty, or elimination as the Government agencies like to call it. The chips pick up all of the data transmitted by Wi-Fi too. This means that they process and retain every bit of educational data that is transmitted, ensuring that no one misses any input.'

Jane stopped. She closed her eyes, breathing deeply a few times. She clenched her fists then unclenched them. She repeated this manoeuvre a few times in an effort to calm herself, before continuing. 'I was shocked by what I'd discovered,' she said. 'But the biggest shock was yet to come, for I later found out that these microchips can be remotely incapacitated. Such an action brings instant terminal illness to anyone who is in arrears with their health insurance. Even more frighteningly, I found out that the chips can be terminated – again by remote control – at any time in a person's life, exploding inside their brain and bringing instant death. So despite no one dying from natural causes …'

'Does that mean that some people can live forever?' interrupted Zoe, aghast at the thought.

'Only if you are rich and powerful,' snapped Jane, annoyed that Zoe had again interrupted her flow.

'How can you do that?' Zoe said indignantly. 'Surely whether you have money or not, you grow up, you can't get ill so you can't die, therefore you must live forever?'

'Not at all. This situation is so different,' stated Jane, somewhat aggressively. 'Politicians and extremely rich people can live forever. They can get transplants of artificially created body organs – including skin – so they never die, nor do they age. If you'll let me finish my story, that's what I'm trying to explain. The microchip enables the State to end someone's life programme, whenever that person ceases to be of use to the State and the economy.'

'Are you saying that the Government kill people?' asked Zoe, horrified at what she was hearing.

'Governments have always killed people,' Jane answered. 'Usually through wars, but sometimes in other ways too. But as I've explained, by using microchips our Government controls everyone right from birth. They also decide when you should die. Yet none of the general public is aware of this. I'd like to tell them, but it's doubtful if it could be proved anyway.'

Zoe shuddered. She tried to imagine such an inhumane existence, and also what it might feel like to have the power of life and death over fellow citizens. *What kind of person did you have to be to do that job?*

Pre-empting Zoe's thoughts, Jane said, 'The people who terminate the lives of others are also programmed by the State. They are scared of losing their own lives. That's why they carry out their orders. They tend not to think about the job they do. After all, it's hardly a subject for discussion among work colleagues is it? Only the people on the small globe have complete immunity and immortality. They can live their lives without fear, unless they lose their wealth or do something to harm or embarrass the Government.'

'Tell me more about your accident and what followed,' encouraged Zoe, trying to get Jane back on track so she could ask her about the time machine again.

Jane spoke softly as she carried on her story. 'When I banged my head, it must have caused my microchip to malfunction. So, as a result of my accident I was free to think and act as I wished, free from the threat of dying by Government decree. Since then I've pretended to be like everyone else so as not to arouse suspicion. It was hard but I managed. Every day I half expected to be arrested, but it seemed that the malfunction had gone unnoticed. Then last week, the Security Police decided to have a mass screening programme at the university. They checked everyone with their updated hand held scanners. Of course nothing registered for me, so I was arrested.

'The police checked Government records, which revealed that I'd died ten years ago. That was the time of my accident when my chips stopped working. I've been in here for just over a week now, while the authorities decide what to do with me. I wasn't allowed to go to my trial, but it was decided in my absence that as my chips couldn't be replaced, I was to be sent to Lowlands and left down there to die naturally. I think they would have liked to have killed me, especially as records show that I was already dead. But I suspect they saw deportation as a better option, because if they had decided to kill me it might have aroused suspicion among my work colleagues, as I hadn't broken any law.'

When Jane had finished her story, Zoe sat in silence. She was shocked. *How could any Government allow children to be specifically created to parental design or microchip people's brains, so that all individuality and creativity was removed? How could they kill a person on some whim, when someone who didn't even know that person has decided they were no longer of use? How could any human throw another human away like an old dishcloth in the*

151

twilight of their life? Whatever happened to creating a loving, caring and free society?

Zoe felt scared. She thought about what would happen to her if the police found out what Jane had told her. She reached for Jane's hand.

'It's not too bad down there,' Zoe said, 'if you find the right people. Look Jane, I'll give you some names and some directions to find the place I lived in. If you tell the people there that you know me, I'm sure they'll look after you.'

She gave Jane details of Lake and the whereabouts of the camp before squeezing her hand. Zoe then drew a deep breath before asking, 'By the way, do you still have your pass for the time machine?'

'Yes,' Jane replied, 'but it's useless, as my authorisation has probably been wiped from it. I guess it's now just a blank disc.'

'Can I have it?' asked Zoe.

'Yes, I suppose so,' said Jane hesitantly, rummaging in her pockets before handing a metal diamond shaped object to Zoe. 'But as I said, it's useless.'

'It might not be,' said Zoe, her mind already thinking that Zak may well be able to utilise the defunct authorisation disc. She stuffed it into her pocket, saying 'Thanks, I think we ought to try to get some sleep now, it's very late.'

CHAPTER FOURTEEN

Zoe and Jane lay back on their respective bunks. Zoe closed her eyes, even though she knew she wouldn't sleep tonight. How could she? She was too excited following her discovery that there was a way to get off this planet and back to her own time.

She decided that once she got out of this police cell, she would try to find Zak. Hopefully, he would be able to find a way of reactivating Jane's pass so they could get home to Zoe's family. Suppressing her excitement she lay back, desperately willing sleep to come to her so she had strength to look for Zak tomorrow when she was released.

After a short time she began to drift off. Suddenly, the cell door burst open and two policemen entered. They hauled her from her bed, dragging her into the room in which she'd previously been interviewed.

One of the officers stood in front of Zoe, he spoke. 'Zoe Marshall,' he said. 'You have been found guilty of trying to use a credit disc that belongs to Victoria Boswell. We have no record of you ever being an official resident in the South. We therefore believe you are an intruder from Lowlands, so we are sending you back there. If you come here again without permission, you will be executed. Come with us, your transport is waiting.'

Zoe sat up with a start. She couldn't believe what had been said. She'd only just got here, now she was being deported. She'd briefly thought there might be a slim chance of being sent back, but only as a worst case scenario. She hadn't really expected it, for what she assumed the authorities would see as a relatively minor offence, or even an oversight, on her part. In fact, deep down she'd believed she could talk her way out of any potential punitive action. Zoe was shocked. She was angry too, and in her anger her thoughts turned to her supposed ally. *Where was Zak? Why hadn't he come to find her?*

He's set me up, she thought. *He's found out about the time machine at the university. He's planning to go back without me, so he can get to his space ship. He's going to take the children's souls back to his planet. I bet he planned this all along. I wouldn't put it past him to make sure I'd leave my disc in the gallery, giving him the chance to leave me behind when I went back for it. Then he arranged for someone to try to rob me and called the police, knowing that they'd send me back to Lowlands, allowing him to make his escape. I knew I shouldn't have trusted him. Come to think of it, he's a shape shifter. He might even have been one of the robbers.*

At that moment Zoe hated Zak. She was determined that she wasn't going to go without a fight. That would mean he had won. One outcome of his victory would mean that she would remain stranded in a time and place she had no desire to stay in. Zoe tried to put her bitter negative thoughts about Zak on hold as she confronted the two policemen in a last ditch effort to overturn her deportation.

'Listen,' she said in an assertive tone. 'I told the officer who interviewed me that I got confused when those thieves were arrested. I was upset and disorientated, so when the policeman asked my name I blurted out the name of someone I was thinking about at that time. It was a mistake that's all, brought about by the state of fear I was in at the time. I *am* Victoria Boswell. It says so on my credit disc, how else would I have got the disc?'

'You stole it,' said one of the officers.

'But I didn't, it's mine. If you do a body scan you will see it matches the DNA on my disc,' implored Zoe, her voice now betraying the desperation she was feeling.

The two officers remained unmoved. They seemed immune to her pleas as they stood impassively beside her.

The second officer spoke. 'We have no facilities or personnel to carry out body scanning at this late hour in this building,' he said. 'Anyway, it's irrelevant. The case against you has already been confirmed. Your punishment is decided. It is now our duty to implement the sentence. We are taking you back to Lowlands, where you belong. You will be transported immediately from the Security Police HQ, so come on. We will escort you there on the mobile walkway. When we arrive you will be despatched by transporter beam to Lowlands.'

The officer's voice was cold and dispassionate as he spoke. Zoe, now in tears, made one last effort to save herself. 'They have body scanning facilities in the Security Police HQ,' she cried. 'You can do a scan there. Then you will see that I *am* Victoria Boswell.'

'You are wasting time,' said the officer, ignoring Zoe's desperate request for justice. He led her outside onto the mobile pavement. The two men held onto Zoe's arms, swiftly propelling her into the security police building once they reached their destination. Zoe was taken by lift to the fourth floor. As they stepped out of the lift, Zoe saw the transportation booth in the far corner. It was similar to the others that she'd travelled in during her short stay in the South. When she got inside she noticed that this one had no list of street names or places, merely two buttons marked Lowlands and South.

There was no machine to take credit cards in this one either. Zoe correctly guessed the booth must be for police use only, probably for their forays into Lowlands as they searched for people to take prisoner. It was clearly also used for deportations.

Zoe suddenly remembered that her credit disc contained her photo. She pointed this out to the policemen.

'That's no evidence,' said one of them, while setting the transporter in motion. 'Pictures can easily be substituted or faked. People who steal credit discs often take their own photograph, then try to claim the disc is theirs.'

The two police officers made the trip to Lowlands with Zoe. The short journey was made in silence. She was shoved out of the booth as soon as it materialised on the real planet Earth below. It was almost dawn, and in the half-light Zoe could see she had been dumped alongside a large bush which grew on the side of a hilly area. This in turn was overgrown with grass and surrounded by trees.

The force of the push sent Zoe sprawling to the ground. She lay there, listening as the door to the transporter slammed loudly behind her with the unfriendly custodians inside, preparing the return to their homeland.

When Zoe was sure that the machine had whisked her escorts safely back to the South, she went across to the bush where she searched around for a while. It took some time but eventually she found what she was looking for.

The transporter booth was very cleverly disguised. It was hidden inside an artificial tree trunk behind the bush. The trunk was clearly designed to blend in with the surroundings with a door handle fashioned to make it look like a twisted knot in the wood. Zoe closed her fingers around it and pulled. Nothing happened! She tried again, still no movement. On the third attempt she pushed instead of pulling. The door opened inwardly, revealing the layout of buttons she'd seen on the downward journey. Zoe smiled with satisfaction as she closed the door. She now needed to make sure she would be able to recognise this place in the future, when she made her next venture into the South. Taking a broken branch that lay close by, she laid it at an angle in the shrubbery after first snapping off a large twig which she used to scratch two small letters into the false tree trunk.

Now it will look as if someone has carved their initials into the bark, so if the police see it when they come down here they won't get suspicious, Zoe thought. *I'll know where to find it when I'm ready. Now all I need to do is find some way of marking my route, so I can find my way back here.*

Zoe searched around for something suitable to serve her purpose. After a while she saw a broken piece of slate lying in the undergrowth. Picking it up, she moved across to the nearest tree where she scratched a Z into the bark.

'That'll do,' she said, feeling a tingle of excitement run through her as she thought about a quick return to the orb that was once again hanging in the sky above. A trip she hoped would lead her to the time machine that lay somewhere on its surface, offering her the chance to go back to her family. Her immediate work done, Zoe curled up beneath the bush, where she slept uneasily until the brightness of the sunshine awoke her.

Hunger gnawed at Zoe's stomach on awakening. She wasn't sure if any of the berries that grew on nearby bushes were suitable for eating, so she decided to try to find Lake. *I can stay in the settlement for a while until its safe for me to return to the South,* she thought.

Zoe made her mark on every tree she passed as she wandered through the forest. She had no idea where she was or where she was going. She had decided it was too dangerous for her to go back to the South just yet. The security police would surely be looking out for her. If she was seen she would be killed. She needed time to think things through and come up with a proper plan.

Heading in what she believed was the general direction of Lake's village, Zoe made up her mind to follow the river, if she could find it. She'd been walking for about thirty minutes when she espied a group of people ahead in the distance. She hurried towards the group, hoping it was Lake, or at least someone from the settlement. Remembering her experience with the dog pack, she resisted the urge to call out. She had no intention of gaining attention until she was close enough to be sure they were people she knew.

As she drew near to the group, Zoe could see them clearly. She didn't recognise anyone, so being unsure if she would meet with friendliness or hostility, she slowed her walk to a steadier pace as she dropped in behind them to observe what they were doing.

She'd barely walked a few metres when she caught a brief glimpse of two tall figures in her peripheral vision. They appeared to Zoe as no more than two silhouettes as they leapt from behind a tree and lunged at her. Her sighting of them came far too late for her to run. She half turned but they were quickly upon her, dragging her to the ground. She tried to fight them off, kicking out and punching as she rolled around on the dusty dirt path. Her attackers were too strong though. Despite Zoe's brave efforts she was quickly overpowered.

Her assailants turned out to be two young men, clad in animal skins. Their faces were painted with streaks and patterns of various hues. Both men had drawings on their foreheads depicting eyes and hands. The pair moved swiftly. The taller of the two men bound Zoe's hands behind her back with plant vines and slender petioles torn from nearby vegetation.

One of them spoke. 'Look what we've got here, Marcus,' he said. 'We've caught ourselves a Southerner! I think we should kill her!'

'Wait Stefan,' the other man replied. 'Let's not be hasty. I think we should take her back to camp so the others can help decide what to do with her. If we don't kill her, who knows? Maybe we can trade her in for something useful?'

The man named Stefan considered this idea for a moment, then confirmed his agreement with a double nod of his head. 'Okay,' he said. Then he grinned, adding, 'And if we can't trade her, *then* we'll kill her.'

'I'm not a Southerner,' protested Zoe. 'I'm not anything. I don't belong here or up there.'

She lifted her head to indicate the gleaming planet above them.

Stefan grinned again. 'Your protests won't cut any ice with us, dear. Look at your clothes. *They're* not from down here. I bet they come from London. Anyway, we've not seen you around in Lowlands before. I'd say that you came down from the South in one of those transporter things, so you can argue all you like but in my book that makes you a Southerner!' he growled.

'No,' said Zoe desperately. 'You're wrong … you're so wrong. I've been here before. I lived with a group of people by the river … with Heron, Rainbow and Lake. You must know them.'

'Never heard of them,' said Stefan. 'Not that it would make any difference if we had. We don't care about other groups. Come to that we don't care that much for our own group either. Marcus and me go our own way. We can be very persuasive. The other group members usually go along with what we say. It's easier that way. It cuts out the fights, and no one gets hurt.'

He gave a big smirk in Zoe's direction before adding, 'So I guess that means your fate depends entirely on us.'

Stefan laughed loudly as he said this. He turned to Marcus, chuckling, and saw his laughter was reciprocated.

'Come on,' Stefan said. 'I'm getting bored now. Let's get her back to camp and get this settled quickly.'

Each of them grabbed an arm, dragging Zoe along the pathway that led through the forest. Zoe had no choice but to go with them. But as they lugged her through the forest she was alert to her surroundings, sketching a map in her head so she could remember her way back to the artificial tree. Simultaneously, she was looking for something that was familiar to her. Her mind was further focussed on finding a chance to escape.

Zoe didn't recognize the part of the forest they were in. She assumed it wasn't an area she'd visited before. All the same she reckoned that Lake's camp couldn't be far away. So if there was a chance to run she figured she could find her way there.

The trio continued for a while, getting deeper into the wood. It was dark and cold now. The trees were very close together, preventing sunlight from penetrating the thick branches and foliage. Zoe shivered in the cool air. She felt the prickling of gooseflesh on her hands and arms, which she had managed to keep moving from side to side behind her back in an attempt to free the bonds that bound her wrists.

After a lot of wriggling and twisting Zoe could feel the vines begin to slacken. Her fingers grasped at the loosening tendrils, gripping the strands tightly to prevent them falling to the ground. She didn't want their laxity to be seen by her captors. She was pleased to have her hands untied. It meant that if she did come across an escape route she could let the vines go and make a run for it, with hands free to help her along.

Another fifteen minutes went by. Stefan and Marcus had barely spoken to each other during the journey. Zoe would have preferred them to be chatting so that they wouldn't be concentrating on her so much. Her desire for a distraction was heightened when she glimpsed a sudden opportunity ahead.

The trees were beginning to thin out now. Through a gap Zoe saw the outline of what appeared to be a building. From the limited view she had, she could see it was made of red brick. It was obviously old, but still seemed to be in reasonable condition. The visible part of the building comprised of two storeys. The brickwork perimeter sprawled across a substantial area of land. Part of the roof was missing as were several of the windows, but the shell looked solid enough. The windows that remained either hung loosely from the frames or had huge cracks zig-zagging across what was left of the filthy glass. Zoe estimated it had been built around the latter part of the twentieth century. Somewhere in the back of her mind the layout seemed familiar to her.

I wonder what it was, she thought, as she pondered her getaway. *More importantly, will it provide me with a suitable hiding place?*

Zoe decided to take her chance. Shaking off the loose

bonds that had hung limply around her wrists for the latter part of her unpleasant experience at the hands of her abductors, she flung them forcefully towards Stefan and Marcus. The action momentarily threw them off guard. Her two captors stepped back as the vines came at them, giving Zoe the split second start she needed. She bounded forward, head down as she charged full pelt towards the building. Giving a quick glance over her shoulder, she could see the two men in hot pursuit, but importantly for Zoe she had gained a valuable start on them, as she sped in the direction of what she hoped would be her sanctuary.

CHAPTER FIFTEEN

When Zoe reached the red brick building, her eyes were already focussed on the point of entrance. Without breaking her stride she kicked out at the door, which was really no more than a lump of rotting wood hanging loosely on frail, rusty hinges. The structure disintegrated in a sawdust cloud of wood splinters as Zoe's foot connected with it. She wafted her hand at the rising dust cloud to try to disperse it, but with little success. Zoe coughed as the fine powder thrown up by the detritus from the shattered door hit the back of her throat, but she continued her run with the minimum of hesitation.

Inside the building, Zoe slowed a little to take in her surroundings. The interior seemed familiar to her too. She could feel something stirring in the deep recesses of her brain, telling her she'd seen buildings like this in 2015. Perhaps she'd even been inside one. The interior was open plan with lots of floor space. A few smaller rooms could be seen annexed off the perimeter of the main central area. In front of her a part demolished concrete staircase led to a first floor balcony, where Zoe could see more small rooms. She knew she should be able to identify the place but it just wouldn't come to mind. Her memory ran through a list of possibilities. *A school perhaps? An office? A Doctor's surgery or Health*

Centre? She told herself it wasn't important at this moment, all that mattered was that she found a hiding place quickly as the crashing noise from the entrance told her that Stefan and Marcus had arrived.

'Where do I go?' Zoe panted, talking to herself as she ran. 'One of the small rooms maybe? No, that's probably too easy for them to locate. Upstairs? No, I might get cornered and trapped up there. I'll just have to keep running in the hope that I can get away from them.'

Zoe raced through the building, looking for somewhere suitable to secrete herself away. At first she couldn't see any likely place. Then she saw a staircase leading to the floor below. 'A basement,' she gasped. 'That could have possibilities. It might even have another exit.'

Zoe ran down the stairs. The route did indeed lead into a basement, one that seemed to cover a large area which would approximate in size with the upper level she had just left. It was very dark down there, but a small shaft of light from outside filtered in through a patch of missing brickwork giving a glimpse of her surroundings. She saw that the basement consisted of one long, wide room containing a large number of objects. She could see outline silhouettes of some of these objects, which at first glance appeared to be tall boxes. When she got nearer Zoe saw that they were metal cabinets, stretching back in rows as far as she was able to see in the gloom. Each cabinet had several wide drawers. They looked similar to the metal filing cabinets Zoe remembered from college, but these were much taller. The drawers were larger and deeper too.

Zoe grabbed at the nearest cabinet. She tried to pull open one of the drawers but it was locked. Curiosity aroused, she momentarily forgot about her pursuers as she tried to open more drawers. But they were all locked too.

'Damn,' she cursed disappointedly.

Zoe could hear Stefan and Marcus stomping about above her, slamming doors and moving rubble as they searched for their quarry in each of the small rooms. She knew she had to hide, but she was intrigued by what might be in the cabinets. The main thought that ran through her head was *it must be something important, otherwise why would they be locked.* Her inquisitiveness quickly got the better of her. Zoe decided she had time to try one or two more before her pursuers finished their business upstairs. On her fifth attempt she struck lucky; one of the drawers had a faulty lock that quickly yielded to Zoe's strong tugs and yanks. She let out a sigh that was a cross between triumph and contentment as the drawer slid open. Reaching inside, she drew out one of the many packaged objects that were crammed tightly together within. The parcel was big. It was heavy too. She carried the item into the thin beam of sunlight, where she saw that it was a package wrapped in a material similar to polythene.

Zoe's fingers scraped and scrabbled at the wrapping, which initially resisted her fevered pulling and probing. Just as it seemed she would have to replace the package unopened she found a small overlap which she assumed to be a seal. Sliding her finger beneath the flap she gently moved it from side to side, pushing upwards as she did so. One edge of the package opened up enough for Zoe to take out one of its contents. She held it up to her face in the murkiness. It was a book. An edition of an Encyclopaedia. The book looked to be in good condition. The protective covering had clearly done its job well.

Zoe quickly slipped the book back into its membrane sheath before placing it back in the cabinet. She closed the drawer as silently as she could. She was excited by her find. Her thoughts were racing with possibilities.

Books, she thought, remembering now where she'd seen similar buildings before. *This must have been a library. I guess the staff locked away all of the books in some kind of plastic wrapping to preserve them. They must have been here for hundreds of years, but they can still be used. In the right hands, these books could offer a gateway to a better Lowlands. I can't wait to…*

The rest of Zoe's thoughts were swiftly abandoned as she heard the sound of footsteps coming down the stairs. She looked urgently about her for a suitable hiding place, cursing herself for spending so much time on opening the cabinets when she should have been trying to escape from her pursuers. It was difficult to move about freely, in the almost total darkness that now engulfed the room. Zoe stumbled about for a bit, unable to find a place where she felt she wouldn't be seen. The footsteps were getting closer.

She was now at the far end of the basement in the darkest spot, where cabinets had been piled high in a haphazard formation that would have done credit to anyone building a maze. Zoe spotted a gap between two adjacent cabinets. She ducked into it, crouching down behind the furthest one. Unable to see out from her hiding place she squatted low, scarcely daring to breathe as she heard the footsteps stop at the foot of the stairs, before they slowly began to cross the room.

Zoe heard the sound of cabinets being pushed aside, accompanied by sporadic grunting and cursing from her pursuers. She had been so preoccupied with what was inside the cabinets, that she hadn't looked to see if there was another way out of the basement. She was certain that the two people who were hunting her would find her. But she tried to shut out the images that had formed in her mind of what they might do to her when they did.

Sitting back on her haunches as she waited in silence, Zoe heard another noise amid the banging and crashing of metal that came from the far side of the room. It was a different, softer sound. Much lower in tone. It was barely audible at first, above the clanging and scraping of metal as each cabinet was crudely shoved aside. Yet she could tell that whatever was making the sound was close by.

Zoe's ears had picked up the second noise immediately. Then as the volume increased she became more aware of its presence. It was a hissing sound – that was continuous in both its projection and its noise level – reminiscent of air leaking from an airbed or tyre. She cocked her head to one side, listening. It was very close now. Whatever was creating the sound seemed to be moving towards her. Zoe's curiosity grew until it got the better of her. Thinking that her stalkers might be using something to aid their search, she raised herself slightly, lifting her head to look in the direction of the sibilance. When she saw the real source of the noise she instantly froze!

Above her head, sliding across the top of the cabinets was a very large snake. It was no ordinary snake either, certainly not the kind Zoe had ever seen in Britain outside of a zoo. It was a constrictor. Zoe wasn't sure if it was a python, a boa, or an anaconda. Her knowledge of snakes wasn't that good. She didn't really care either. All she knew was that these snakes crushed their prey to death rather than poison it. Pressing herself closer to the side of the cabinet Zoe held her breath, hoping the reptile wouldn't see her.

While she was watching the snake, Zoe was also thinking about Marcus and Stefan. They were in this room too, so any noise or movement she made would give away her hiding place. Zoe couldn't decide which would be worse, death by a crushing snake or whatever fate her pursuers had in mind for her if they caught her. The snake was very close now. Zoe held her breath as the creature abruptly changed direction, veering towards her as if it had seen her. The reptile swiftly slithered into the gap between the two cabinets where Zoe crouched, its eyes seemingly fixed on the squatting girl.

The situation presented a real dilemma for Zoe. If she ran, she risked being caught by Stefan and Marcus, if she stayed the snake would get her. She had to make a quick decision. Zoe decided to run. *At least this way,* she thought, *I have a chance of escaping.* She tried to stand up. Instantly she felt something wrapping around her ankle, dragging her backwards and downwards. She looked down. The snake had begun to coil itself around her lower leg, quickly pulling itself higher as it sought to get sufficient purchase on her body to allow it to climb up to her waist or neck, from where it would complete its deadly business by squeezing and crushing the life from her.

Zoe grabbed frenziedly at the slithering reptile, pulling and clawing as she tried to prise it away from her legs. Fortunately for her, the snake hadn't yet got a firm enough grip on her body for it to successfully withstand her frantic attempts to free herself. Zoe used every bit of strength she could muster as she struggled with the creature. It was the first time her fingers had come into contact with a snake. She was surprised how dry and smooth its skin was – in contrast to its appearance – but this was no time for nature study. She tugged hard, giving an almighty yank at the rippling body that was attempting to bind itself firmly around her legs. Zoe then hit the serpent hard, once, twice, followed by a third time as desperation began to mount inside her head. Through these coordinated, combative efforts she managed to stop the creature's progress. It retreated slightly, but still hung loosely around her left ankle waiting for a second chance to envelop and devour her. Zoe reflected that if it did so she wouldn't have the strength to resist a second time given the effort she had just put into freeing herself. It was only a matter of time before her strength ran out completely.

'Where do you think she is?' It was Marcus.

'She's got to be in this building somewhere, so keep looking,' was Stefan's response. 'She won't be in here though, not with all this junk about. There's no room to go any further forward, look at it. We might as well go. Come on let's try upstairs again.'

Their voices were accompanied by another bout of loud banging as the pair pushed over more cabinets in their attempts to get to the stairs so they could continue their pursuit of Zoe. The noise they made was enough to distract the snake, which slackened its grip on Zoe still further. It soon relinquished its hold completely, retreating to the top of the nearest cabinet. From this fairly lofty vantage point, the reptile raised its heavily patterned head to search for the source of the noise.

Still cowering in her hiding place, Zoe heard the two sets of footsteps cross the floor again. This time they were heading away from her. The softened thud of leather clad feet gradually receded as the men left the basement, heading upstairs. Zoe's body ached from being twisted into such a small space. Fighting the snake while still crouching between two cabinets hadn't helped either. She didn't really want to stand up yet, in case Stefan and Marcus were waiting at the top of the stairs for her to try to make her escape. However, she needed to stretch herself before cramp set in. She also wanted to get as far away from the snake as she could. It was the latter wish that was the deciding factor. Zoe leapt from her hiding place. She sprinted to the door, where she stopped for a moment to rub her legs until some feeling came back into them. After this she ventured into the corridor, creeping along with her back to the edge of the wall where the shadows were deepest. At the bottom of the stairs Zoe gingerly stood up straight, arching her back and flexing her shoulders to try to get her muscles working properly again.

There was silence as she inched her way upstairs. At the top she furtively stuck her head over the staircase to look into the main part of the library. Zoe wasn't able to see much in the dim light, but nonetheless decided to risk a move into the next room. Stealthily manoeuvring her way along the wall towards the entrance she stopped every few feet to listen. She couldn't hear any sound to suggest that her pursuers might be near so she continued to edge forward, following what she hoped was her escape route. It was only a short distance now to the doorway, with every step taking her nearer to freedom. Zoe was so close she could see outside. There was no sign of either man so she took a deep breath before making a dash for the exit. Before she knew it she was in daylight again. Thin shafts of sunlight speared through the trees, even though the main part of the forest was in shade. Zoe bounded down the steps. Once clear of the building, she headed for the cover of the trees. She slowed a little, breathing a sigh of relief as the shadows in the forest enveloped her.

'Gotcha!'

The single word rang loud and clear in her ear. At the same time a hand clamped firmly on her shoulder. It was accompanied by an arm sliding around her neck and pulling tightly across her throat. Zoe turned her head as much as she was able to without choking. She saw Stefan's grinning face leering at her. Marcus stood behind him.

'I told you we'd find her, didn't I?' Stefan gloated as he glanced at Marcus. 'All we had to do was to be patient. Now we can carry on from where we left off.'

Stefan's grip on Zoe tightened as Marcus temporarily left him to go into the nearby trees. He soon returned carrying more plant vines and tendrils. This time he bound her more securely, tying the tendrils around her ankles and legs in a criss-cross pattern that was so tight Zoe worried it might interfere with her blood circulation. Stefan relaxed his grip once Marcus had again displayed his binding skills on Zoe's arms and hands. She was now properly trussed up, unable to move her arms or legs.

'Let's see you escape from *that*!' snarled Marcus when he had finished.

The two men carried Zoe deep into the wood. Neither said a word until they reached their camp, where they dumped her unceremoniously on the floor of a small, crudely built mud hut.

'You can stay there until we decide what to do with you,' growled Stefan. 'But whatever that is, I promise you it won't be pleasant.'

Marcus nodded his agreement, treating Zoe to a glimpse of broken and missing teeth as he opened his mouth wide in a sneering smirk. On hitting the ground, Zoe's vine-bound body rolled across the rough dirt floor until it came to rest on an uneven patch of soil.

The two men laughed loudly together before leaving the hut. Zoe lay on the floor for a while unable to move. It was very uncomfortable. Although scared, her mind was still focussed on getting back to the South, but first she had to get out of her current predicament. Stefan and Marcus left her alone for some time, so she had plenty of opportunity to think. She thought about Zak, wondering if he was trying to find her or whether he had chosen to ignore her and try to find his own way back to his planet, leaving Zoe to her fate on Lowlands.

It was the latter part of this thought that worried Zoe most. Not for the first time she had visions of Zak resurfacing as Kazzaar in 2012. If he did so he could easily find his spacecraft with the children's souls still intact. If that happened, nothing could stop him returning to his planet and putting his plans to colonise the Earth into practice. If his people did take over the Earth, then this future time she was now living in wouldn't exist in its present form. Zoe thought of what might happen then, *will everything disappear, including me? Or will I suddenly find myself in a future World controlled by aliens?* One thing she could be sure of was that if either of her hypotheses – or some other unusual event – happened while she was still in 3015, she'd know for certain that Zak had betrayed her.

At that same moment, up in the South, Zak Araz was thinking about Zoe. She hadn't yet been in her apartment. He had searched everywhere – in every possible guise he could think of – without finding her. He was missing her, and he too was worried. One of his concerns was that Zoe had somehow found a time machine then used it to get back home, leaving him stranded in this unfriendly, alien World.

Back in Lowlands Zoe struggled hard to free herself from the vines that imprisoned her, but they stubbornly resisted her efforts. Stefan and Marcus had made sure there was to be no second escape. Her wrists hurt, so did her legs. Numbness was beginning to set into all of her joints. As she futilely wrestled with her bonds, she heard a noise outside the hut. She looked up. Stefan and Marcus both stood in the doorway. Stefan leered as he approached her.

'Well my dear. It's time for you to face the people of the village. Time for them to deliver their verdict on your future.' The two men pulled Zoe roughly to her feet.

'I've done nothing wrong,' she protested. 'I've told you, I'm not from the South. I'm not even from this time. I came to this World by accident. Check it out. I lived in Lowlands for a while with a group of people before I went to the South to try to get home, then I got deported back here. Please … you've got to believe me. I've done nothing wrong. Just find Lake … or Heron … or Rainbow, they will all confirm my story.'

'We've already told you we don't know anyone by those names,' said Marcus. 'We have our own community. That's all we care about. We know people in the South don't like us. They don't want us around. They send soldiers down to hunt us, kill us, or take us to their planet. That's why we take our revenge on any spies we catch.'

'But I'm not a spy,' pleaded Zoe. 'I've told you and I'll keep on telling you because it's true!'

Stefan grinned sadistically. 'It's not up to you is it? It's up to the people in the village. Well, it's up to us really. They will just do as they're told. But you only need to look at the facts. You suddenly appeared in Lowlands, no one has seen you before, and you're wearing clothes that are not made down here. All of which clearly says that you are from the South. So in our book that makes you a spy.'

'I'm not! I'm not!' screamed Zoe. 'What do I have to do to convince you?'

'It's not us you have to convince,' said Marcus, shrugging his shoulders.

He helped Stefan to hoist Zoe across his shoulders. She was immediately carried outside into a cleared area where she could see the villagers all seated on the ground in a circle. Zoe was thrown to the floor in the middle of the group. She could feel everyone staring at her. Stefan began to address the crowd.

He put forward the case that she had come down from the South to spy on them, intending to return there with information that would lead to soldiers invading and killing all of the villagers. The crowd bayed loudly, applauding every word as he spoke. Zoe already had a sinking feeling inside which got worse as the noise from the group continued to rise to a crescendo. When Stefan had finished speaking, he told Zoe that she was now to be questioned by the villagers.

She did her best, answering questions that were fired at her, denying accusations, trying to explain why she was here. But no one was listening. Soon Stefan – who seemed to be both prosecutor and judge – announced a guilty verdict.

The anger Zoe felt at what she deemed to be an unjust verdict and a farce of a trial, was replaced by despair. This was quickly followed by terror as Stefan delivered her sentence.

'You have been found guilty of spying,' he announced triumphantly, the glee in his voice overriding the solemnity of his words. 'Your punishment will be the same as it is for all spies. You will die by the traditional method we use for secret agents and traitors. You will be burned at the stake.'

Zoe was shocked but she was still able to shout out. 'You can't do that. It's barbaric. It's inhuman.'

'On the contrary,' countered Stefan. 'We *can* do that. As for the fact that you think it's barbaric, well whether it is or not doesn't matter, we'll still do it. It will deter other spies from coming down here. It will also give the villagers a bit of entertainment.'

'But I'm innocent,' screamed Zoe. 'How many more times do I have to keep telling you that?'

'Only until the fire consumes you,' Stefan stated coldly, then pointing to two young male villagers, he ordered, 'Take her away. Stay with her. Guard her well. We must prepare the site for the execution.'

The crowd cheered wildly as Zoe, still securely bound, was taken away. She was roughly bundled into the same crude mud hut as before. The two men stood outside at the entrance, regularly sticking their heads into the room to check she remained there, even though there was little chance of her escaping.

CHAPTER SIXTEEN

Zoe spent another sleepless, uncomfortable night on the rough floor of the hut in which she was imprisoned. The tightness of the bonds on her wrists and legs cut into her skin. It hurt, but she had no time to think about the pain as a multitude of disturbing thoughts tumbled non-stop through her head. She tried desperately to think of some way to get out of her dilemma, but was unable to see any means of escape. Knowing that this would probably be the last night of her life, her thoughts once again turned to her family and friends. She reflected on how none of them would know she had died, nor the process by which she had perished. It comforted her little to think that the people close to her probably believed she had died a thousand years back when she disappeared into the time vortex. As morning approached, Zoe thought about Zak Araz and hated him more than ever.

The next day dawned far too quickly for Zoe. The morning sun had barely risen – casting its light only briefly from behind rolling black clouds – as she was blindfolded, then carried from the hut by her two guardians. They lifted her struggling body into the cleared area in which she'd faced the hostile crowd on the previous day.

The villagers had gathered in their numbers again,

but this time they were in festive mood as they prepared to enjoy the spectacle that was about to unfold before them. It took some time for everyone to arrive and settle, so Zoe was kept in suspense for a while longer before her blindfold was removed. When it was finally taken away, the horde of people who were assembled around the clearing gave a loud cheer.

Even though the crowd was large – and noisy – Zoe didn't pay them much attention. Her eyes and mind were focussed on the centrepiece of the clearing. Right in the middle stood a huge bonfire construction made up of tree branches, twigs and leaves. The hastily-put-together creation towered menacingly above her. Zoe felt an urge to look at it despite the fear and revulsion inside her. She raised her head slowly as she took in the width and height of the pile of dry kindling that was seemingly just waiting for her to scale its peak before it burst into life. Zoe's eyes scanned upwards to the very top of the pile, where they became transfixed. She was horror-stricken, not so much by the crudely built mound of wood as by the macabre structure that stood prominently at the summit of what was to be her funeral pyre.

At the very pinnacle she could see a small wooden platform on which stood a vertical post complete with a noose for her head. Further down the upright stake were what looked to be manacles for her hands and feet. All of these attachments were made from plant tendrils and osier. Zoe guessed they would be difficult to break free from, especially if tied by Stefan or Marcus.

She felt really despondent. Not for the first time,

terror gripped her insides as she was hauled up to the platform by Marcus. He secured her to the wooden post, placing her head inside the noose. Zoe – having by now abandoned all thoughts of escape – tried not to think of the terrible fate that awaited her, hoping only that it would be over quickly. She wished that she would faint, so as not to be conscious of the pain that she knew would soon consume her. She gasped loudly, visibly fighting for breath as panic began to build inside her. The watching crowd roared loudly, but Zoe was oblivious to their noise. All she could hear was her rapidly beating heart – a heart that she knew would soon be still and silent within the cinders that would be all that remained of her incinerated dead body. Her head was filled with thoughts of the terrible death that was now only moments away. She knew this was the end. This time there was no one to save her.

Zoe's spirit sank to rock bottom as she looked down. Stefan stood at the base of the construction with a flaming wooden torch in his hand. He stepped forward, grinning maniacally up at her as he thrust the torch forcefully into the bonfire. The dry kindling and leaves immediately burst into flame as the fire took on life, spreading quickly in the stiff breeze that had suddenly sprung up as if eager to play its own part in Zoe's imminent execution.

Zoe could already feel the heat, even though she was much higher than the fire. She saw the flames begin to dance as they leapt across the wooden pyre, licking and flicking like snake tongues. Red and orange fingers of fire reached out – grabbing at everything within range as they spiralled and stretched, extending like blazing giant tentacles – eager to greedily consume every single object that lay in their path. Higher and higher the fiery fingers rose as they moved fervently towards the summit, where Zoe coughed and choked. The acrid smoke had begun to surround her, clutching, clawing at the inside of her throat. It forced her into a coughing fit that racked her hacking aching body. The sky – already heavy and darkened by cloud – was soon pitch black from the thick billowing smoke. It was as if nightfall had come early, or the planet itself was in mourning for Zoe's imminent fate.

Soon the flames were so close to Zoe that had she been able to move her hands she could have touched them. It was incredibly hot. Zoe could feel the prickling on her skin. Soon it would start to peel and burn. Her mind couldn't focus now. She was terrified. Images flickered through her brain. She saw her mum, her dad, her brother. She briefly wondered what kind of life they would have, wondered if they missed her and wondered if they even thought about her. More vivid mental pictures followed, tumbling through her head at a rapid pace in unhindered, uncontrolled sequences. She saw her college, her course, her training, the career she might have had. It was all gone now. She was about to die a horrible death all alone one thousand years into her future. Even Kazzaar – alias Zak – who had been her enemy then briefly an ally, wouldn't know what had happened to her. Neither would Lake or Rainbow. Zoe remembered Hoblues High School, Amy, Simran, Daniel, her teachers. She saw the safari park, the time vortex, Benson and Professor Tompkins. The pictures stopped. Then the tears came. Zoe had never been so scared in all of her life, nor had she ever felt so lonely. She sobbed uncontrollably as the flames reached the platform from where they would begin the final leg of their journey up the wooden stake to which she was tied.

Zoe felt faint. She could feel her consciousness beginning to dwindle. She struggled to catch her breath as the choking black smoke filtered deep into her lungs. The tears rolling down her cheeks formed tiny pink rivulets on her soot-blackened face. Closing her eyes, she prayed that the end would come soon so that the pain she was already suffering wouldn't be prolonged. Zoe had never thought about death. It wasn't a priority when you were young – unless you had suffered bereavement – and if she *had* thought about it, then this wasn't exactly what she would have chosen for her own demise.

A loud, fierce explosion disrupted Zoe's thoughts, dragging her insentient mind back to the reality that currently surrounded her. She opened her eyes quickly to see that the sky – previously indiscernible in the swirling black smoke – was now brilliantly illuminated. She could see dark silhouettes of the trees that surrounded the clearing. They appeared starkly profiled against the radiant light. The arboreal ensemble stood brooding and magisterial, like a panel of judges or jurists sitting in condemnation of those participating in the grisly scenario being played out in the clearing. The brightness in the sky lasted only a few seconds before darkness descended once again. Zoe looked down to check on the state of the blaze below her. The flames still danced unforgivingly just below her feet, but it wasn't the fire that had lit up the sky. It was lightning.

More loud bangs interspersed with several deep rumbles reverberated around the clearing, as thunder rolled across the heavens in a percussion accompaniment to the ragged, jagged forks of electricity that intermittently sliced through the dark sky as easily as a hot knife through butter. To the watching villagers, the dazzling bolts of discharged energy – which rent the sky with haphazard patterns of light – looked every bit as menacing as the brooding black clouds that hung low above the clearing. Zoe suddenly found the will to raise herself up so she could watch this natural phenomenon that hadn't changed in millions of years. It was as if all of the ancient gods of this partially abandoned and much neglected planet had risen together, intent on avenging all past injustices by venting their anger at the outrageous misdeed that was taking place beneath them.

Something hard and wet splattered against Zoe's face. Then another. Then another. Then there were lots of them. Hard, cold little pellets that stung sharply as they made contact with her skin, rapidly increasing in volume until not just her face but her whole body was consumed. The objects became softer despite increasing in size. They were wet too. It was raining! Zoe had never found rain more welcome. She felt her hopes rise as huge raindrops splashed onto her face, arms and legs, plopping loudly onto the smouldering wooden platform beneath her feet. It wasn't just raining. It was bucketing down.

The watching villagers ran for cover as the storm

lashed across the clearing. Many of them clasped their hands over their ears as they ran, trying to keep out the sound of thunder. Zoe wondered *did the fleeing people think this was a normal storm. Or did some of them perhaps think it was some sort of divine retribution for what had happened to her? Maybe some thought it was the people in the South punishing them for what they were doing to one of the southern citizens?* Whatever they thought, she didn't care. She stood atop the charred platform, still alone, but no longer in fear of dying. Below her the flames were losing their power. The brightness beneath her diminished as the fire was slowly extinguished by the force of the torrential downpour.

Zoe could still taste the smoke. Still feel it biting at the back of her throat as it bristled and prickled inside her chest. But now the fire was out, she was not going to burn. She dismissed a fleeting, morbid thought that the smoke might have damaged her lungs to the extent that she would die anyway. Instead, she chose to concentrate on how she could take advantage of this unexpected, but welcome, intervention by the elements.

The heat from the fire had frayed her bonds, weakening them so that she was no longer unable to move. Zoe escaped from imprisonment with a few tugs and twists that helped the smouldering tendrils irrevocably relinquish their hold on her. She stepped free, scrambling down from what was left of the bonfire. She banged her knee as she did so, managing to cut her hand too when moving a charred piece of timber that barred her way. Zoe shook her hand vigorously to clear the few spots of loose blood before continuing her descent. When she reached level ground she looked around for Stefan and Marcus, half expecting them to jump out and take her prisoner again. But they were nowhere to be seen. Zoe ran into the forest where the trees provided much needed cover. Lightning was still ripping across the sky but now the illumination was a bit further away, although the rain hammered down as fiercely as before.

Zoe kept on running. She had no idea where she was heading. She wanted to get as far away as possible from Stefan and Marcus. After a while she couldn't run any more. She was exhausted. She leaned against a tree breathing deeply. Zoe found herself gasping. She couldn't get her breath. She stood for a while, coughing continually as her exertions caught up with her. When her breathing had returned to something near to normal, the battering that her lungs had taken from the smoke became evident from the pain she felt in her chest. It was at this point that Zoe heard a distant noise. It was a continuous roaring sound, a bit similar to the noise she remembered from her childhood on the occasions she had held a seashell to her ears. Instinctively her body became taut again at the unexpected clamour. She listened carefully, cupping her hand to her ear. Still shaky from her brush with death, Zoe hoped it wasn't caused by anyone from the village from which she'd just escaped. She held her breath, then moving further into the forest she sighed in relief as she heard the loud sound of rushing water drowning out the noise of raindrops pattering on leaves.

It's a river, she thought. *If it's the one that goes by Lake's village then maybe I can find my way there later, but for now I must rest.*

Zoe guessed that it was probably late afternoon by now, even though prevailing darkness was still shutting out any sunshine above the lowering clouds.

Her spirits were raised somewhat at the thought of finding her old village. But she needed to rest. She was exhausted. Zoe looked around for somewhere suitable to lie down for a while, or possibly spend the night. She saw a grassy bank rising ahead of her so she climbed to the top. From there – by assessing the noise level of the water – she was able to judge that the river was very close. She didn't want to fall in, certainly not in the darkness. Standing on the knoll, she peered into the gloom. From her elevated position, Zoe could just about make out that the bank she was standing on roughly formed a right angle with an adjacent bank. Both sloped downwards to form a hollow that was overhung by branches of nearby trees. It wasn't exactly a trench, but it was probably as near as she would find to one in the circumstances. More importantly it didn't look as if the rain had got in, so it might offer her a suitable shelter for the night.

Zoe carefully clambered down the bank to avoid slipping on the wet grass. The rain had now abated into a fine drizzle. At the bottom of the hillock she was pleased to find that the overhanging branches were of sufficient density to offer a large dry area of ground beneath them, as well as continued shelter from the watery precipitation. Crawling into the naturally formed cradle at the base of the two banks, Zoe lay on the ground. She pulled her jacket tightly around her, shaping her body into the foetal position as she settled into the temporary sanctuary offered by the trees. It wasn't long before her body relaxed enough to allow her to drift off to sleep.

Zoe slept for two days. It was a sleep plagued with tortured dreams, as Stefan, Marcus, the snake, the security police and Kazzaar all put in an appearance at various times during her slumbers. But despite this subconscious confusion she didn't wake up until the very early hours of the morning two days later. When she did it was still dark.

At first Zoe couldn't recall where she was. But her brain clicked into gear as it put the pieces together, remembering and making sense of the reason she now found herself lying under a clear starry night sky at the bottom of an embankment with a canopy of trees as her only cover. She lay for a while staring at the stars. Then her gaze fell upon the twinkling orb that was the South. The planet cast its light towards the land below, but the illumination was little more than moderate. The artificial orb glowed, but the effect of its light on the Earth's surface was insignificant when compared to Zoe's memory of the full moonlight she recalled from growing up on Earth. Zoe looked for the moon now. There it was. A quarter moon with light limited at the best of times. Its time honoured illumination now partially eclipsed by a man-made satellite that hung above the real Earth's surface. The sight made Zoe wistful. Yet somehow she found even a quarter moon to be reassuring in her current situation.

Turning her attention to the South, she wondered if Zak was still up there or had he found the time machine and gone back to the Earth of her time? Sighing, she thought *I need to get back up there as soon as I can.*

Zoe turned onto her side, curling her body up once more so she could enjoy another period of sleep – hopefully less troubled than her last one – before daylight arrived. Suddenly, she became aware of something pressing against her back. Turning her head to find out what it was, she was stunned to see a human face looking straight back into hers. Instantly Zoe's body froze. She screamed loudly as her mind shot into overdrive.

CHAPTER SEVENTEEN

Zoe quickly turned her head away so that she wasn't looking at the face. She tried to convince herself it was a dream. She told herself that the face wasn't really there. The pretence didn't work though. With her heart in her mouth she risked a further quick peek over her shoulder. The face was still there, staring straight into hers with deep dark wide open eyes, its mouth agape in a sinister rictus grin. Zoe turned away again from the spine-chilling sight. Her mind was struggling to make sense of what she saw as the cruel irony of her current situation. *If I'm not dreaming then it has to be either Stefan or Marcus,* she thought, her body now shaking violently with fear. *They've found me! After all I've gone through they've found me! The rain came and saved my life and I thought I was safe. I've run for miles. Now they've caught up with me again!*

Zoe's spirits sank to their lowest level. She knew there would be no escape if they had caught her for the third time. She didn't have the will or motivation to run again. Besides, she was lying down so she couldn't run even if she wanted to. *Just my luck,* she thought. *I was sure I'd escaped from them. I've made it this far. I've got to the river so I must be quite near to Lake's village. It's beyond belief that they've found me again. I should have carried on running and not stopped to sleep. There won't be another chance of escape.*

They'll kill me for sure this time. She closed her eyes and waited for one of the men to speak, or grab hold of her.

Zoe lay there cowering for a while but nothing happened. There was no word or movement behind her and no one laid a hand on her. *That's strange* she thought. *They are unusually quiet. I would have expected one of them to have said something or made a move by now.* She decided to risk yet another look. She glanced furtively behind her, making a momentary appraisal of the situation which quickly allayed any fears about the presence of her previous captors. What she did see however brought new concerns, forcing Zoe to turn completely in order to contemplate the full horror of who was currently sharing her sleeping quarters. It wasn't Stefan or Marcus. In fact it wasn't even a face, though it had been once. Zoe's relief at the absence of her recent torturers was quickly overtaken by revulsion and horror at the sight that now confronted her. She was stunned to find herself staring into two empty eye sockets that were part of a human skull!

The white skull bone gleamed in the reflection from the pale light cast by the planet above. Zoe closed her eyes. She took a deep breath, then with eyes opened again – this time even wider – she risked a further, longer, look at the object. Zoe could clearly see that it wasn't *just* a skull! There was a full human skeleton attached to it! She caught sight of another one, then another, then another. She seemed to be surrounded by human skeletons. Not only that, she could also see lots of loose bones and unattached skulls scattered around various places on the embankment.

Zoe sat up quickly, heart pounding like a steam hammer. As she did so one of the skeletons leapt from the top of the bank, almost landing on top of her. She screamed loudly again, but this time she passed out.

When Zoe regained consciousness it was daylight. She was still surrounded by skeletons, but they were motionless. She was certain that they hadn't been there on the night she'd chosen this resting place or she wouldn't have stayed. *So, how have they got here?* She mused.

Gingerly Zoe got to her feet, scrambling up the slope until she reached the level ground at the top of the embankment. It was there that she got the first inkling of what had happened. The heavy rain had forced the river to burst its banks. Flood water covered much of the surrounding ground. There were pieces of stone scattered all around. Small bits, as well as large chunks that seemed to have been stuck into the ground at oblique angles. Zoe picked up one of the pieces that lay nearby. There was a name and a date scratched into the surface. She picked up another one, it was similar. Looking around she could see more names and dates etched onto the other stones too. Zoe sighed. She guessed that this place must have been an ancient graveyard. The surging floodwater had obviously disturbed the shallow graves, carrying the bones and full skeletons along the bank before dumping them in the hollow. Zoe gave an involuntary shudder as she considered the poor dead people whose final resting place had been so rudely disturbed, people whose bones had been dragged from their ultimate sanctuary to be deposited unceremoniously and sacrilegiously into the sheltered nook in which she had been sleeping.

There was nothing Zoe could do about interring the bones in their original burial place, however much she might want to do so. She crossed herself, saying a silent prayer for the souls of the poor departed. Then she walked the short distance to the river.

Before starting her trek along the wet muddy bank Zoe stood for a while looking up and down the course of the river. She was trying to see if anything looked familiar, but nothing registered. She tried to work out where Lake's village might be in relation to the settlement where Stefan and Marcus had tried to burn her, but again drew a blank. Zoe soon gave up trying. More in hope than certainty, she decided to head westward by following the flow of the river.

The rain – long since ceased in its precipitation – had caused substantial flooding, but nevertheless Zoe managed to find the path that ran along the river bank. Luckily it was still navigable with care, so she decided to risk walking it as she continued her quest to find Lake's settlement. The river gushed rapidly alongside her as she made her way along the path. The water level was still very high, with white water rapids cascading over the rocks and the broken trees – felled by the ferocious storm – that now protruded into the river. The rushing water roared loudly as it rolled powerfully along its well established route. It was fierce and uncontrolled, threatening to break over the banks at any moment. Zoe decided to keep as far away from the edge as the path would allow. She didn't want to fall in or become victim to a freak wave. If either event occurred, she knew she would be immediately washed away in the savage, merciless current. That would mean certain death, which would be an irony – as well as a disaster - especially as she'd managed to evade the death by fire, arranged for her by Stefan and Marcus.

The journey wasn't easy. On the way Zoe encountered more flooded areas, all of which added time and distance to her trip. She frequently found herself having to take evasive action by using other pathways that steered her away from her intended route, before bringing her back to re-join the river further along. Zoe's lungs still hurt as she breathed, but regardless of this she continued, not wanting to stop until she reached her destination. Her perseverance paid dividends when she reached a part of the river that she recognised. It was the place where she used to bathe and wash her clothes. Zoe felt excited, yet scared at the same time. Despite the short time since she was last here, she wondered how her presence would be received in the camp.

It was just a brief walk to the place where Zoe had spent so much time when first arriving in this time zone. As she walked into the village clearing several heads turned to look at her. Zoe scanned the faces for signs of recognition. She instantly knew everyone there. Several people smiled or waved in greeting. Then a figure broke from the main group. It ran across the clearing towards her, calling out as it ran.

'Zoe? … Zoe? … Is it you? What are you doing back here?'

The figure stopped in front of Zoe. 'I can't believe you're back. But why are you so dirty?'

It was Lake. She flung her arms around Zoe enveloping her in a warm welcoming hug, which took Zoe's already labouring breath completely away. When a coughing spluttering Zoe had finally extricated herself from Lake's bear-like hug, she was bombarded with questions which were fired in such a rapid stream that she had no time to answer one before the next one was upon her.

'Wait, wait, slow down,' gasped Zoe. 'I'll tell you everything when I get the chance, but first I need to wash. I also need to maybe get something to eat and drink? I'm hungry and I stink!'

Hours later Zoe – appetite sated, thirst quenched, and dressed in clean if oversized clothes borrowed from one of the villagers – leaned back as she finished the tale of her adventures since leaving the group only a few days ago. There had been gasps, squeals, hands clasped together, or clamped over mouths as the group listened to Zoe relating her tale about the South, her deportation, her brush with death at the hands of Stefan and Marcus, and her experience of waking up next to the skeletons.

'Are you going to stay with us now?' asked Rainbow.

Zoe smiled apologetically. 'For a little while perhaps,' she said. 'But not for too long. I have to go back.'

Zoe saw a look of disappointment flicker across Lake's face as she sat opposite her. Zoe took her by the hand as she said, 'Lake, somewhere up on that planet there is a time machine that might be able to get me home. I have to find it. It's my only chance to get back to my family.'

She asked about the village where they had tried to burn her to death.

It was Heron who answered. 'We know where it is,' he said. 'But we keep away from it. Most of the villagers are fine, but those two – Stefan and Marcus, you say – must be the ones who have been controlling and terrorising everyone around this part of Lowlands. They are always declaring war on other settlements. Both of them are nasty pieces of work. There is no chance of peace while they are around. I think the other villagers are scared of them.'

'They are,' agreed Zoe. 'Not one of them tried to stop my execution. In fact it seemed to me that they enjoyed it. They certainly shouted and cheered enough when the fire was lit. However, if as you say they are scared of those two, then I suppose it must be difficult to protest. I guess it's safer for them to go along with what is happening, whether you agree with it or not.'

Just then Zoe spotted a face she knew, but the last time she'd seen this face its owner had been talking to her in the short time they had shared a police cell. It was Jane.

Zoe went over to talk to her. 'Hallo,' she said. 'I see you managed to find your way here.'

'They found me actually,' replied Jane after returning Zoe's greeting. 'I was deported the day after you went. I was wandering about trying to find my way to this place as you suggested, when I met someone from the camp here. You were right, they are looking after me. I've been made to feel very welcome. I've actually changed my name to Bluebell so I can fit in. I did toy with the idea of calling myself Oak as I wanted a name that suggested strength and longevity. But I had a rethink, then decided that I didn't want my new name to sound as if it might have come from a piece of furniture or a door.'

Zoe was unable to suppress a little smile as she thought that Jane obviously hadn't had the same considerations about the name Bluebell. It might be the name of a beautiful flower that heralded the imminent arrival of summer, but in Zoe's mind it summoned up images of a number of farmyard animals and dairy herds.

'Talking of names,' Jane added, 'I thought you told me your name was Victoria Boswell? Everyone here seems to know you as Zoe. Did you change *your* name too?'

Zoe briefly explained the mix-up over names that led to her being arrested and how that had come about. When she had finished Lake sidled up to her.

'You're definitely going back then?' she whispered.

Zoe nodded. 'I have to,' she said.

Heron and Rainbow approached her. Heron spoke. 'Zoe,' he said. 'Now that you've been up to the South what do you think we should do? Should we try to get up there ourselves so we can change the way people see us? Maybe try to get them to stop sending the soldiers down here to harm us?'

'Jane, sorry … Bluebell, has also been up there,' said

Zoe, 'for much longer than me too. She'll tell you everything you want to know about the people and what they do, but from my short time there, my advice would be to ignore them. I think you should rebuild a new World down here. There's no freedom up there, no respect, for people or for life, both are easily expendable in that place. The only things they care about are money and power. It's not a place where you should be. You don't belong there, you lot are far too nice. Stay here. You can start all over again, learn how to build, how to create energy so you can tap into electricity, how to use natural gasses, find medicines, you can also learn other farming techniques to support the ones you use at present. If you can do that, there's every possibility you could prolong your current expected life span. You can create a proper society, encourage your children to take your work on through their lives too so that the Earth can live again. This time in peace and harmony with everyone being equal. You can learn from the mistakes of the past.'

'How can we do this?' asked Heron. 'We have no formal education, and no information about what has worked or what didn't work in the past. We have some knowledge of our recent heritage, but insufficient history of the planet to understand it or avoid making similar mistakes to those our ancestors might have made. We don't know how to create or use things that might provide opportunities to improve our World.'

'I will show you,' said Zoe, 'but first we have to go to that other village. I discovered something near there that I'm certain you can use to help you rebuild this planet.'

'It is dangerous to go there,' said Heron.

'Maybe,' said Zoe, 'but it is not impossible. If you want to progress as a race, you need help. Besides, someone has to stand up to those bullies Stefan and Marcus, or they will stop you from ever being able to make life better for anyone. You can't let bullies rule you, that's what's happening up there.' Zoe pointed to the South. 'It's not a good place to live. Ask Bluebell.'

Zoe looked around the group. 'So will you come with me to that village?'

Heron looked to the others for his answer. He was met with nodding heads all round.

'Okay,' he said, 'but we must be careful. It is late now. Zoe also needs to take it easy for a while so that her lungs can recuperate. We will go when she is recovered.'

It was a further four weeks before Zoe had recovered sufficiently to go back to find the library. She hadn't anticipated it would take that long, but her lungs had been in a worse state than she'd imagined. She had spent many days in bed rest, while the sunshine and fresh air outdoors had also played a crucial part in her period of convalescence.

On the day they left to retrace Zoe's steps from the time when she'd cheated death by fire, she led the group along the river bank to find the library. The river had subsided from the raging torrent it had been when Zoe made her journey into a calming flow of gentle rippling water. The path had dried considerably, although there was still some mud about.

When they reached the grassy knoll near the

sheltered hollow, Zoe saw that the skeletons were still there. The sight of all of those bones still made her feel uneasy, but she was glad they hadn't been washed away in the floodwaters, or taken by animals.

Heron placed a hand on her arm. 'We must stop a while. We should bury these people,' he said. 'It is the right thing to do. Even if we did not know them we should show them respect, especially in death.'

He motioned to the others. Soon everyone was working hard, using whatever they could find to utilise as tools, as they dug into the still soft earth to make fresh graves for the remains of what were once living human beings. They chose a spot well away from the previous graveyard to try to avoid future disturbance from flood waters. When they had finished, they all stood in silence for a while in memory of the deceased.

When the time came to move on, Zoe couldn't remember the way to the village. When she had been running away from the place, she hadn't been in a position to take much notice of her surroundings. It hadn't really been her priority. She guessed the blank space within her mind might also be at least partly due to her brain trying to shut out bad memories of that day. Fortunately Heron did know the way, so the group now followed him with Zoe walking alongside Lake and Bluebell.

As they drew near to the village, Heron motioned everyone to slow down. He signalled for silence then broke off a large branch, trimming the twigs and buds from it by running his hands up and down the main shaft.

'We may need weapons,' he said quietly. 'Arm yourselves just in case.'

The others followed suit, grabbing whatever they could, to use as weapons. Then, led by Heron they marched into the village.

There were a number of people about, mostly going about their daily routines. Surprise was evident on many faces when Heron entered the clearing, accompanied by his band of followers. There was no resistance. In fact quite the opposite. One of the villagers informed Heron that Stefan and Marcus had been taken by the security police on the night of the fire. The villagers were really quite pleased to see the pair go, as they had terrorised everyone. It seemed that for some time they had been ruling, persecuting and controlling the tribe in tyrannical fashion. The two of them had brought fear to everyone in the group. They had also brought death to anyone brave enough to offer a challenge.

The villagers now offered refreshments to their guests. Zoe also received countless apologies for the way in which she had been treated on her previous encounter with the group. Afterwards, when old wounds had been partially healed – with potential new friendships and co-operatives being formed – Heron and the group left.

Zoe took over at the head of the group, eagerly leading the way to the library she'd found, after warning the others of the possible presence of a snake inside the building. In the basement she located the unlocked cabinet. There was no sign of the reptile. Zoe quickly opened up the parcel that she'd briefly examined on her last visit.

'Look,' she said, holding a large tome aloft. 'Books! These can be the key to your future. They will tell you all you need to know. There are plenty of books here, all well preserved. I don't know what's in the other cabinets but if the contents are similar, there will be sufficient information to enable you to learn the history of your planet. With that you can rebuild your World. You can learn how to make and build things, grow more crops and flowers, feed yourselves in different ways and educate your children with greater knowledge. You should also be able to find several different forms of energy. In fact you can do anything you want. You can make Earth a proper planet again, but this time without the greed and war that previously existed, just as I said you could. Come on, let's get the other cabinets open.'

Everyone got busy with the weapons they'd fashioned, but this time they were used as makeshift tools to break the locks on the cabinets. Zoe was proved to be right. The other cabinets did more contain books. There were lots of them, fact and fiction. There were books of many different types.

Bluebell offered to help the group too as she had knowledge from her role in the South. She also had information from her historical trips back in time. The group members took as many of the items as they could carry back to camp with them. They made their plans to transport the rest of their potentially precious find back to their village over the next few days.

Back at camp, Zoe sought out Lake. 'I'm going back up there,' she said pointing to the sphere in the sky above her. 'I have to find that time machine. I want to go home.'

'I'm not sure *what* I want anymore,' sighed Lake. 'I've always thought that there was a better way, hoped that we could change our lives, improve our lifestyle, maybe extend our life expectancy … part of me thought that if I could get to the South, then like you I would find the answers and get what I want.'

'That place isn't for you, Lake,' Zoe said softly. 'Really it isn't. Please believe me you wouldn't want to be up there. I don't want to be there, but I have to go. I have to find a way home.'

'What about me?' cried Lake. 'I missed you when you went there the first time, even though it was just a few days before you came back. How will I manage now without you?'

'You still have everyone else here,' said Zoe. 'Bluebell is here now too. I'm sure she could do with a good friend like you.'

'I know,' said Lake. 'I will try to be a friend to her and help her to settle in, but if I'm honest, I have to say that I've never had a friend like *you* before. I was so pleased when you returned. Please Zoe, stay here. Help us as we rebuild Lowlands.'

'I can't,' whispered Zoe. 'You know that, Lake. It would never work out. It might be okay to begin with, but I would always be missing my family… always wondering if I could have got back to them … always worrying that by staying here I had allowed Kazzaar to find the time machine, using it to get back to my World before taking the souls of those children to his own planet. On second thoughts, if he did that I wouldn't be wondering any more as nothing of what is here today would exist, because his race would then colonise Earth. If that occurred, there would be no you, no me, none of your people or anyone you recognise. There would be no South or Lowlands, and whilst you may think that's a good idea, just think what might be in its place. There would probably be an alien occupation that steals the souls from your children. I can't let that happen. I've got to try to get back, Lake. I've got to try to stop him.'

Tears began to form in Lake's eyes as Zoe spoke.

'Don't cry,' said Zoe comfortingly. 'Be brave. Be magnificent. Change your own World. Make it something to be proud of. Work together. You can use those books to build something special. You can build hospitals, schools … anything you want. Just go for it!'

'Do you really think that's possible?' asked Lake.

Zoe nodded. 'It's been done before,' she said. 'So why not again?'

Lake ran a hand across her face to wipe away her tears. She hugged Zoe as she whispered, 'Thank you.'

Zoe smiled. 'That's okay.' She said, adding, 'I will miss you too, Lake. I've enjoyed the time I've spent here. You have helped me a lot, you've also guided me through a very dark, scary time in my life. I wouldn't have managed it without you … You know – when I do get back to the South – if I can't get home for any reason, then as I promised you before I will return here. Then I will stay with all of you and help you in your quest to build a new World. But for now I have to try to get home. My home is one thousand years in the past. Lake, you know I need to be with my family. So if there's any chance of a return I have to try and find it, but whatever happens I will always remember you and care about you, and the others too. So I'll have to say goodbye to you all ... yet again.'

CHAPTER EIGHTEEN

Two nights later Zoe left the camp to head towards the settlement in which she had suffered so much pain. To her relief, her lungs were now fully operational again. She was dressed in the clothes she had arrived in from the South. Lake had washed them thoroughly in the river, as well as executing a few minor repairs. She had then pressed the garments using large flat stones. They looked far from brand new, but were relatively smart again in readiness for Zoe's planned re-entry into life on planet South.

She had chosen to return under cover of night, to avoid running into the daytime patrols who used the transporter booths. It had taken a long time for her to arrive at this decision. She was conscious of the fact that night time use of the transporter would be likely to raise suspicion at security police headquarters, as it was normally only used in daylight hours. However, on balance Zoe believed it was the right choice, as darkness provided her with a better chance of keeping out of sight once she got there. She also knew – from the time she got deported – that staff levels in the headquarters were much lower at night.

One thing that did concern Zoe was the thought of the wild animals that roamed the forest at night, hunting for prey. After much deliberation, she decided it was a risk she had to take if she wanted to get to the South under cover of darkness. The pale moon hung limply in the sky as Zoe walked the river path. She had chosen this route because she reasoned that fewer animals would be likely to hunt by the river than in the woodland. Of course, there was always the chance she might happen upon something slaking its thirst at the water's edge. Zoe made up her mind that she would deal with any situation as it arose, but if faced with imminent danger her plan B might involve taking a chance on using the river to swim to safety.

The moon seemed to be somehow dwarfed by the relative proximity of the artificial planet. The man-made sphere seemed to absorb whatever moonlight there was, giving rise to blackness all along the waterside path that Zoe trod. Somewhere in the distance, she could see twin shafts of bright light cutting swathes across the backdrop of the night sky, forming a symbolic bridge between the South and Lowlands. Zoe thought about the hidden staircase that lay within each beam, a staircase that had not so long ago provided her with the means to make her first visit to the new planet. Tonight she could ignore the beams. She had no need of the staircase now.

Luck was with Zoe on her journey, and she made her destination without encountering any of the nocturnal creatures she had been worried about. Despite the darkness she had managed to find the village, which she bypassed as she headed in the direction of the deserted library. From there – with a little difficulty and the odd detour – she eventually located the first of the trees that formed the marked trail she had left when she arrived in the transporter.

Zoe followed the trail until she came to the angular branch that indicated the whereabouts of the artificial tree with the two letters she had scratched into the surface. She quickly found the booth, went in, and pressed the button marked *south.* Seconds later she arrived in the police headquarters from whence she'd been roughly despatched not long ago. She hoped that by now the police would have forgotten what Zoe Marshall looked like. If not, she would be really up against it, as anonymity was key to her plan to rehabilitate herself in the South.

The transporter had stopped in a different part of the building to the place she had arrived with Zak when they had climbed through the beam of light. However, Zoe was aware that there would probably be security cameras focussed on the booth and everyone who used it. She guessed that security personnel would be alerted whenever the booth returned so they could ensure that no one from Lowlands was able to use it to sneak into the South. She further assumed that security surveillance would be heightened by the transporter returning at such a late hour, particularly as no officers would be on Lowlands patrol duty at this time of night.

Zoe hoped there wouldn't be a policeman waiting for her when the door opened. She needed time to make her escape. She looked around the interior of the booth. There was nowhere to hide in there, so she would be a sitting duck if anyone was waiting. Zoe thought she ought to try and take some form of action that might just give her even a slight advantage in such a scenario. She pulled her jacket up until it covered her face, leaving a small gap around her eyes so she could see where she was going. Next, she lay flat on the floor near to the door but towards the side it would slide to when it opened.

Zoe held her breath as the door opened. She couldn't see anyone waiting so, crawling along the floor, she slowly eased her body outside into the terminal bay. Creeping along the edge of the walls – where there was very little light – she managed to reach a door. Zoe stood up intent on opening it, but her heart sank as she saw the security lock could only be actioned by an official code. She had forgotten that she and Zak had used stolen ID discs to exit the terminal when they'd arrived before. Cursing under her breath, she slumped back to the floor as she tried to think of a way round her problem.

Lying there in the shadows, Zoe suddenly heard the sound of voices. Before she could move, the door began to open. She stood up quickly, flattening herself against the wall as she did so. Luckily for her, she was behind the opening door as two people dressed in security police uniforms emerged. They were deep in conversation and didn't bother to look back as they headed toward the transporter booth. Zoe seized the opportunity to slip unnoticed through the gap created by the slowly closing door.

She found herself in a corridor that had several entrances and exits, all of which were clearly marked. Keeping her face covered, Zoe headed for one marked *General Public Exit to Street*. On reaching it she ran down the stairs that lay beyond the exit. Very soon she found herself on the street outside. She felt both relieved and elated.

'Now for part two of my plan,' she muttered, bracing herself for what was to come. 'Hopefully it will go as well as part one.'

Standing on the moving pavement, Zoe gathered her thoughts. It was still dark. She couldn't yet carry out the next part of her plan. It was too soon after the transporter had arrived, and it was likely that the two officers she had evaded were looking for the intruder. *I need to wait until morning to allay any suspicion. But what can I do until then? I don't know where my apartment is and I don't know where Zak is, but I need to find somewhere to wait. I can't stay on this pavement all night, the cameras will notice me if I keep going round and round. It wouldn't be long before the police arrived to see what I was doing.* Zoe's thoughts did little to comfort her in her impatience.

She stayed on the pavement for a while trying to decide where she could go for the next few hours. Before long the pavement passed through an area that looked familiar to Zoe. She recognised it immediately. *It's the building where I waited for Zak when he went to get clothes for us,* she thought. *There's a toilet in there. I can wait there until it's time to go.* Zoe leapt from the pavement, found her way into the building then settled herself down inside a cubicle. She sat there in a state of excitement mixed with apprehension, waiting for the moment when she could leave to put part two of her plan into action.

When that time arrived she left the toilet, heading for the offices of the street police. When she got there, Zoe began to feel less confident than when she had left security police headquarters. She felt her heart rate increase slightly as panic began to rise in her throat. Negative thoughts began to invade her head. *What if the plan doesn't work? What if the police don't believe me? What if they are expecting me to come back and are looking out for me?* She stood outside the police offices for ten minutes or so, calming herself while simultaneously trying to convince herself that her plan was a good one without any reason for suspicion. Finally, she plucked up sufficient courage to go in.

At the desk Zoe took a deep breath before speaking to the officer on duty. 'Excuse me,' she said hesitantly. Then, drawing herself up to her full height she raised her voice. In a far more confident tone Zoe continued with the speech she had rehearsed many times in her head.

'My name is Victoria Boswell. I've had my ID disc stolen. Can you please tell me if it has been handed in here?'

The officer looked at her blankly. Zoe repeated her request.

The officer looked her up and down, his face exhibiting the semblance of a sneer. 'We don't deal with that here, we are the Street Police,' he said haughtily. 'You should know the procedure. It's the Security Police HQ that handles ID issues. We handle crime and prosecution.'

Zoe felt her heart sink into her stomach, but she was determined not to let the officer put her off. She stood tall, looking him straight in the eye before saying 'I know that.' It was a lie but Zoe continued, knowing he wouldn't be able to tell. 'But the person who stole my ID was arrested by police from this station, so I assumed that you'd be dealing with it and that perhaps the ID disc would still be here.'

The officer remained unmoved. 'Procedures are procedures,' he said slowly, giving Zoe a look that suggested he viewed her as some kind of imbecile. 'We may arrest ID thieves, but I've already told you that ID issues are dealt with by Security Police. You'll have to go there.'

For a moment Zoe was reminded of DI Chalk whom she met back in Cristelee in 2012. He too was a stickler for the rules, never paying attention to anyone's opinions if they didn't match his own. She knew she wouldn't get anywhere by arguing her point with this officer. She tutted loudly, tossed her head, turned on her heel and then marched out of the building in an act of defiance she hoped would mask her blushes from the staring, head-shaking deskman.

Outside, Zoe leaned against the building as she took time to regain her composure. This was going to be more difficult than she thought. She didn't really want to go back to security police headquarters, as she was worried that someone might recognize her from the night she arrived with Zak, even though she'd worn a helmet on that occasion. There might even be camera footage of her most recent arrival. Either way it would be a risk. She didn't want to face any awkward questions. The wrong answers could result in her death. However, if her plan was to work and she was to take her place as a resident in the South, she had to go through with it.

Ignoring her concerns and drawing on her inner

strength, Zoe headed for the security police headquarters. She was very nervous as she entered the building, sure that the duty officer would hear her heart thumping as she approached him. Her stomach was performing somersaults. It felt as if she was on a roller coaster.

'Yes Miss?' the officer asked, raising his eyebrows, as Zoe stopped at his desk.

Zoe repeated the virtuoso performance she had perfected for the "we deal with crime and prosecution" policeman.

'My name is Victoria Boswell,' she stated in an assertive manner, 'I've had my ID stolen.'

'Just wait for a moment Miss Boswell,' said the officer as his fingers sped across the keyboard in front of him. 'Yes, here we are Victoria Boswell, ID stolen by Zoe Marshall who was subsequently deported to Lowlands.'

He rubbed his chin, uttering several mmm sounds then he said. 'You've taken your time coming in for this. It was stolen several weeks ago. How have you managed without it?'

There was now a hint of suspicion in his voice. Zoe knew she had to get this just right otherwise she was in trouble. 'I'm sorry,' she simpered. 'But I've not felt well for the past few weeks. I've stayed in bed in my apartment, so I've not needed my disc. This is the first day I've been out. I couldn't send any of my friends here, because you wouldn't have been able to give my ID to them, so I had to wait. I'm sorry if this has caused you a problem.'

As soon as she uttered the words Zoe realised she

had made another mistake. She remembered that no-one got ill anymore in this modern germ free world.

She took instant steps to try to rectify the situation. 'Of course,' she continued with her lies. 'When I say I haven't felt well I don't mean that I've been properly ill. I guess I must have eaten something that my body reacted to in a negative way, making me feel tired and lethargic. As a result I took to my bed. It sort of escalated from there. It actually went beyond what I intended, but you know how easy it is to slip into a pattern of living. I guess I got used to resting. I'm sorry. I'm a bit of a wimp really. I should have come here earlier.'

Zoe pouted, fluttering her eye lashes in a rather pathetic attempt to look sorrowful. She was hoping to elicit some sympathy from the officer, but it was a waste of time as he didn't even appear to be paying any attention to her. He was scanning through his electronic data. Eventually he looked up.

'Well, our records do show that that there has been no DNA camera recognition of Victoria Boswell for several weeks. But there is still the question of how do I know you really are Victoria Boswell?' he asked, suspicion firmly registered on his face.

'I am her … I am her!' said Zoe earnestly. 'But you have my ID so I can't really prove it can I?'

'Yes you can,' replied the officer, who was now glaring at Zoe as if he thought she was stupid.

Zoe felt uncomfortable with his eyes boring into her. She stepped back from the desk before speaking again.

'How?' she asked.

'Body scan,' was the reply.

Zoe stiffened. Her mind filled with pictures of being sent back to Lowlands again, just as before when she attempted to retrieve her ID – claiming to be Victoria Boswell after mistakenly introducing herself as Zoe Marshall. Then she remembered she hadn't been given a body scan on that occasion. A scan now *would* show that she was Victoria Boswell, because that was the name in which Zak had registered her ID. She relaxed a little as she said confidently 'Of course, sorry I'd forgotten for a moment in my confusion. Scan me. It will prove that I am who I say I am.'

The officer jerked his head in the direction of a door in the wall opposite.

'In there!' he ordered.

Zoe went into the room. It was tiny and cramped. A young woman sat at a small table. She stood up at Zoe's entrance, crossed the room to the girl, before leading her gently by the arm to a red circle painted on the floor. Above this Zoe saw a small circular grille embedded into the ceiling.

'Stand there!' the woman instructed. 'Don't move or you'll ruin the scan.'

The woman returned to her table, where she fiddled with a dial that was set deep into the table top. Zoe assumed that this activated the scanner as she immediately heard a slight buzzing sound above her head. A faint ripple of warmth passed through her body. Within a matter of seconds, the woman told her she could go back to the officer in the next room.

As Zoe approached him, the officer slapped her ID disc onto the counter.

'Here,' he said sullenly. 'The scan confirms that you are Victoria Boswell. I suggest you look after this a bit better in the future.'

Zoe was about to say that she *had* looked after it but someone stole it from her in a robbery. However, she decided to remain silent as she wanted to get out of this place as quickly as possible. The last thing she needed was a prolonged lecture or debate with a policeman.

'I need your signature to say you've got it back,' said the officer brusquely, thrusting an electronic pad and pencil in front of Zoe as he spoke. 'I also need to log it out on the computer after you've filled in that form … hurry up, I go off duty in ten minutes.'

Zoe scanned the form on the electronic tablet. It asked for her name, address, date of birth and signature.

Address! she thought filled with alarm once again. *I don't know my address. Zak organised the accommodation. He was going to take me when we left the historical site. I've never even been there. I have the key but I have no idea where it is! Nor do I know what date of birth he registered!*

Now she had her ID in her hand, Zoe thought about making a run for it, but dismissed the idea quickly. To do so would certainly raise suspicion, probably resulting in her being asked a whole range of questions that she couldn't answer without getting herself locked up, deported, or killed.

She stared about wildly, desperately trying to think of a way out of this nightmare scenario. Then she noticed that the officer had moved away from his computer screen to fetch something from the far side of the room. Zoe glanced at the screen. Her heart skipped a beat as she saw her name, address and date of birth displayed in full view.

Leaning forward across the desk so she could see the screen display more clearly, Zoe strained her eyes to pick out every number and every letter. It was hard, as the font on the screen was small. But she succeeded, in spite of the choking feeling of panic that ran riot inside her as her eyes frequently darted from screen to officer and back, while she simultaneously read the information and monitored his whereabouts. When the officer returned to his post, Zoe handed him the tablet with all sections completed. Despite her anxiety, she had still managed to make a mental note of her new address. Now all she had to do was to find it!

Zoe sighed in relief as she left the building. She felt jubilant. Not only had she got her ID back, she also knew where she lived. More importantly she could now find Zak, if he was still here.

With the aid of the transport booths – as well as a few helpful commuters on the moving pavements – Zoe succeeded in finding her way to the apartment block in which she now apparently lived. After a short search of the floors she located her flat. At the door Zoe fished out the small triangular key – which Zak had given to her – from where it had stayed throughout her recent ordeal, on a short length of thin metal that she'd placed around her neck like a homemade necklace. With trembling fingers, Zoe placed the key into the automated slit at the side of the door. She held her breath, then gave a long deep sigh of relief as the door panel slid open to allow her entry.

Once inside, Zoe wandered around exploring her apartment. It was smart and clean, but very basic. There was a lounge and dining area combined, with a sliding partition at the far end of the room that opened at the touch of a button to reveal a single bed. Alongside this was a small wardrobe – which Zak had filled with various clothes for her – and a bedside cabinet. A separate bathroom – that was extremely tiny – housed a toilet, sink and shower unit. Despite its small size, the room had facilities for showering with or without clothes. It also included an overhead drier, which was similar to the wall-mounted ones she'd encountered in public toilets in her own time. This drier was fixed into the ceiling in the form of a large disc which was clearly designed to dry the whole body rather than just hands. Everything in the room was compacted, all operated by the slightest touch.

Zoe looked around for the kitchen. She found it quite by accident. She opened what she thought was a cupboard in the dining area to find it was a fully automated kitchen. Well, it was automated in as much as it produced food chosen from a fixed menu, again by touch selection. The food arrived down a plastic chute in the form of tablet, liquid, powder, or cube, depending on what was ordered. There were no pots, pans, or cooking facilities.

The décor in the apartment was drab. Every room was decorated with pale cream coloured paint which covered all of the walls and ceilings. The furniture was sparse. There were two foldaway dining chairs, a small foldaway table, and two easy chairs. Television and computer screens were set deep into one wall. Zoe pushed the button to switch on the TV. She found that there was just one news channel, with a second channel reserved for light entertainment. The computer screen had only a direct feed into educational programmes. It couldn't be used for any other purpose.

Zoe sighed. The whole place had an impersonal, institutionalised feel about it. As she stood surveying her new home the doorbell buzzed, startling her. She warily made her way to the front door, where she spied the security camera. Zoe clicked it on to see who was outside. To her surprise and partial relief she saw Zak Araz standing at her door. She opened the door, inviting him to enter.

'Zoe,' Zak began. 'It's good to see ...'

That was as far as he got. Zoe exploded into a tirade of accusations. 'Don't you say it's good to see me!' she yelled. 'Where have you been? Why didn't you come to help me? I bet you set this whole thing up to get me out of the way so you could try to find your way back to 2015 – or wherever it is that you want to go – without me.'

'Whoa, stop, calm down,' pleaded Zak. 'I didn't set you up. I *have* been looking for you. In fact I went back to the booth at the art gallery, but you'd gone. Then I went to the police station. They told me they had Victoria Boswell's ID but couldn't find her. I had to get out of there pretty smartly or they might have arrested me on suspicion of abducting or even murdering you. How did they manage to get your ID disc?'

Zoe, having calmed down a little, told her story of

the robbery and her mistake in giving the wrong name at the police station.

Zak shook his head. He smiled. 'I never thought to ask about Zoe Marshall,' he said. 'For two reasons. Firstly, I couldn't remember your surname. And secondly, I didn't think you would be stupid enough to use your real name after I told you not to. Particularly when you are trying to retrieve an ID disc that is in the name of Victoria Boswell!'

Zoe blushed deeply. 'I know,' she said quietly. 'It wasn't the brightest thing to do, was it?'

Zak shook his head, still smiling.

Zoe went on to tell him about being deported along with the story of her escapades in Lowlands. She continued with the tale of her return to the South, then retrieving her ID. She finished by telling him of her conversation with Jane where she found out about the existence of a time machine. She showed him the now defunct authorisation pass that Jane had given to her.

Zak took the pass. He examined it carefully. 'I'll keep hold of this,' he said. 'I can visit the university in disguise. I'll try to find out where the machine is located, and check out how to access it. Then I can make us both the necessary authorisation that will let us use it to get back to your time.'

'What if we can't use it?' asked Zoe.

'Then we need to look for alternatives,' Zak answered.

'Can't you do something?' Zoe queried. 'After all, you managed to turn back time on Earth. Can't you do the same here?'

Zak shook his head. 'I was lucky on Earth. I had access to a collection of materials that I could adapt to make the equipment I needed. I also had a group of monkeys who were a willing bunch of workers. Then there was the cover of the trees which provided the seclusion needed to assemble and hide the apparatus and instruments. Of course it all came to nothing because you and your colleagues stopped me, which incidentally is why we are here in this place.'

Zak grinned as he saw Zoe glaring at him. 'Just joking about the last bit,' he said. 'But the truth, is I couldn't build anything similar here because of the reasons I've given you. I don't have the use of any of those things here and there isn't the privacy here that I found there. So, if we can't use this time machine we are stuck, until I can find a different solution.'

'Well, we'd better keep our fingers crossed that you can make the authorisation pass work,' snapped Zoe.

After Zak had left, Zoe chose something from the food menu, quickly swallowing the mix of liquid and tablets that was dispersed by the machine in the kitchen. She pulled a face at the taste. Then she had a shower, after which she decided to go to bed.

Once in bed Zoe lay awake for a while pondering the dilemma she'd had ever since Jane had told her about the time machine. She desperately wanted to get back to 2015 to be with her family and to continue her life there. Yet the only way she could achieve this was if Zak was with her. He had already attempted to action his plan to colonise the Earth with his own species once. Then he'd tried to destroy the planet with a combination of his force field, time reversal and his use of computer games in order to control the people of Cristelee.

When she had fallen through the time vortex with Zak, the World had become a safer place. Now she risked exposing it to grave danger – perhaps total destruction – if she attained her greatest wish by managing to get back to her family. Zoe decided this probably wasn't the best time to think about her problem as she was tired. She settled herself down to sleep. She slept reasonably well until she awoke in the early hours of the morning with another disturbing thought running through her head.

I've told Zak about the time machine. I've also given him Jane's authorisation, Zoe thought. *What if he finds the machine and does something to make the authorisation work again? He's a shape shifter. He can easily become Jane. Then he could use the machine to go back to his spaceship, leaving me here until I die.*

CHAPTER NINETEEN

Shoving the discomforting thought to the back of her mind, Zoe sought to return to her slumbers. She did doze off fairly quickly, but it wasn't long before she was awakened again. This time by the sound of someone at her door. The repeated fervent staccato rasping of the buzzer was accompanied by a frenzied loud knocking.

Zoe awoke immediately. 'Alright' she yelled. 'I'm on my way. Don't knock the door down.' Bleary eyed, Zoe crawled out of bed, throwing a long robe loosely around her shoulders as she plodded across the floor to the door.

Despite her anger, the doubts she'd had about Zak during the early hours faded from her mind. *This must be him,* she thought. *I was wrong about him leaving. He's come to take me to the time machine. But he didn't have to wake me so early by making such a noise.*

Zoe was so certain that the person at her door was Zak, she didn't bother to use the door cam. The loud knocking continued as she approached. Now severely irritated by the banging and what she perceived as Zak's impatience, she yelled, 'For goodness sake! I've already said I'm on my way. Stop the noise, I'm here. I'm opening the door. Just wait. What's so urgent anyway?'

Still half asleep she pressed the button that opened the door. The door swung aside. Zoe was about to let her anger loose on Zak, only to step back in alarm as four people began to force their way inside. Zoe tried to push the door shut, but the quartet were too strong for her and she was quickly shoved aside. The interlopers stood in the hallway. They had guns, which were now pointing directly at Zoe. She could see that each of the intruders wore a security police uniform. Before she could say anything Zoe was grabbed by one of the police officers, who pinioned her arms behind her back. The tallest of the four figures spoke. Zoe couldn't see his face through the black visored helmet he wore, but she could tell he was male from his voice.

'Victoria Boswell, I am arresting you in connection with the disappearance and possible murder of Security Agent D1104. You do not have to say anything at this moment, but if you do it will be used in evidence against you.'

Even in her shock at the accusations, Zoe was able to note the slight difference in the police caution, to the one she remembered from the many police dramas she had watched on TV. The word *will* rather than *may* in respect of any statement being used as evidence wasn't the most important thing in her current predicament. Nonetheless she took heed of it, as it suggested the police might already have made up their minds about her guilt. It didn't bode well for what might follow. In fact – given her previous experience in the police headquarters – the whole scenario brought a chill to her heart.

'What's this all about? I don't know any Security Police agent,' Zoe asked, struggling to regain some composure.

'We'll deal with it when we get to Police Headquarters,' said the policeman.

'Can I go and get dressed?' asked Zoe.

The tall man nodded. He indicated to another member of the group – whom Zoe could now see was female – to go with her.

'Stay with her while she gets dressed. Make sure she doesn't escape,' the tall man commanded.

The two people holding Zoe's arms relaxed their grip to allow her to go into the bedroom area. She was closely followed by her female chaperone.

As she dressed, Zoe tried to stem the flow of negative thoughts that were racing through her brain. She was struggling to get to grips with what was happening to her as she contemplated the scene that was being played out in her flat.

How have the security police found me and why send four officers to arrest me? Why do they think that one of their agents going missing has anything to do with me? How can they think that Victoria Boswell – a non-existent resident of modern day London and the South – has killed him or her? More importantly, what do they intend to do to me now?

This last thought played on Zoe's mind. She was familiar with the way police forces worked and how they went about their enquiries, from the time she'd spent with DI Benson. She had some idea of how the legal system worked too, but her knowledge had been gleaned in 2015.

I'm now in 3015 and in a completely different World, she thought. *I have no idea how anything works here. I know nothing about the police or the law other than the little that*

Jane told me. Do they still have proper trials in court? Or are people found guilty – even without evidence – on the say so of someone in power? That certainly happened to me when they thought I was Zoe Marshall, who had supposedly stolen Victoria Boswell's ID. I could be in real trouble here. Not only am I ignorant of the law and the police, I don't know anyone else on this entire planet, nor do I know anything about the background that Zak invented for Victoria, so what do I say if I'm questioned about it?

The thought of Zak Araz set off another chain of deliberation for Zoe.

Wait a minute, she mused. *I do know someone else here. But he's an alien … Well I suppose I am too in a strange kind of way, but he's the real deal. I was hoping that he would be my passage out of here, although his past record suggests that he's hardly trustworthy. In fact where is he now? He lives on the floor above. He must have heard the commotion, so he must know the police are here. Yet he hasn't come to see what's happening or to check if I'm okay. Why isn't he here to help me? It's strange that the police have come to arrest me on the morning after I move in here. Just after I told Zak about the time machine. If I am suspected of murder, why didn't they arrest me yesterday when I got my ID back? It wouldn't surprise me in the least to find that Zak has set this whole thing up?* She paused in her thinking, clenching her fists as a whole new chapter of suspicion began to seep into her brain. *Yes, of course. That's it. I was right after all when I worried he would leave me after I gave him the information about the time machine along with Jane's authorisation pass. He's gone to the university so he can use the machine to travel back to his spaceship without interference from me. He's created this scenario as a diversion to allow him time to escape. I suppose it's possible that he's come to some arrangement with the police so they will help him get back to 2015 in exchange for him incriminating me?*

Either way he gets to go back to my time zone unchallenged, leaving the way clear for him to return home with the children's souls, so he can then lead his people to take over the Earth!

Zoe's heart sank to rock bottom at these depressing thoughts, the theme of which had now become a familiar pattern for her. Yet the fact that she had been wrong on every past occasion she'd envisaged this particular outcome of events never entered her head in her present state of confusion and despair. Her suspicion of Zak ran deep, a consequence of which meant the notion that Zak Araz was plotting to leave her here was never far below the surface in her mind. So certain had she become in her subconscious belief, that all evidence to the contrary was ignored.

Zoe was now fully dressed. She had chosen a very modern outfit from the collection that Zak had placed in her wardrobe. She wore a dark green collarless jacket, cutaway near the waist, and a calf length matching skirt. The material was inlaid with an indistinct helical pattern of the same colour, and was synthetically made from a substance that was unknown to Zoe. She had selected a pale green, high necked shirt and flat black shoes, as an accompaniment to her costume. She had decided that if she was going on trial, she wanted to look smart in order to appear more credible in court.

The policewoman took a firm hold on Zoe's arm and pushed her towards the door. As they left the bedroom,

Zoe was immediately grabbed and handcuffed by one of the other officers before being led outside onto the moving pavement. At the corner of the street she was bundled into one of the booths. This one was different again from the others that she had travelled in. It was much smaller, with opaque windows set in a metallic outside frame that was dark blue. There was a logo on the door that she saw comprised the letters SSP intertwined together. Zoe stood between the policewoman and a male officer. She was surprised to see all five of them were able to fit comfortably inside.

She watched as the lead officer pushed one of a number of buttons on the wall panel. There was a loud hissing noise as the booth sealed itself hydraulically. He pressed another button. Almost in the blink of an eye Zoe found herself being pushed out of the booth, into the familiarity of the police headquarters where she'd arrived on both occasions she'd come to the South.

She was propelled rapidly to the reception desk, where she was searched, photographed, and body scanned by an officer who moved a hand held scanner up around her frame. Her ID disc was taken from her, before being scrutinised and placed in the custody of the desk sergeant. Finally she was handed an electronic tablet on which the charges against her appeared. Zoe started to plead her innocence, but was cut short by an officer who led her away to a room where she was imprisoned in solitude.

The room bore little resemblance to the old fashioned police cells that Zoe remembered from her time with DI Benson, but she guessed it was a cell nevertheless, as it was similar to the room she'd been in with Jane. There was a washbasin and toilet, but only one bed. The room was heated or cooled – depending upon the interior temperature – through vents that were set high in the walls. Zoe thought it seemed comfortable enough given it was a cell, but she noted that the door was electronically secured. She also noticed that her every move was observed and monitored by a discreetly placed camera.

Zoe spent the whole day in the cell. Food was brought in regularly, but no one spoke to her. When she asked questions of the officers she was ignored. The day passed slowly and Zoe's mood grew darker with every passing hour.

When night time arrived, Zoe found it hard to get to sleep, as she always did since being in this strange world. She felt very alone. Not for the first time she thought about her family, again despairing of ever having any further contact with them. In fact she thought that given her current situation there was a good chance she might never get to see the outside world again. She did sleep, but intermittently. In the early hours of the morning whilst in the throes of a terrible nightmare Zoe was roused to consciousness by the sound of a voice in her ear. It said.

'Don't worry. I'll get you out of here.'

She sprang up in bed and looked all around her. There was no one there.

'The voice must have been part of my dream.' she mumbled, sleepily rubbing her eyes. She shook her head to try to clear her confusion. 'I wish I could have a nice dream for a change'

That was the end of sleep for Zoe that night. Her brain wouldn't switch off from the mass of thoughts. She lay on the bed for the next few hours, wondering what the day ahead had in store for her. A policeman brought breakfast, but Zoe had no appetite for the liquefied mush and assorted cubes that were laid before her. It was late in the morning when they came for her. She was taken to an interrogation room where she was questioned, after again before being informed of the charges against her. There were six officers in the room with Zoe. They were all dressed in police uniforms. They sat on soft chairs arranged in an arc around a table. Each officer had an electronic pad before them from which they occasionally read, tapping in their own notes too as the interview progressed.

Zoe sat on a hard chair facing the sextet. The seat was extremely uncomfortable, forcing her to squirm and shift about on her bottom throughout the time she was being questioned.

The interview began with one of the officers informing Zoe of why she had been arrested. 'Victoria Boswell,' he said. 'We have reason to believe that you have committed a very serious crime. If you are found guilty you will be sentenced to death.'

Zoe inhaled deeply at the officer's words. Her head began to spin. *Death!* The police had previously threatened her with execution if she ever came back to this planet. She'd considered it a possibility in this case too, but had then dismissed it as highly improbable. She remembered what Jane had told her about the cruel ways of people in authority in the South. Now she could see it for herself. She knew for certain that she was facing a death penalty. There was nothing to lose, so Zoe decided to go on the offensive.

'What am I supposed to have done?' she asked boldly, her voice tone reflecting none of the fear she was feeling inside.

A second officer spoke. 'You have murdered one of our agents,' he said coldly.

'That's nonsense,' snapped Zoe. 'Why would I want to do that? I don't even know any of your agents.'

'Agent D1104 was on a mission to Lowlands several months back. He was with agent C2217. They both signed in as present when they returned to headquarters after their excursion. Both logged reports of their journey and mission outcome. Then both signed off duty before going home.' This time it was another officer speaking.

Zoe swivelled her head to look at him. She stared him straight in the eye as she spoke, 'So what has that to do with me?'

A fourth officer took up the charge. 'He never returned,' he said. 'Neither of them showed up for duty on the following day so we tried to contact them … but without success. We knew something was wrong because our street and building monitors have been unable to pinpoint their movements since not long after they left headquarters. We were even more concerned when we checked the DNA reading taken on agent D1104's return and found it didn't match anything we have on our records. We haven't as yet been able to trace either agent. But two days ago we got a lead. Well, at least on agent D1104. It's quite funny really, in a strange way. We were about to file the case in our missing, presumed dead case files, when we got a body scan which matched the scan taken on D1104's return from that final duty in Lowlands.'

'If you've got a match then he can't be dead. So why am I here? What has all this got to do with me?' challenged Zoe defiantly.

'The match wasn't with the DNA of agent D1104. It was with the body scan you gave the other day when you claimed your lost ID.' It was the fifth officer this time who leaned forward to speak, thrusting his chin out as his finger pointed accusingly at Zoe. 'It wasn't agent D1104 who came back and filed that report. It was you!'

'No!' said Zoe emphatically.

'Yes it was,' said the sixth interrogator quietly. 'We know it was you. The other body scan was fine, so we know you came back with agent C2217. We think you got friendly with 2217 when he was down in Lowlands. The two of you then conspired together to get rid of agent D1104. Agent 2217 smuggled you into the South. He also arranged an ID disc for you so you could stay here. So tell us. Where is agent C2217? We know he's hiding somewhere. We think you know where he is. It will save *us* a lot of time, and *you* a lot of trouble if you tell us.'

'I have no idea what you are talking about,' Zoe bluffed. 'I don't know any agent C2217 or agent D1104. Maybe the people who stole my ID set this up.'

'Nice try,' said the officer who had spoken first. 'But it wasn't the ID disc that betrayed you, it was your bone structure and DNA which is recorded on our data base.

That proved to be a clear match with the bone and DNA recorded by the scanner when agent D1104 returned to headquarters on that night. How do you explain that?'

Zoe couldn't explain it. In fact she knew it to be true. She slumped back in the chair close to tears. She was terrified of what might happen next.

The policeman continued. 'After we got your DNA reading we dug a little deeper. We found there is no record of you on our microchip database. In fact there is no record of you living in the South until a few months ago. Your appearance here coincides with our databank being hacked into. Coincidentally, on exactly the same day as agent D1104 went missing. On that day two new identities were created in the South, yours and a Zak Araz, whom we assume to be agent C2217 under an alias. We hadn't originally been able to detect these new identities otherwise we would have had a DNA match to you and agent D1104 much earlier. Whoever created them was very clever, and obviously had an extremely sophisticated working knowledge of our systems. This further suggests that agent C2217 is involved as he was studying advanced computer technology in his spare time.'

The officer leaned in towards Zoe then in a voice filled with menace said, 'We are taking you back to your cell for now. I suggest that you use the rest of today to think over your position. When we come back into this room this evening you will tell us everything, including what you have done with agent D1104 as well as the whereabouts of agent C2217. Failure to do so will result in a decision that you are guilty of not one murder but two. In accordance with our law, that will result in you being be put to death – by laser rays at midnight tonight.'

Zoe made one last attempt to save herself. 'Surely I'm entitled to a trial? A lawyer too?' she asked brazenly. When no reply was forthcoming, she repeated her demands. 'What about my trial?'

'*This* is your trial,' said the officer unflinchingly. 'We make decisions based on evidence, and in this case all of the evidence points to you being guilty. The matching body scan result from your entry to the South as agent D1104 – coupled with those taken during your visit to our headquarters to claim your stolen ID – is irrefutable. The fact that our agent D1104 is missing and you returned in his place – using his ID – suggests that he is dead. So you must have either killed him or you are an accessory to his killing. Therefore, you are guilty of causing his death. There can be no argument with that conclusion.'

He stood up, walked across to Zoe, took her by the arm and led her back to her cell where he locked her in. Zoe's heart was thumping inside her chest. Her mind was numb. She couldn't think of any way out of this. She was definitely going to die tonight. The thought of this left her feeling very, very scared.

Zoe sat on the bed in her prison cell. She couldn't think straight. She had been so near to getting back home. She'd regained her ID. She'd managed to get into her apartment. Had she got to the university, it might have led to her going home to her family. She had been very close. Now she was back in police custody and about to be executed.

A tear trickled down Zoe's cheek at the thought of what lay ahead. For the first time in her short life, confidence completely deserted her as she pondered her pending execution. She was resigned to the fact that she couldn't now get out of this predicament. There was nothing left for her to do. Zoe lay back on the bed and wept.

CHAPTER TWENTY

'Zoe, don't cry. Stay strong. Trust me. I'll get you out of here soon then we can get you home.'

The voice startled Zoe. She stopped crying. Looking up she saw Zak Araz. He was dressed in a security police uniform.

'How on Earth did you manage to get in here?' asked Zoe, once she got over the shock of seeing him. She was suddenly filled with a feeling that all hope was not after all lost.

'Small flying creatures and insects can get anywhere,' answered Zak, smiling. 'Even in a place that has tight security. After getting in, it was easy to then become a policeman, especially in a police station. I can't stay long now, as the cameras are watching me. I just came in to say don't despair. I'm going to take you to the university. We are going to find the time machine. Then you and I are going back to your home.'

Zoe wiped away the remains of her tears. She gave Zak a weak smile. 'How?' was all she said.

'You have to trust me,' said Zak. 'I won't let them kill you. Be patient. Just wait here. I will be back to get you out as soon as I can. But, when I do come back you might not recognise me. So you'll have to play along with whatever I say.'

Zoe smiled – nodding her head vigorously in both relief and acceptance – as Zak disappeared just as quickly as he had appeared. At the same time she saw a small beetle scuttle across the floor, before it crawled beneath the tiny gap at the bottom of the door and vanished.

Half an hour later the cell door opened. Another police officer appeared. Zoe recognised him as one of the six men who had been in the interrogation room. He was carrying an automated key card.

'Come with me,' he ordered.

Zoe hesitated, remaining on the bunk bed. The officer jerked his head in the direction of the open cell door.

'Come with me,' he repeated.

Zoe remembered what Zak had said, but she was unsure if he was taking on the guise of this officer or if the man standing before her was a real policeman.

'Where are we going?' she asked.

'Home,' replied the officer quietly. He gave a huge theatrical wink as he spoke.

The man headed for the door. Zoe suddenly felt alive and excited. Now convinced that this officer *was* Zak she quickly followed him, looking from side to side to see if any other official was about. There was no one.

The officer led Zoe to the front desk, where he quickly made a few adjustments to the data on the computer screen. Then using the key card he walked to the main entrance with Zoe following him. Once they were outside the building, Zak pulled her into a nearby alleyway. He spoke to her in a voice that was both soft and urgent.

'Zoe you really do have to trust me now. There is only one way we can get to the university in time to find the time machine before officers come looking for you. We have to fly.'

'Fly,' echoed Zoe, looking puzzled.

Zak touched her arm gently. 'I'm going to change into a very large bird of prey … a condor,' he explained. 'That's a species that were never seen in the wild in this part of your World at any time. The sight of such a large creature is bound to attract attention, especially as all birds have been eliminated from this planet. However, we have to get to our destination as soon as we can, which means I have to make myself into a bird that is big enough *and* strong enough to carry a human. Once you are on my back, you will need to hold on tightly. I will take us to the university using the quickest route.'

'Why can't we use the transporter beams in the teleports?' asked Zoe, who was feeling a little apprehensive about sitting on the back of a flying bird as it soared over the rooftops.

'Because the police will be monitoring the booths. They will also set the scanners on every building to attune with your DNA. Your body scan will show up if we use any of the booths, or any conventional form of transport come to that. The police will then know where we are heading. They will be there waiting for us when we arrive,' explained Zak. 'This way we can fly above the scanner beams. They won't be expecting us to fly so there's a good chance we won't be seen … well I guess we will be seen … we'll be pointed at too. But no one will know it's you.'

Zoe smiled nervously as Zak closed his eyes. He screwed up his face in concentration. A few seconds passed then a large condor appeared where the police officer had stood. Zoe climbed nervously onto the creature's back. She clung tightly to the feathers at the nape of the bird's neck.

Zoe held her breath as the giant bird took off, flapping its huge wings as it soared skywards. She was scared. It was a precarious position to find herself in, hanging onto the neck of this great creature as it flew slowly, silently and quite majestically upwards into the new London skyline.

Zoe looked down at the landscape beneath her. Her fears increased as she saw how tall the buildings were. But she was also fascinated by the scene that had unfolded below. From her lofty viewpoint she could make out the lie of the land for a long way ahead. She could also see the real planet Earth some way beneath her. It was a very strange feeling, quite a weird, almost surreal experience and the unusual beauty of it took her breath away.

Zoe's pleasant reflections were brought to an abrupt end as the bird circled once then plunged rapidly downwards. It slowed as it neared the ground before settling back into the alley that the pair had left only moments ago. Zoe leapt from the condor's back. As she balanced herself uneasily on her somewhat unsteady feet, Zak reappeared as himself. She looked at him quizzically.

'That's not going to work,' Zak said, shaking his head. 'The condor's body isn't strong enough to support your weight. It was as much as I could do to get to that height on take-off. If I hadn't come straight back down we would have plummeted to the ground out of control, probably with very dire consequences.'

Zoe glared at him. 'Are you saying that I'm overweight?' she snapped.

'No, of course not,' replied Zak, laughing. 'But as the condor I am going to have to use my wings to climb and fly. The wing span of this species varies, but is generally between 7 to 12 feet. That's good for condors in their natural environment as they use thermals to soar to great heights. There are no thermals here so that means the wings have to work harder. Also, condors don't normally carry people on their backs. That's because people are too heavy. I made a mistake. I drew on my knowledge of your planet but I came up with the wrong answer. I'm sorry Zoe. I can't think of any other bird I could become that would be strong enough to carry you. Do you know of a bird on your planet that is big enough and would also be strong enough to carry a human on its back?'

Zoe shook her head. Then with a mischievous grin she said, 'There's the ostrich. That's the biggest bird on my planet.'

Zak's face lit up. 'I can remember the ostrich from when I learned about your planet back in your time,' he said. 'Give me a moment to think about shape and size.'

In a matter of seconds an ostrich stood before Zoe. It ran up and down flapping its wings. Then the ostrich vanished and Zak was there again. 'This is difficult,' he said. 'How does this bird manage to fly?'

'I was just winding you up,' said Zoe. 'Ostriches can't fly. They can run fast though. But I don't think we'll get very far with you running through these moving streets as an ostrich, especially with me on your back.'

'This is no time for joking,' said Zak sternly. 'The Security Police have probably discovered by now that you are missing. We are only a few yards from their headquarters. Someone may also have seen the condor and reported it, even though we were in the air for such a short time. The police could be here any moment. Just be quiet while I think. I have to find a creature that can fly and is big enough to do what we want. Let me dig deep into my memory banks to search the natural history of your planet to see if I can find a solution to our problem.'

After a few minutes Zak spoke again. 'I think I've got it,' he said. 'It's a little unusual, but the only flying creature I can be certain will be strong enough to support your weight while flying is one that died out on your planet a long time ago.'

'What's that?' asked Zoe. Then when Zak told her what he had in mind, she wished she hadn't asked.

'It was known as a pteranodon, and it lived in the cretaceous period some 75 million years back. The male had a wingspan of around 18 feet, so if I become that creature I should be able to carry you,' Zak explained.

'I've not heard of that species before,' said Zoe, half-quizzically.

'You probably know it as a pterodactyl,' Zak replied, 'which is really a bit of a misnomer. All of the prehistoric flying creatures are often mistakenly lumped together in one group – and then categorised as pterodactyls – when there is actually more than one species.'

'A pterodactyl?' Zoe gasped, completely ignoring Zak's elaborate elucidation, 'You have got to be joking! That will draw even more attention than the condor.'

'Probably,' said Zak. 'But it's all we've got, so we'll have to be quick. Wait there. I have to go deep into my body's resources and into my mind in order to become such a large, extinct creature. I only hope that I can do it.'

Zak closed his eyes. He hunched his body, simultaneously twisting his face in a grimace of supreme concentration. Zoe could see him straining every part of himself as he strove to become this nightmare creature from the past. Zak twisted his neck around and up, as he stretched his body to its limits. Suddenly his appearance began to change. Zoe was fascinated. She had never watched him change his shape before. He had always transmuted so quickly. She could see the leathery skin slowly spreading across his body. The pointed head was next to materialise, quickly followed by the long papery wings. When the short strong legs with slightly webbed feet – which were equipped with menacing talons – appeared, the image was complete. There right in front of her stood, what she still believed to be, a real live pterodactyl. Zoe wasted no time in climbing onto its back. She found a small leathery protrusion at the centre of the creature's back between its shoulders, which she grasped firmly with both hands. Straight away the pteranodon took off, flying high into the sky above the alleyway. Zoe clung on tightly to the leathery knob she had grabbed, flattening herself along the creature's back to assist with aerodynamics as well as to avoid detection by anyone on the streets below.

As the prehistoric bird wheeled and soared above the concrete metropolis, Zoe was vaguely aware of people looking up. She could see some of them pointing at the unfamiliar sight they were witnessing in the skies above. She couldn't help but wonder what it might be like for them to see such a primeval creature flying high above their city. She guessed it would be awesome, and probably scary too, especially as there hadn't even been a sighting of any bird in the city for centuries. Looking down from her lofty perch Zoe saw a number of flashes from ground level. She assumed it was people taking photographs of the bizarre phenomenon that had materialised above them. It took some time before she realised that the flashes weren't from cameras. They were from weapons. Tasers, lasers, and destabilising guns that were being fired by the security police with the sole purpose of bringing her and Zak to the ground.

'So much for your idea that no one would see us,' Zoe shouted to Zak. 'The police are shooting at us. You'll need to watch out. We don't want to get hit.'

Zak lurched suddenly to the left as he zigzagged to avoid the gunfire. The movement caught Zoe by surprise. She lost her grip, slipping from the pteranodon's back and plummeting towards the ground below. Her mind raced ahead as she thought of the moment when her body would hit the ground. She would surely die, shattered and broken beyond recognition. Zoe considered the irony. She had escaped death by fire. Zak had also saved her from the dog pack, the two policemen on Lowlands and execution by laser. Now – just when she was so close to finding the machine that might take her back home – it seemed that she *was* going to die a painful death after all, smashed to bits on a moving pavement after falling from a long extinct animal. Zoe – in what she deemed to be her final moments – couldn't decide which of the deadly scenarios she'd been faced with since she arrived in this world was the least desirable.

She felt tears pricking her eyes again as her thoughts briefly drifted again to her family. Zoe braced her body for the impact as she neared the ground. She could see the group of policemen gathered on the moving pavement very clearly now. It seemed that they had stopped the mechanism that brought about the pavement's movement. The men were crouching motionless as they primed their weapons for a second salvo. Zoe flinched, closing her eyes as the ground zoomed nearer. She could now clearly see the tiny black holes in the end of the guns, from which the charges were fired. *They surely won't miss their target at this range?* Zoe thought, despairingly. *So I'll probably die before I hit the pavement, anyway.* She braced herself in readiness, for whatever death fate had decreed. Then, she felt something hard digging into her shoulder.

It was a talon. Zak, in his guise as the great ancient dinosaur, had swooped down low. He stretched out one of the massive claws, expertly catching Zoe's tumbling body before holding it steady. He then dug a second talon into her other shoulder. Zoe breathed a sigh of relief, hoping that he wouldn't now drop her. The pteranodon – using its massive leathery body to shield Zoe from the weapon fire – began to climb once more, dragging and lifting its precious cargo higher and higher as it doggedly made its way to the university buildings which were now within its sight. The prospect of freedom was now very near.

Zoe's body hung limply beneath the creature's powerful legs. Her mind had regained both sanity and clarity as she silently expressed her gratitude to Zak with a wave of her hand.

The giant tan coloured bird soon began its descent towards the university buildings, carrying Zoe across the perimeter walls. It dropped slowly and silently towards the courtyard where it hovered just above a lawned area, opening both sets of claws to allow Zoe to make the short downward leap to the ground. She landed in a heap on the grass. The pteranodon settled beside her, before quickly changing shape to become Zak Araz again.

'Are you alright?' Zak asked.

Zoe nodded, picking herself up she brushed grass off her clothes. 'Yes,' she gasped. 'A bit out of breath from the flight, but I'll cope.'

'That was a bit scary back there,' said Zak. 'I thought I'd lost you.'

Zoe pursed her lips and emitted a low whistle. 'Yes,' she said. 'Me too. But thanks to you I survived. It seems to have become a bit of a habit eh?'

Zak smiled. 'Follow me,' he said. 'Don't say a word to anyone. If someone talks to you, just nod or shake your head. If you *are* forced to answer, say as little as possible.'

Zoe gave him a mock salute. 'Will do,' she confirmed, adding 'How are we going to get inside?'

'Leave that to me,' Zak replied. 'I've been busy working on passes for both entry and use of the time machine. We should be okay but stick close to me. If anything goes wrong, I'll get us out of there.'

Zoe wasn't sure whether she should be pleased or worried by Zak's words. She smiled at Zak then simply said, 'Lead on.'

Zak set off across the courtyard in the direction of the main building. Zoe tucked in behind, following closely in his footsteps. It was only a short distance, but Zoe kept her head down for the most part as she didn't want her face to be seen on any CCTV screen inside the university grounds, in case the security police had issued her picture as that of a wanted criminal.

She did glance up once or twice to look at Zak. On one of those occasions she was forced to do a double take. Instead of the usual figure of Zak walking in front of her she glimpsed what could only be described as a blob of pale jelly. Zoe blinked hard, but when she looked again there was Zak striding way ahead of her.

That's funny, Zoe thought. *For a moment there I could have sworn I was walking behind a jelly. My eyes must be playing tricks. I guess I'm tired and stressed from my ordeal with the police and from the trauma of the journey here. The sooner we get to that time machine the better. If I get caught again, there will be no reprieve. I'll definitely be killed.*

Zoe quickened her step to catch up with Zak just as

they arrived at the main entrance. Zak grabbed at the door handle. He tried to turn it but there was no movement as the door stubbornly refused to open.

'It's locked,' he whispered to Zoe.

Zak pressed the doorbell panel. The loud buzzing of the bell could be heard echoing inside the building. It wasn't long before footsteps sounded from the other side of the door. A small hatch slid open and a face appeared. The face had hard, unblinking eyes that conveyed an unspoken message that no one was welcome here and no one was to be trusted. Zoe could feel the eyes boring into her as Zak spoke to the man behind them.

'We were told to come here,' he said in a respectful yet assertive voice. 'We are students of history. We need to finalise our essays and complete our revision for the forthcoming exams. I have authorisation from the college authorities, including identity discs.'

Zak pushed the forged documents through the hatch. The pair waited as the man inspected them. Zoe held her breath. She was concerned that her identity authorisation – which showed her to be Victoria Boswell – would ring alarm bells. If so it might lead to her being apprehended by the university security guards, who would surely keep her prisoner until the security police arrived to take her away. The more she thought about it, the drier her mouth got. Her breathing quickened. She felt her heart fluttering. An imaginary lump appeared in her throat, making it hard for her to swallow. Then she remembered that the police still had her ID disc. They had taken it from her when they interviewed her about the loss of their agent.

So where has the new one come from? she puzzled.

Meanwhile, Zak stood there calmly. He looked to be full of confidence as the small file of documents was perused by the gatekeeper. Zoe tried outwardly to imitate his certain manner, but it was very difficult as her insides were churning so much. She was sure that they were going to get found out. But Zak had done a good job. The forgeries easily passed scrutiny.

The guard opened the door, indicating for Zak and Zoe to enter. He pointed the way down a nearby corridor.

'The library is at the end of that corridor, on the right,' he said. 'You will find all you need in there. You are not allowed to enter any other rooms.'

'Thank you,' said Zak, retrieving the authorisation and ID documents from the man.

He beckoned for Zoe to follow him. As they made their way to the library Zoe whispered to Zak. 'How did you get my ID? It's still with the police.'

'New names, new ID,' replied Zak. 'I'm Charles Dickens and you are Jane Austen. I remembered the names from the knowledge I acquired whilst on your planet. They are good, yes?'

'Not really,' hissed Zoe. 'They are the names of famous authors from years back. You may not have noticed but we are about to enter a historical library. What if they have books by these people? Won't they be suspicious?'

Zak shrugged. He whispered, 'There will be many people whose names are the same, don't worry.'

Zoe felt far from reassured by Zak's casual attitude

to what she saw as a potential banana skin, but she at least took comfort from him being there.

Soon the two of them were in the university library. It was a room that was stacked full with electronic books, readers, computer screens and keyboards. There was no one else present.

Zak motioned for Zoe to keep quiet by placing a finger on his lips. He sat down at a keyboard, opened up a programme on the nearby screen. He wrote in the smallest font available. *I am going to find out all about this time machine and its exact location. Don't speak, just sit at a computer. Look as if you are working. There are probably cameras and microphones everywhere. We are being monitored.*

Zak had turned the screen at an acute angle to allow Zoe to read his message without it being picked up on camera. Zoe had to strain her eyes to read the words. She nodded when she had finished reading. Zak immediately erased the message from the screen.

Zoe sat down at the computer opposite Zak. She logged on, opening up a programme as if she was studying. But she wasn't interested in the words or pictures on her computer screen. Her eyes were on Zak as his fingers sped over the keyboard at an incredible speed. He shook his head, sighing occasionally when his attempt to access the information he wanted was unsuccessful, but he carried on determinedly.

Zoe was shocked when Zak suddenly disappeared. In his place – for the second time inside a matter of minutes – sat an amorphous, translucent cream-coloured blob of jelly like substance. Then, just as quickly the blob became Zak again. This happened several more times as they sat there. Zoe's curiosity was raised, particularly as she'd seen this same blob appear earlier. She was more than a little alarmed by these sporadic transmutations. She stared at Zak, raising then lowering her eyebrows to indicate her confusion.

He simply mouthed, 'I will explain later,' then continued his work.

In less than ten minutes, Zak had switched off his computer. He motioned Zoe to do the same with hers. When this was done he stood up – jerking his head for Zoe to follow him – then he left the library.

Zoe was by his side in the corridor as he bent low, whispering, 'The time machine is in the Practical History Department in a room called the Time Gallery. I have studied its construction, dimensions, and its systems. I now fully understand how it functions. I have also activated an authorisation for Charles Dickens and Jane Austen to use the machine once for educational purposes. We need to go quickly before the guard comes to check where we are, as the security cameras will show that we have left the library. I also suspect that the Security Police may be on their way.'

'Okay,' Zoe breathed. Her body shaking with excitement. *Or was it fear?* 'But quickly, before we go tell me why you keep changing into that thing I saw in the library there? What if the guard has seen it on the CCTV screen? You could have put us in even more danger. What is it anyway? It looked as if you were changing into a large wobbly jelly. Are you planning something? Is that it? Are you planning to leave me here and escape by becoming a transparent mass so you can hide from the guards?'

Zak looked at Zoe with eyes that were filled with both sorrow and distress.

'I'm not leaving you Zoe,' he said quietly and deliberately. 'I'm dying.'

CHAPTER TWENTY-ONE

'Dying?' gasped Zoe, shocked by Zak's statement. 'I didn't think you could die … well … I suppose I never really thought about it. Can you? Die I mean.'

Zak nodded.

'How come it's happening now?' Zoe asked. 'What's causing it?'

Zak spoke quickly. 'We need to hurry but I'll tell you as we walk. You know that I am a shape shifter. Well, back on my own planet we can change shape as many times as we wish, as long as we nourish our bodies with proper food and other produce from our World. That includes the special chemical I told you about, ZzP2. Unfortunately I haven't managed to get either of these things since I've been on your planet, or up here in your future World. That wouldn't normally be too much of a problem as our bodies are adaptable. This flexibility enables us to absorb food from other Worlds. But we can only do this for so long. It's now been more than three of your Earth years since I ate properly and in that time I've changed shape so many times that my internal organs are now malfunctioning. When I became the pteranodon, it took so much effort that the strain on my body was too much. Although we have the capacity, we are not normally meant to become creatures of that size.

It was too much for my internal organs to cope with. They were already struggling to survive the demands I placed on them by being a variety of snakes, insects, and the moth larva, since I arrived on your planet. Anything that small also pushes my powers to their limits.

'The shapeless jelly mass, as you described it, is what I look like on the inside. My organs are constructed from a semi-liquid pulp to allow the flexibility we need when we change shape. They can then become rigid to form a bone structure in whatever shape I have chosen to be. At the moment my body is undernourished and exhausted. It is finding it very hard to perform even the simplest of tasks, as my organs have been overstretched and overworked well beyond their normal capacity. In fact, I suspect they are almost ready to give up. Three Earth years is not really that long in my own time zone, but here on Earth it is and that is what my organs are programmed to respond to ... I am keeping my body going on mental strength at the moment, a combination of concentration and willpower. I have very little time left unless I can get back to my space craft, where I have an emergency supply of ZzP2. That would be enough to get me home at least. But I have to go back to 2012 so I can ingest the chemical as quickly as possible otherwise I will die. Meanwhile, I hope I don't have to change shape anymore as I suspect that might just be one step too far.'

Zoe was saddened by what Zak – or Kazzaar to give him his real name – had just told her. They'd been through a lot together and in a strange kind of way she'd grown to like him, even though she still didn't fully trust him. She didn't know what to say to him now, so she stood in silence for a moment staring sympathetically into his face. Then she placed her hand on his.

'Come on, we must hurry,' whispered Zak urgently. 'The guard will be here soon. For sure he will try to stop us using the time machine. It's possible that he may have access to some mechanism that will shut it down.'

Zak took off again down the corridor at a fast pace. Zoe struggled to keep up with him. The blob reappeared twice on the journey, before Zak – still fortunately in human form – stopped outside a large door marked *Department of Practical History.*

'This is it,' he said, turning the handle.

The door didn't move.

'It's locked,' said Zoe, her disappointment spilling out in her voice. She had forgotten that Zak had got them through locked doors before.

'Don't worry,' Zak responded, taking out the ID discs. He inserted them into the small aperture on the panel mounted on the wall nearby. The door immediately slid aside without a sound. Zak retrieved the discs. He entered the room first, with Zoe trailing in his wake. But it was Zoe who spotted the Time Gallery first.

'There,' she said pointing.

Zak repeated his previous actions with the two discs. In a matter of seconds they were standing in front of a gleaming silver machine. The contraption looked solid enough. It was cylindrical in shape, narrowing at top and bottom. Zoe thought the middle area resembled an ultra large water cylinder. Zak ran his hands over the shiny exterior, searching for any clue that would show him how to gain entry to the object that he and Zoe both hoped would facilitate their escape from this unfriendly world.

The repetitive shrieking of an alarm siren suddenly broke through the silence, interrupting Zak's search. A look of unease appeared on Zoe's face. Anxiety rose inside her again. The wailing siren seemed to increase in decibels as a television in the corner of the room burst into life. The screen relayed pictures of armed security policemen – accompanied by university security guards – charging into the main building. A second TV screen showed a number of them swarming along the corridors on their way to the gallery. At the same time a disembodied voice which seemed to be coming through the walls gave out a grim warning.

'Stay where you are! You are surrounded by armed police. To run would be foolish. It would only result in your death. There is no escape. Stay there we are coming for you.'

'The police are here,' said Zoe, breathlessly. 'Quick, how do we open this thing?'

Zak was desperately looking around the room. Zoe followed suit. They both saw what they were looking for at the same time, as two pairs of eyes simultaneously settled on a miniature computer, set deep into one of the surrounding wall panels.

Zak was quickly across the room. He had already logged in before Zoe had time to move. Ten seconds later he pumped the air with his fist. 'Yeeesss!' he shouted triumphantly.

The silver cylinder immediately emitted a whirring sound, which quickly changed into a suitably contented purr as the front panels parted to reveal its inner secrets. Zoe and Zak hastened into the inner chamber. Jane had been right. There wasn't much room inside. In fact, the two of them were a bit cramped in there together, but that didn't matter. Zak quickly found what he wanted. It was the door control panel. He reached for the button to close the doors on the time machine just as the security police burst into the room.

When the first two policemen saw Zak and Zoe inside the capsule they immediately opened fire. This was rapidly followed by other police and guards letting rip with their own weapons. A stream of laser and electronic beams sped from the guns aimed towards the pair inside the time machine. Zoe instinctively ducked, closing her eyes as she waited for the power charges to strike. But she hadn't reckoned on Zak's lightning reflexes. Even as he ducked too, his hand shot out towards the control panel. His finger plunged downwards onto the button marked CLOSE DOORS. The machine vibrated and shook as the killer beams bounced harmlessly off the silver metal on the now firmly closed doors.

Zoe grinned at Zak. 'That was a close call,' she said. 'I seem to have had a lot of those since I've known you.'

Zak grinned back. 'I'll set the date controls then, shall I?' he said.

But Zoe was already at the panel. She scanned the instructions, quickly confirming Jane's information that a maximum of three dates could be entered to allow for research of different time zones in any one journey. The dates didn't have to be entered at the same time. One date could be punched in on entry with the others being set after the capsule had arrived in the first time zone, should it be required.

Zoe hadn't got an extended stay disc, so she knew that the machine would only allow a maximum of thirty minutes in her own time zone before it returned to 3015, whatever date she set. On entry to the capsule she had grabbed control of the time panels because of what Zak had said as they left the library. When he talked about dying he'd said he had to get back to 2012, but Zoe was determined to go to 2015. Before Zak could stop her she had punched the numbers 2015 into the date panel. She then set the day and month so she would arrive on the day before she fell into the time vortex. Zak stared at Zoe. She shrugged her shoulders, then pressed the start button.

The noise from the guns outside were drowned out as the time machine sprang into life, emitting a low whine which rapidly built to a screaming crescendo as power increased. The outer walls began to shake slightly as the vibrations built. Then, with a final lengthy tremor the machine began its journey back through history with its passengers safely settled inside. Time whizzed past outside of the spinning cylinder, with each year registering on the interior screens. Zoe watched them intently. She was fascinated as well as excited, yet part of her was unable to accept that when the doors opened in a little while she would be back in her own time.

The journey wasn't unpleasant, despite a spasmodic

shuddering that occasionally rattled the outer walls as the machine gathered speed. Zoe found herself thinking that being cooped up in this metal container as it spun round must be akin to being inside a giant food blender, but without the mess and maceration.

This light-hearted thought was soon replaced by darker, more sinister concerns. She was aware that she was approaching what was a pivotal point in her relationship with Kazzaar. She was still worried about his motives and his intentions. It was imperative that she stayed in charge of the date control panel. Zoe knew this situation couldn't go on for ever. Very soon she would have to make a crucial choice. A choice that could, literally, preserve or destroy the Earth.

She had been dreading this day. Although desperately wanting to be back home with her family, she had always known that if she got her wish it would come with major consequences. Whatever these were, they were directly linked to the actions and intentions of the alien Kazzaar. Zoe now found herself holding the key that would determine the way in which those actions might unfold.

Zoe's head was spinning. She'd grown to like Kazzaar, and she owed him her life – on more than one occasion too – but she was still conscious of the fact that he'd stolen souls from children. He had planned to take over the Earth too. Then – as Zak Araz – he'd threatened her, using a troop of monkeys in an attempt to inflict harm on not only her, but DI Benson and Professor Tompkins too. He had also been prepared to destroy the Earth and the Universe in his attempts to regenerate his evil plan. She was further aware that at no time had he expressed any remorse for what he had done. Her mind was awhirl with thoughts.

Only today Kazzaar has told me he is dying. But can I believe him? After all, he is a shape shifter, so he could just be changing into that jelly like thing in order to fool me and convince me that he is dying. For all I know, it could be part of his strategy to enable him to achieve his ambitions to take over the planet.

Zoe thought about the World she had just left behind. *It was so different from the one she'd grown up in. The World in 3015 was a nightmare come true. It was straight out of science fiction. There was nothing about it that showed any sign of warmth or humanity – except for the people she had lived with in Lowlands.*

She tried to imagine what it would be like living in the South. An image of Jane sprang into her head. *Poor Jane,* Zoe thought. *She gave her entire working life to Government research, then when they discovered she was different – and as such they couldn't control her – she was banished to a planet that was primitive, dangerous and dying, where they hoped she would be killed. I really hope Lake and the others can develop Lowlands into a proper place for people to live and grow up in.*

Zoe looked across at Kazzaar. He saw her looking so he gave her a reassuring smile. 'Anything wrong?' he asked.

'No,' said Zoe, turning her face away.

She knew that was a lie. In fact *everything* was wrong. She looked at Kazzaar again. 'Do you think the future is fixed or can it be changed?' she asked.

Kazzaar looked slightly puzzled at the question, but he answered.

'I believe it can be changed. For example, take a ruler, or a warrior, whose life is dominated by war. It would be normal for such a person to kill his enemies on sight. Yet supposing one day he had the chance to kill someone but he let them go free. The future would change because that person was still alive. It might only make a small difference, but it would still make a difference. Firstly because it would affect the reputation for ruthlessness that the ruler had established. No longer would people regard him as showing no mercy. That would change the way his enemies saw him, which might increase the risk of him being attacked, or conversely it might mean he would be seen as someone who is more amenable to compromise and consequently wars might be avoided. Secondly, there would now be a person alive in the World who should have died. The person whom he had let go free might then decide to lead a revolution, overthrowing the leader. He would thus become the new ruler. He might then be a far more ruthless and uncaring ruler than the one he deposed, or he could be a compassionate, caring leader. Either way there would be changes. So the initial action of sparing that man's life would be significant. It would have far-reaching consequences for every person in the nation, which could result in living conditions becoming better or worse. There would also be some ripple effect on the rest of the World. But although I think the future *can* be changed, I guess you can never be certain of what consequences will result from your actions in doing so.

Sometimes however, you just have to trust yourself and your instincts. You have to take a chance and make that leap into the dark.'

Zoe said nothing. She was thinking hard about what Kazzaar had said. *It's a pretty extreme example but I can see his point. I guess we all have a choice in whatever we do and say. Sometimes we make good choices that help a situation, sometimes we make bad ones that make it worse. But nonetheless we still have a choice, and whatever choices we do make in life the future is affected. Not just for us but for other people too. It's like throwing a pebble into a river. Everything we do produces ripples which spread far and wide. Those ripples will impact on infinite numbers of other people, including strangers, as well as on any number of events. It's also true that every word we speak and every action we undertake has a consequence. I know too that we often have to make choices based on nothing more than what we feel inside. Yet sometimes if we do make wrong choices, we may get the chance to make better ones at some time in the future. These will hopefully redeem any damaging effects arising from our original decision.*

Unfortunately, I don't get a second chance in what I have to do in a few minutes. I must make a choice which will have severe ramifications for the future of planet Earth, if I get it wrong. Zoe closed her eyes and took a long deep breath as the ultimate thought entered her head. *It's the biggest decision I have ever had to make and if I am really honest with myself, I truly don't know what to do.*

Zoe was faced with a real dilemma. She couldn't *make* Kazzaar get out in 2015. He wouldn't go. If she left him, she'd have to trust him to do as he promised. If she stayed with him to make sure he did go straight back to his own planet, she still might not be able to stop him. In which case he might get his humanoids to take her soul too. In any case, if Zoe did go back to 2012 to let him out there, she might not be able to get back to 2015 again due to the thirty minute restriction imposed by the time machine. She would have to relive those three years again. That wouldn't be easy if the World was under the rule of Kazzaar's people – which it may well be if she let him go back. Even if it wasn't under his rule, Zoe would have to go back to school and repeat her last years there before starting all over again at college. Returning to school would be difficult, not so much from a schoolwork perspective, but how would she explain her physical growth of the past three years?

The future of planet Earth was in Zoe's hands. She was alone in making her choice, but she hadn't got a clue which course of action to decide upon. Zoe had briefly thought about killing Kazzaar during their time travelling journey. She had even considered staying in the time machine with him until the last possible second before it returned to 3015 then rushing out, leaving it to take Kazzaar back to the future where he couldn't do any harm to the current planet. In this situation he would probably die anyway, due to lack of ZzP2. However either action would be cruel and heartless. Zoe knew deep down that neither would happen.

The time machine was now silent. It had come to the end of its journey. They had arrived in 2015, according to the screen. She had less than half an hour to make her decision. For the umpteenth time since entering the machine Zoe began a conversation inside her head as she once again sifted through her thoughts to try to find a solution.

What if Kazzaar didn't keep his word? I could set the machine for 2012 but as it can be set for a third date too he could reset the date after I've left. This would take him beyond 2012 to wherever he wants to be. He could go back to the time when he had his ship filled with children's souls. If he does this he could take them back to his planet. The Earth would then be doomed. He could go back even further, taking more souls or he could colonise the planet well before my time. If either of those things happen, then all I've gone through in 2015 and 3015 will have been for nothing. The work of Benson and Professor Tompkins will have been wasted too. In the event of such a scenario, whatever I do now will alter nothing. It will mean that when I open this door in a minute I'll find that the human race has become slaves to aliens from the planet Zaarl.

Zoe sucked breath deep into her lungs as she pondered her predicament. If the aliens were here now, what kind of World would she find when she stepped out of the time machine? She made up her mind that if she did find a completely different World dominated by Kazzaar's species, she would try to rush back into the machine before it sped off with Kazzaar. Once there, she could try to reset the date for a time when she and her family were happy, perhaps when she was still a young child. Then she could at least enjoy some quality time with her family before Kazzaar put in an appearance on Earth. Zoe shuddered at the mere thought of a World run by aliens. She then remembered the World she'd just left, a World ruled by human beings. She thought *could a World run by aliens be worse than that?*

Zoe further pondered on whether taking the machine back to such a time could possibly provide a solution to the problem anyway, as Kazzaar would have to go back with her too. Without his supply of ZzP2 he would die. She could then grow up again in the company of her parents with no threat to the planet.

Zoe initially warmed to this plan of action but quickly saw the major flaw as she thought that if Kazzaar got desperate he could kill her then take the machine back to 2012 anyway. She also thought of the shock her parents would get if – at her current age of nineteen – she turned up in their house at a time when she should have been nine.

That would take some explaining, she thought smiling inwardly. *What would I say? Oh I'm sorry I've aged ten years, but I've had a really hard day at school Mum? Anyway, my younger self would probably be at home too, and we couldn't have me meeting myself in two different time zones. It might prove to be a phenomenon that is calamitous for the planet. But seriously, it's a straight choice now. I either have to go back to 2012 with Kazzaar, or if I stay here I have to trust him and hope that he doesn't betray my trust.*

'Well?' Kazzaar's voice broke into Zoe's ruminations, bringing her back to the reality of her current predicament.

'Sorry,' said Zoe. 'I was just thinking … maybe I should go back to 2012 with you and go through my last years at school again.' She smiled. 'I might even get better grades this time'

'You don't trust me?' It was more of a statement than a question. Kazzaar looked mournfully at Zoe as he spoke.

Zoe hesitated. 'How can I … really?' her voice was edgy, unsure. 'After what you did when we were enemies in my World.'

'I can understand that,' Kazzaar replied. 'But haven't I made it up to you with the help and support I've given to you when we were stranded in 3015? Don't I deserve your trust?'

'I suppose so,' said Zoe tentatively, 'but …'

'But what?' asked Kazzaar.

Zoe raised her eyes to look into his. 'When we were in the university you told me you were dying. Then you said you had a supply of ZzP2 in your spacecraft,' she said. 'Is that what you stole from those children? Are you going back to the time before I came into your spaceship so you can use the chemicals you extracted? You are, aren't you? You're still going ahead with your plan.'

Zoe's voice had got louder and more urgent as her statement progressed from question to accusation. Kazzaar's face remained impassive throughout the whole time Zoe was expressing her views. When he answered her, his voice was quiet but filled with passion.

'No!' he said emphatically. 'You've got it all wrong, Zoe. Our spacecraft all carry a special emergency pack of ZzP2 in case we get stranded on some planet where there is no substitute. It's not the souls of the children, I promise you. It's nothing to do with them. I'm not taking them with me. How could I? You released them when you came into my spacecraft. Remember? Listen to me. I'm not trying to fool you. I really am dying.'

Zoe stood, finger poised above the button marked *open doors.* Her mind was still clouded with doubt. She told herself. *He's lied to me before, so how do I know he's not lying now?*

'I give you my word, Zoe,' Kazzaar pleaded, as if reading her thoughts. 'In fact I will go further and swear on the life of all of my people that when you leave this machine, I will take it back to the moment I first arrived on your planet. Then I will retrieve my spacecraft, take the ZzP2, and return immediately to Zaarl, without any souls or samples. You must believe and trust me, Zoe. I know you don't want to go through the last three years again.'

Zoe thought for a moment, then said, 'We only have fifteen minutes left now before this capsule will be recalled to 3015. If I make a date setting on this control panel for 2012, you could still change it after I leave. I am grateful Kazzaar, really, really grateful for what you have done for me. Without your help I would have died on that planet. So it's thanks to you that I am still here and able to go back to my family. But I also have to think about *this* planet ... and all the people who live on it. I don't want to see them as slaves ... or see them die. Nor do I want to live in a World where no one has hope or aspirations, where the sole purpose of human life is to have babies to feed the needs of an alien race who rule over us. I know you said there would be no illness or unhappiness, but being ill and being unhappy is part of being who we are. It is an essential part of being human. Learning to deal with things that leave us unhappy makes us stronger, better people and being ill helps us to understand about caring and compassion. It also teaches us that we are vulnerable and finite in our lifespan. From these things we learn about ourselves and the need to treat people kindly while we can. I don't want anything to change that.'

Zoe gave him a pleading look. 'I know from what we've just seen of the future it doesn't look as if it will get better, but 3015 is a long way ahead and the human race still has time to learn and change. You said yourself the future can be changed, so please, Zak or Kazzaar, or whoever you are, can't you see that we can progress?'

Kazzaar smiled. 'I've found all of that out in my time on Earth, also in my time with you in 3015, Zoe,' he said. 'That's why I no longer have any desire for my people to come here. When I get back to my planet I will tell them it's not a place where they could live. You humans are a strange breed, a weird mix of angst and joy, war and peace, enmity and amity, selfishness and selflessness. It is far too confusing for us to contend with. We are a peace-loving people who – despite our advanced technology and our dying planet – just like to lead simple, uncomplicated lives. You are a relatively young species who are still learning. I think we should leave you to learn in your own time. I promise you that once I've got my spacecraft back I will go home and you won't see me or my people again.'

Kazzaar smiled again. 'Anyway,' he continued. 'On a personal level, you have already thwarted me twice. I have no appetite for a third battle, especially after the one we've just been through together … united … *And* we escaped. So please trust me. Please believe me, Zoe.

Let me go to my craft. I promise you won't see me again. I will tell them that planet Earth is not a suitable place for them.'

Zoe mulled over what Kazzaar had said. The time control showed that there were now just eight minutes before the machine returned to 3015. She had to make her decision. Zoe looked deep into Kazzaar's eyes as her brain processed the statement he'd just made. Then she held out her hand.

'Okay,' she said. 'I'll trust you … I guess. So it's goodbye … good luck … and thanks for looking out for me back there. Thanks too for getting me back home safely. I hope you do manage to find a new home for your people. I also hope you will find one soon. I don't want you, or them, to die with your planet.'

Kazzaar took the proffered hand. He shook it warmly. 'Goodbye, Zoe,' he said smiling. He told Zoe the exact date he'd first arrived on Earth. She punched it into the alternative date panel in the time machine. Afterwards, she pressed her finger on the button controlling the doors. They slid open with a hiss. Then, Zoe walked out without looking back.

CHAPTER TWENTY-TWO

Standing outside the time machine, Zoe took a while to get her bearings. She appeared to be in an underground cavern. It was dark and cold. The walls were covered in foul-smelling black stains which had spread themselves outwards as they jostled for room with a multitude of sprawling damp patches that appeared at various points across the grim grey stone. The air was dank and fetid, making breathing unpleasant. Zoe could see moss growing in the corners of the rock walls. She was disappointed. She had expected to see something more recognisable. A small part of her wished she hadn't left the time machine, which was now quickly dematerialising behind her. She heard the slight whirring noise, turning in time to see the blur of silver as it faded from view. Zoe suddenly felt very alone and very vulnerable.

For the first time since she'd fallen into the time vortex she was completely on her own. She had no idea where she was. She'd put her trust in Jane's story about a machine that could travel through time. *What if it was just that – a story? What if it merely took you to another part of the same building? Or somewhere else on the planet?* Zoe decided that the first thing she had to do was to get out of this place, so she could find out exactly what World lay outside.

At first glance there didn't appear to be any entrance. The cavern wasn't massive. In fact it was only about the size of her mother's living room at home. Zoe stood for a while, shivering. She looked about her taking in the surroundings whilst at the same time trying to figure out how she could get out of this cold, stinking grotto.

A bigger part of her was fearful of what she might find when she did get out. The nagging worries that initially manifested themselves the moment the machine vanished haunted her thoughts. Until she discovered what was outside the cave, she couldn't be sure that what she'd just travelled in was really a time machine. She only had the word of Jane and – to a lesser extent – Kazzaar. For all she knew she was still in the year 3015, either somewhere deep down in the bowels of the man-made planet or back on Lowlands in some subterranean prison.

Zoe suddenly became aware of muffled voices. At least they seemed to be human. She held her breath as she tried to listen to what was being said. The voices were clearer now. They seemed to be coming from the other side of the cavern wall that Zoe was leaning against. It took a while for her to realise that there was a thin aperture in the rock through which the sound was travelling.

She ran over to the opening. It was tall and very narrow, stretching from floor to ceiling. The gap looked to be just about big enough for her to squeeze through if she breathed in very deeply. With a combination of squashing, elongating and twisting her limbs and torso, Zoe succeeded in making it through to the other side.

When she emerged from the slender opening, Zoe flexed herself. Her body ached with the effort of squeezing herself through the tiny aperture. Pressing gently onto the parts where she imagined bruises would later appear, she imagined this was what it must feel like to be put through a mangle. Standing up fully, Zoe saw a small group of people some way ahead of her. She could only see their backs as they walked, chattering loudly to each other. It was their voices she had heard from inside the cavern. She hadn't been able to properly hear the words they had spoken, but from the rear view she had of them, their clothes seemed to indicate that she could well be back in her own time.

Zoe saw that she had emerged into what appeared to be some sort of dungeon, which according to a sign on the nearby wall was in fact part of a public exhibition. Somehow it looked familiar to her. She thought long and hard before she remembered where she had seen it before. It had been when she was in primary school. She had come here once with a party of classmates. Recognition brought relief to Zoe as her previous concerns and doubts disappeared. She now knew where she was. She was inside the Tower of London.

Zoe remembered that Jane had said the time machine locks itself onto the nearest fixed point. *If it is on a fixed site and time merely passes around it, then its position on the future planet known as the South must directly align with this dungeon in the Tower of London.* Zoe thought. *It's quite spooky really, when you think that I only met Jane in the first place after I'd been arrested on a visit to the London buildings that included this Tower.*

She made a mental note of the whereabouts of the exhibition, even marking the aperture by scratching the wall around it with a loose piece of stone that lay nearby. She thought that by doing so she might be able to locate the time machine in future if the need ever arose. Not that Zoe imagined that the machine would be there waiting for her if she ever chose to come here to find it. Nor could she envisage any circumstances in which she might want to return to 3015. *But who knows?* she thought. *Perhaps one day I'll come here again to try to find it. Maybe there's a mechanism behind the aperture that could be used to summon the machine from its future mooring point?*

After she had marked the entrance, Zoe followed the crowd of visitors. Soon she stood outside in the grounds of the Tower, watching the ravens swooping and fighting for food in the sunlight. It was strange to be standing there. Her thoughts drifted back to when she was standing in this same building back on the South. *It was shortly after that I left my ID credit disc in the gallery, then got robbed and arrested. How strange life is. If those events hadn't happened then I would never have met Jane. Then I wouldn't have found out about the time machine. I'd have still been lost in the future instead of being here back in the England that I know in 2015 … at least I hope it's 2015!*

Zoe left the grounds of the Tower. She walked the short distance along the path to Tower Bridge. The River Thames was glistening as the sun danced on the water. For the first time in ages she felt good. She was back in her own World. Zoe decided she'd had enough excitement and adventure for now, all she wanted to do was to go home to her family to continue what passed for normality in her life.

As she wandered onto the London streets it was quite a culture shock – a relief too – for her to see the familiar scene of scurrying commuters rushing along on crowded pavements. Alongside the scampering pedestrians the roads were clogged with vehicles that stopped, then started, then crawled along in a single line that was occasionally broken as an impatient driver tried to cut into the small gap that opened when someone was a little slow to accelerate. Zoe threaded her way between two slow moving cars thinking *at least they are mobile*.

It was good to see these familiar sights again after the moving pavements and static cars of the South, or the overgrown open green spaces in Lowlands. The noise, the smell of petrol and diesel fumes, allied to the general bustle of hordes of people seemed to be welcoming Zoe home. She didn't know London well, but she assumed that what she was seeing was a normal day in the capital. It certainly looked as if Kazzaar had kept his word. Everything seemed as it was when she'd left. A glance at the date of a newspaper that lay on a nearby news stand confirmed to her that she was indeed in the year 2015. She briefly thought about Kazzaar and hoped he had managed to find his way home safely.

Zoe stood on the street looking about her as she tried to figure out her exact whereabouts in London. She was conscious of people staring at her. At first she thought it was because she was just standing still whilst everyone else rushed about, but then she realised it was the way she was dressed. She was still wearing the clothes she'd put on when she was arrested by the southern security police. They were smart and clean but given that they had been designed in 3015 she guessed that they were far too futuristic, even for a fashion centre like London.

Zoe suddenly remembered that she had no money. She had no mobile phone either. London was around a hundred miles or so from Cristelee. It was certainly too far for her to walk. She wandered around aimlessly for a while trying to think of how she could get home.

'I can't believe this,' she muttered to herself. 'In the past months I've travelled in time and space to 3015. I've made the trip from Lowlands to the South – twice. I've travelled back to 2015 in a time machine. Now I'm here in my own time zone again, I can't even get from London to Cristelee.'

Zoe did think about finding a public phone where she could make a reverse charge call to her mum. She could ask mum to come to London to collect her. The idea was quickly discarded though, as she imagined the conversation that would take place between them about why Zoe had decided to go to London with no money, leaving her unable to get back home.

Zoe was so absorbed in her thinking she had no idea of how far she'd walked, or of where she was. She was about to cross a busy road with the traffic lights on red when she noticed a lorry waiting at the lights. It was just an ordinary lorry but what caught Zoe's attention was the writing on the side of the driver's cab. The vehicle was from a haulage company based in Cristelee. Zoe looked at the driver. To her delight it was a female. Waving her arms wildly, Zoe ran across to the lorry. She hammered on the passenger door. The driver wound down the window.

'Look I'm sorry to be a nuisance, but I've been to a fancy dress party here in London where someone has stolen my purse, my mobile, and my weekend case,' Zoe lied. 'I have no money and no phone. All I have with me are these weird clothes that I wore to the party. I live in Cristelee so I need to get home. Is there any chance you can give me a lift please?'

'We're not supposed to give lifts,' said the driver. 'You could be a decoy for a hijacker.'

'I promise you I'm not,' cried Zoe. 'I'm just someone who badly needs to get home as soon as possible but has no money to do so.'

'I could lose my job if I'm seen with anyone in my cab,' the driver argued.

'Oh please help me,' pleaded Zoe. 'I'll be discreet. I'll crouch down on the floor or even go in the back of the lorry so I won't be seen. Please … The lights are going to change any second now then I'll be stuck here.'

Two hours later Zoe climbed down from the lorry in the centre of Cristelee. After thanking the driver she headed for her home. As she passed the police station she decided to go in to tell DI Benson that she was back, and let him know that Kazzaar had returned to his own planet.

At the reception desk she asked if she could speak to DI Benson.

'We don't have a DI Benson here, Miss,' said the civilian clerk. 'We do have a DS Benson. He's assistant to DI Chalk. That's DS Benson over there.'

She pointed to a man who sat talking to a woman on the opposite side of the reception area. He looked up as he heard his name. Zoe recognised him straight away. It *was* Benson. She was disappointed when he showed no sign of recognition towards her and turned away. She was about to call out his name when it all fell into place in her head.

DI Chalk ... DS Benson, she thought. *They were the two policemen originally in charge of the case when those children were disappearing, but Chalk later got taken off the case with Benson taking over. Now Kazzaar has gone home, Benson doesn't know me because none of it happened. The children didn't disappear, so there was no case. Benson and I never met. There was no safari park incident and no time vortex, even though I lived through both. There is no Soul Snatcher. Kazzaar has gone, so I guess, technically he was never here.*

Zoe turned back to face the clerk again. 'No, it's okay,' she said. 'It isn't him.'

With a final glance at Benson, Zoe left the police station. As she walked in the direction of her home, the euphoria she had felt when she discovered she was back in 2015 abated. She suddenly felt disappointed and a little annoyed. Everything was as it should be, but she knew different. Kazzaar had existed, children did disappear, some of her friends included. Zoe thought, *I did fall into the time vortex, and haven't I just spent the most horrific period of my life in that terrible World in the future. I still have to live with that. How can I ever explain it or get anyone to understand how I feel. It's going to be really hard to settle again, pretending I've been here all of the time, but for everyone's sake I'm going to have to do that.*

275

By the time she arrived home, Zoe had managed to bury her disappointment and annoyance beneath the joy she was feeling at the thought of seeing her family again. When she got to the house, she remembered she hadn't got a key. Fortunately for her the door was unlocked. Zoe entered by the front door. She could see her mother in the kitchen, but Zoe popped her head around the door to the lounge first to say hello to her dad and brother. She was pleased to see that they were both back to their normal selves. The hypnotic effect from the computer game had worn off. Or more likely it had never taken place. After a quick exchange of greetings she went into the kitchen. Her mother looked up as Zoe walked in.

'Hello love,' said Mrs Marshall. 'How's your day been?'

Zoe ran across the room. She flung her arms around her mother. 'Oh Mum,' she cried. 'It's so good to see you and to be home again.'

Mrs Marshall pulled away from her daughter. 'What on earth is the matter with you?' she asked. 'It's only a few hours since I last saw you. You've only *been* at college too. Anyone would think you'd been in outer space and hadn't seen me in ages. Get off me, you big soft thing.'

Zoe smiled. 'I know Mum,' she said, chokingly overwhelmed by the normality of it all. 'But I still missed you. Now what's for tea?'

'I'm making a roast,' said Mrs Marshall. Then she saw what Zoe was wearing.

'Whatever have you got on? Surely you haven't been to college in those clothes? And what have you done to your face? I've haven't seen you without make-up for a long time. I have to say you look quite tanned. Have you been sitting out in the sun?'

'The clothes were for an experiment, Mum,' Zoe lied. 'So too is the lack of make-up. We've been doing it for a while now. We've also been having lectures outside and sitting in the sun at break times. You probably haven't noticed, as I usually put my make up on before I come home.'

'What sort of experiment involves that kind of behaviour?' asked Mrs Marshall.

'It's to see how we cope mentally with the ravages of time,' Zoe continued her lie. 'It's only for a short time but the sun quickly has an effect on our skin and if we don't wear make-up we can get some idea of what it's like to grow old. Then we discuss how this makes us feel. It's for a module called The Psychology of Ageing. I'll go and get changed now and put some moisturiser on. I'll have the make-up on again tomorrow, as the experiment has now finished.'

Mrs Marshall seemed happy to accept Zoe's hastily concocted explanation, much to Zoe's relief. She'd forgotten that her time in Lowlands would have affected her outward appearance. As she looked in the mirror in her bedroom, Zoe hoped that moisturising cream would eventually return her skin to its normal texture.

After tea Zoe sat watching television with her parents and her brother. Now she was home with her family, she felt at peace for the first time in a long while. She had been through things that they would never know about. Things they would never even dream about, or begin to understand if they did. She had been close to death on several occasions too. There had been so many times when she had thought she would never see her family again. Yet she was here with them now, back in her own time.

Zoe was composed and contented as she relaxed in the large comfortable easy chair. From now on she could concentrate on college and her career. She thought now that she could – despite her earlier concerns –try to forget about the past and focus on her future. For the first time in ages, she felt safe and untroubled. She was pleased that there was to be a happy ending after all, despite the heartache and horror she had experienced in 3015.

Had Zoe been around to read the previous day's evening newspaper – which was at that moment forming part of the new lining in the cat's basket – she might not have felt quite so relaxed or comfortable. Near the bottom of page four – almost hidden away next to a large advert filled with offers from a local superstore – was a short news item. The headline to the story read *"Boy and Girl disappear from two different Schools."*